Maaculla

An Optimistic Novel By Chef Saad Ghazi

Copyright
Maaculla

Publisher: Chef Saad Ghazi

www.thecurryguru.com
curryguru@thecurryguru.com

Dedication

The Maaculla once said, we often forget our mother, in the sense that through that beautiful and incredible person we all came to this world. I believed her, because I never had that opportunity of meeting my own mother. Through my wife Karen I experienced mother hood when I watched her with my daughter Saaren. Maaculla is right again, we cannot awe them enough respect, gratitude and love. Although she her self hadn't had any children, through her love and care for us all humans she became Maaculla, the mother of the world. I dedicate my fifty years of efforts to bring this book to reality to all the mothers of the world, with love, respect and gratitude.

Gratitude

I am eternally grateful to my wife Karen for her help with putting this book together. She took on the task of correcting my intelligible early drafts which meant little sense. However, I continued writing because Maculla planted this story inside me whether I wanted it or not. I also became a financial burden to my wife during the writing of it. She also gave me permission to use her image for the cover. I couldn't possibly find a more appropriate image for this book.

I also hope our customers have forgiven me for closing down our restaurants for this. I never disclosed to them the reason for this. I received a lot of disappointed emails & phone calls since then. I hope it was worth it for their sake too. I am grateful for their forgiveness. Nevertheless, I am grateful to Maaculla for trusting me to deliver this valuable message to humanity at the right time. For without people this world has no meaning...Maaculla said.

TOC

Maaculla Part 1
Chapter 1 Who or what is Maaculla
Chapter 2 Saad- How it all began
Chapter 3 What did Saad do then - 1969?
Chapter 4 Can we shift our own energies?
Chapter 5 How Maaculla acquired this ability
Chapter 6 Richard must find a way to go to India
Chapter 7 Robert trains Richard to fly balloon
Chapter 8 The balloon takes off like bird in the sky
Chapter 9 Teaching of the High priest (Maha Guru)
Chapter 10 What Richard need to learn from all this
Chapter 11 Richard & Robert arrived back in Portsmouth
Chapter 12 Richard meets the right girl of his dream
Chapter 13 Green witches hideout
Chapter 14 In Search for Green witch
Chapter 15 The day before the wedding
Chapter 16 Phillip IV of France teamed up with Green witch
Chapter 17 Richard having a second thought about the baby
Chapter 18 Robert is in love
Chapter 19 Rescuing Brigit
Chapter 20 En route to Luxembourg
Chapter 21 Oostende to Portsmouth the ship disappears
Chapter 22 Birth of the Maaculla and the baby Richstella Portsmouth
Chapter 23 Richard and Robert in a military camp
Chapter 24 Robert is showing his family and Brigit around Portsmouth
Chapter 25 Richard and Stella move in to their new home
Chapter 26 Richard starts a program for poor
Chapter 27 Search for Robert and Brigit
Chapter 28 Time to celebrate
Maaculla Part II Present Day
Chapter 29 The real story
Chapter 30 Saad's yearly visit to England - Present day 2016
Chapter 31 Maaculla's message to the population - 1968
Chapter 32 Laws of The Universe
Chapter 33 Why maculae
Chapter 34 Saad is humbled by all this - Present day
Chapter 35 Visit to North Korea
Chapter 36 Attack on the 3 Ex Presidents
Chapter 37 Finally a guidance from Maaculla
Chapter 38 Saad visiting emergency medical holding centre
Chapter 39 A new beginning

Introduction

How would you like to have a world without fear, worry, disease, bullying, jealousy, cheating, robbery, terrorism, dishonest lawyers, politicians or even wars, crimes or natural disaster etc? Does it sound too far fetched to you? Then you should read Maaculla. It is a novel of romance, sex, love, friendship, sacrifice, hope, science and the future rendering of sexuality by The Universe that may be in the future. Through his unique story telling, you will learn about the probability of a perfect world we are destined to live in, and how we are deluded into the world of negativity. If we don't change our course soon, doomsday is waiting for us tomorrow. Everyone should realize this fact by the way things are developing around the world...

As early as 1968, through these words, Maaculla was trying to plant the seed of a unique concept of Global Peace in into the minds of everyone. Through nurturing it to the maturity we could eliminate Crimes and Wars from our world. This could be a watershed moment for the fledgeling human civilization...
And yes, only you can take it to the next step...

MAACULLA PART I

Chapter 1

WHO OR WHAT IS MAACULLA?

Sometimes the most extraordinary things happen to most ordinary people. Saad was one of them. He didn't set out in his life to unravel the mystery of the universe. On the contrary, he was too busy with his cheffing and restaurant businesses. Along the way, he encountered a superhero, Mrs. Griffiths, who introduced him to the most astonishing occurrences. Later he named her Maaculla. *Maa* means mother, and *culla* means everything (the world) in his Sylheti slang: "the Mother of the World. It's the opposite of Dracula, meaning a negative energy, and Maaculla, meaning a positive one. Needless to say, she had superhuman abilities similar to Dracula but in positive ways."

Saad never thought he would come across anybody or anything like this. This kind of story belongs in storybooks—that's what he had believed in his twenty-six years of life so far. He was in limbo. It was difficult to disregard her extraordinary tale, but at the same time, he found it hard to accept. Most importantly, he was finding it difficult to take responsibility for the knowledge Maaculla had given him.

He couldn't explain why she had picked him for this purpose in spite of his reluctance to accept all these extraordinary accounts and the responsibility with it. It had been haunting him for the last fifty years or so. However, after reading this story, one may find it difficult to disregard the following statements, just as he couldn't:

1. That someone can see the spirit of dead people. That someone, by the way, was the Maaculla, the heroin of this book.

2. That sex is more than the urge for pleasure and propagation. It has other purposes, such as energy manipulation so that one can possess superhuman ability.

3. That transgender people are not freaks of nature. On the contrary, they may be the future of human evolution, based on the truth that the universe is infallible.

4. That humans and everything else in the world consist of two energies, negative and positive.

5. That the energies within each of us can be manipulated through virginity. It pays to be a virgin if you are pursuing real power.

6. That the experiences in our life come from our percentage of choices of negative and positive intentions.

7. That the universe randomly chooses anyone to channel most extraordinary knowledge. That is to say, to the universe, there is no difference between the queen of England and the homeless person you might have just passed on the street.

8. That a mass awareness of that negative energy can cause disasters in our life as well as in our environment. In that case we could reverse the effect by creating mass awareness of positive energy in our world.

9. That adversity precedes a positive outcome.

10. That when you forgive others, it is for your own self-protection.

11. That it is also possible for us to know what Maaculla knew as an avatar. She knew what crisis the world would face half a century after her death. We are facing the same crises right now around the world, such as the water crisis, the energy crisis, polar ice melting, severe weather, global warming, sexuality, overpopulation, the influx of homeless and countryless people, overcrowded jails, out-of-control crime, terrorism, and so on. How could she even know their solutions fifty years before all these happened?

12. That the formula for world peace lies within our intentions.

13. That it is possible to be an avatar and foresee the future, as Leonardo da Vinci might have done.

ENCOUNTER WITH THE BROWN-SUITED MAN—1968

This story begins with Saad. He was a restaurateur. The year was 1968. In search of a new location for his family restaurants, Saad visited South Sea, a subdivision of Portsmouth, England, answering an advertisement, a restaurant for sale. He purchased the restaurant from the restaurant owner, Mr. Minhoy. While doing this, he met Mrs. Griffiths (not her real name), who was also the landlady for the restaurant. Mrs. Griffiths lived next door to the restaurant. Saad visited Mrs. Griffiths every day during his stay there. She told him many interesting accounts of her life, the past history of Portsmouth, and many interesting stories about her travels to India and her family ancestry, starting from fourteenth century.

Since his childhood, Saad had been a good listener. He always followed the advice of his grandfather, who told him you should listen more than you talk. That was why God gave us two ears and only one mouth. So he continued listening to Mrs. Griffiths for nine whole months, as if he were possessed by an energy that compelled him to listen. Sometimes he wondered what this was all this about—what had brought him to Portsmouth, and how was he going to remember all this? Most of all, why?

Mrs. Griffiths continued to reveal parts of her life story to Saad. She told him that one of her favorite pastimes was to stand in front of her bay window and watch the traffic go by. A couple of doors away from her house was a bus stop. Every Saturday, she would catch the bus to go to the town centre, where she would do her weekly shopping. The bus driver and the conductor knew Mrs. Griffiths by name. Her house was at the corner of Albert Road and Exmouth Road. On the other corner, by Exmouth Road, was the King's Theatre. One day as usual, Mrs. Griffiths was standing on her favorite spot in front of the bay window watching the traffic go by. She noticed a man wearing a brown suit running out of the theatre and across Albert Road. A moment later, she heard the screeching of brakes as a bus made an emergency stop. Many people came out of the bus and gathered in front of it. It was difficult to see what was going on from inside her house, though it was only a few doors away. She finally went out to investigate. There was a lot of noise and commotion, and people were shaking their heads in disbelief.

The bus driver came over to her as soon as he saw her. He asked, "Mrs. Griffiths, did you see anything? All I know is that this man came running out on to the road out of the blue, and then I braked, but it was too late.
He was obviously distraught."

10

She said, "I'm glad it wasn't him." She pointed across the road at a man wearing a brown suit and tie—the one she had seen few minutes earlier coming out of the theatre and running across the road. At this stage, she had no idea who had gotten run over, as she could see the brown-suited man was standing across the road. She thanked God he was safe.

But to her surprise, the bus driver said, "What man? I don't see anybody there."

All the people from the bus were gathered on this side of the road. No one was over there.

Obviously he couldn't see anyone there.

They walked near the front of the bus, and the driver said, "This is the man who got run over."

He pointed to a man wearing a brown suit lying on the road, with blood gushing out of a head injury. Mrs. Griffiths couldn't believe her eyes. She could still see him across the road. The man then started to walk across the road towards the crowd to investigate the commotion. He couldn't believe his own eyes when he saw himself lying on the road, motionless and bleeding profusely.

He tried to tell everyone, "Look, I'm OK. Nothing's wrong; look at me."

Only Mrs. Griffiths could see and hear him.

The ambulance came, and they covered up the body with a white sheet and took it away on a gurney.

What had happened to the brown-suited man?

WAS MRS. GRIFFITHS, IMAGINING THINGS?

After that incident Mrs. Griffiths continued with her regular routine of a shopping trip into town on the same bus. Every time she got on the bus, there was the brown-suited man sitting across the aisle facing her. The first row of seats by the door on the double-decker bus (for those who are not familiar with England's double-decker buses) is placed horizontally, with seats facing each other across the aisle, one on each side. Each bench could seat four people. All smokers sat upstairs. The bus conductor who collected fares, always said good morning to Mrs. Griffiths. She completely ignored the man, as if he didn't exist. He was still wearing the same brown herringbone woolen suit with a brown tie and a cream-colored shirt. Only Mrs. Griffiths could see him wondering and looking around at everyone.

Three months went by. It was the beginning of the winter season in England. Everyone was wearing warm clothes, sweaters, overcoats, mufflers, hats, and so on. He was still wearing the same brown suit, cream shirt, and brown tie. The temperature or the weather didn't seem to bother him. He was there every Saturday as usual when Mrs. Griffiths went on her shopping trip. This bus route ran past the local cemetery and the pub called the Grave Diggers. There was a bus stop just past the pub, by the cemetery. One Saturday as the bus stopped, an old lady jumped on the bus and sat by the brown-suited man.

She said to him, "Good morning."

The man was startled and almost jumped off his seat.

He asked, "Can you see and hear me? I've been going around on this bus for about three months after my accident. No one could see or hear me until now."

She said wryly, "Of course I can see you and hear you, silly man. I'm one of you."

The man asked, "What do you mean, one of me?"

She said, "Well, our bodies are dead, dear. We are free spirits now."

The man seemed happy meeting her but extremely curious about what she was saying. Mrs. Griffiths overheard the lady suggest to the man that he could get off the bus with her by the abandoned old castle at the end of the bus route. Many of them lived there.

After that day Mrs. Griffiths never saw the man or the lady again.

Why was it that only Mrs. Griffiths could see and hear them?

Chapter 2

SAAD—HOW IT ALL BEGAN

It was quite a humble beginning for this story compared to what was about to unfold to Saad over the next nine months, whether he wanted it or not. He believed it was necessary to mention it all exactly the way it was told to him, simply because he believed there was a message for all of us for now and for our future. Thank goodness he continued (unwillingly) wondering about it for almost fifty years. That led to the most extraordinary series of events. These events are not occurring just for the sake of another story. They contained the knowledge and truth about the fundamentals of the ultimate human journey for happiness, peace, and, most importantly, the survival of the human race. It may also contain the formula and understanding to achieve these goals. Once this awareness is established in everyone's mind, these goals can easily be achieved by separating the good people from the bad ones. In order to achieve that, a war has to be won. A war within each person's mind. A war without any weapons. A war without a visible enemy. A war to end all the wars. An ultimate war. A war to answer all our questions. A war to save humanity. A war to end averting awareness to negativities around the world. A war to stop the self-annihilation of humankind. A war within each of us to make the right choices.

It started out as nothing unusual, like an everyday occurrence in the daily life of any business person in those days. First, a brief account of his family history as it is important for the reader to understand how it all began.

A BRIEF DESCRIPTION OF SAAD'S BACKGROUND—1960

By 1960, Chef Saad's family had acquired a few restaurants up and down England. His uncle Ghuri, his mentor and his guru, started his first restaurant in 1939. As a chef and restaurateur in their family restaurants, Saad was also busy scouting out new locations for expansion. It was out of necessity rather than the ambition of having multiple restaurants around the country. The reason was that unlike today, they had an influx of staff (Sylheti people) who arrived in England during that time. Most of them couldn't speak English, and they were unskilled labours. Saad and his family took on the responsibility of training and finding suitable employment for a large number of them. Most of them knew one another from back home in Sylhet. It was a very small place, and they were related to one another in some way or another. Sylhet is located in the northeastern corner of East Bengal, now known as Bangladesh. Unlike the rest of Bangladesh, its culture grew from the Hindu culture originally, and then Muslim when the Moguls came to India and after the Moguls, the English. The food of the Hindu culture was rich with vegetables and herbs. When Moguls ruled India in the sixteenth century, they introduced the Middle Eastern, Greek, and Italian styles of cooking to India. Then the English imported tea from China, and Sylhet was selected as one of the ideal locations for growing tea because of its climate and hilly land. In a word, the Sylhetis are multicultural people, as they're described in Chef Saad's cookbook, *Indian Food Recipes by the CurryGuru*, on Amazon.

When Uncle Ghuri arrived in Birmingham, England, in 1939, there was no Indian restaurant there. India then was still under British rule. It became independent from British rule in 1947. In 1962, when England issued a deadline for immigrants coming to England from newly independent India, a few thousand Sylhetis arrived in England to beat the deadline by July of that year. Uncle Ghuri had to open a few more restaurants to employ an influx of labor. He remembers they had an extra twenty to thirty people working and living in each restaurant and trained them to work mainly if or when a new restaurant opened up. They could not just turn them away, especially when they all knew one another. Today a Sylheti chef in England is worth his weight in gold.

This is just a brief description of how this story began with Saad. Nothing that exciting—so far.

SAAD MEETS MRS GRIFFITHS, a.k.a. MAACULLA—1968

In 1968, while on a quest for a restaurant, as mentioned earlier, Saad visited South Sea, Portsmouth, Hampshire, about seventy miles from London. He arrived in South Sea at about three in the afternoon and found that the restaurant was closed after lunch. A lady from next door saw him knocking at the door of the restaurant. She thought he was a customer. She informed him that they would be back to open for dinner that night at six o'clock. She asked him if he would like to come back then. Saad had assumed that the owner, Mr. Minhoy, would have waited for him, as he had made an appointment to see the place prior to leaving London. He told the lady his intention to buy the restaurant from Mr. Ng Minhoy. She introduced herself as Mrs. Griffiths (not using her real name), the landlady of the restaurant. Later she explained that she was a widower and that her husband had passed away a few years ago and left her these terraced properties. She turned them into retail shops and was making a comfortable income from them. She invited him in for a cup of tea while he waited, as she still lived next door to the restaurant. After all, he had three hours to kill before Mr. Minhoy would arrive back to open the restaurant for dinner. They spoke for about three hours and had several cups of tea and biscuits. She played some records on her old gramophone. That old gramophone had a cylindrical drum with spikes as a record. She wound the spring inside in order rotate the record, and a prong hit the spikes to play the different notes of the music.

Saad observed that when Mrs. Griffiths was describing some of her past history to him, it seemed that she could see every building, every landscape, every situation and person there. Her eyes would be open, but her focus was as distant as the fourteenth century. It would seem to him as though she were living through that era and the life it offered. As she continued with the storytelling, her expression changed as she described every situation, every person, and every place, similar to a TV screen on which the colour, darkness, and light would change accordingly. Chef Saad would even feel the hot and cold of the weather. He often wondered if there was something she added to the tea to put them both in an unusual trance. Nevertheless, he continued attending her sessions, like a good student preparing for his final exam.

She continued to tell him her life story. Her family had a long history in Portsmouth, going back to the fourteenth century. Her husband was in the British Army. They travelled together around the world. They had no children, so she travelled with him everywhere. That was how she had gathered extensive knowledge about India. Then she told him about her encounter with the brown-suited man.

It was a very strange experience for Saad to meet Mrs. Griffiths like this. It felt as if someone had lured him there and he was in some

15

sort of a trance. The next thing he knew, he was checking in to a bed and breakfast nearby. The following day he met with Minhoy again and then went to a solicitor. He made a deal with him. He paid him for the restaurant from his bank in London. It took him a couple of months to renovate the place into an Indian restaurant and to open for business. He called it the Maharaja on Mrs. Griffith's advice. She remembered a few maharajas she had met during her stay in India.

Saad visited her every day. He didn't know anybody else in South Sea then. All in all, he stayed in Portsmouth for nine months. Every day she spoke about different subjects, such as her life history, her ancestors, her travels, and so on. When he thought back, it felt as if she had been expecting him there and the restaurant was only an excuse. Otherwise how could one explain Saad's next move?

Chapter 3

WHAT DID SAAD DO THEN? 1969

Nine months had passed since Chef Saad arrived in South Sea. Mrs. Griffiths told him that this town was for retired people. They had been around the world, either doing business or serving in the military. By then, she had told him many of the accounts involved in this story. Saad wondered why she was telling him all these stories, and how did she expect him to remember any of them? And why? Some of them were ancient historical facts about Portsmouth, India, and so on, and some of them involved her own life story. Most importantly, some of them were pertinent to the future of humankind! Mrs. Griffiths assured him when he asked that he would remember everything when the time came.

In the meantime, Saad's family in London started to wonder about him. They knew he was travelling a lot, scouting for business locations up and down the country. But this time it had been nine months since anyone had seen or heard from him. The day after Mrs. Griffiths told him the story of brown-suited man, he felt as if his work was done there. The next morning he got up and gave the key to the restaurant to his headwaiter, Majid, and got ready to leave for London, as if he were possessed by an energy or something. He never looked back or came back to South Sea again. Thinking back, he wondered, what happened there? Within a few months of opening the restaurant, he just left and never looked back! He never even called to see how the restaurant was doing. As far as he was concerned, the restaurant belonged to Majid, who later changed the name to Golden Curry Restaurant. Saad never contacted Mrs. Griffiths either! That was in 1969. After that encounter, his life took a different turn. As usual, he was involved in other restaurants, but he kept wondering about Mrs. Griffiths, the brown-suited man and many conversations he had with her.

GOOD-BYE MRS. GRIFFITHS

At the beginning of 1969, as Saad decided to leave Portsmouth, he met Mrs. Griffiths in her drawing room as usual. Saad was silent. He was thinking how to break the news of his departure. As usual, she made tea for them.

Mrs. Griffiths suddenly broke the silence. "So, no 'so long'? Just good-bye, Saad?"

Saad was startled. How did she know?

She was not surprised. As she handed over a cup of tea to him, she leaned forward, and for first time ever, she kissed his third eye. A strong energy ran through his spine down to his tailbone. The next thing he remembered, he was walking into his house in London.

THE PICTURE *THE DEFINITION OF HUMANKIND*

Before he left Portsmouth for good, even though it was totally inexplicable to him, Saad drew a picture on the black wall of the restaurant. He had no training or skill in drawing pictures. At that point he didn't even know what it meant. He just drew it on the spur of the moment. It was supposed to be some kind of equation or solution of some mathematics. At the same time, he kept wondering about the brown-suited man. There had to be some explanation as to why Mrs. Griffiths could see him and the lady while no one else could.

Years went by, and he opened and sold many restaurants. In 1972 he joined his mentor and guru, Uncle Ghuri, for a restaurant in Birmingham. It was a very big Indian restaurant project. It had a theatre, dancing, cabaret, full bar, and so on. During that time, he met his wife, Karen, when he was auditioning artists for a cabaret act. They got married in 1976 and visited Los Angeles during their honeymoon. They fell in love with the lifestyle, the sunshine, beautiful weather and fresh vegetables, and so on. Most importantly, he was looking to create a distance between himself and Portsmouth. Maybe he would be able forget his experiences with Mrs. Griffiths. Out of sight, out of mind. They sold all their restaurants and their house in England and moved to Los Angeles in 1979. They opened their first restaurant in Beverly Hills in 1980, Canard de Bombay. At the same time, they were blessed with a beautiful daughter, Saaren. While he was involved in all these mega projects, in the back of his mind, Saad still wondered about Mrs. Griffiths and the amazing encounter he had had with her. Later he realized that their move to Los Angeles had been in her plan all along.

By then, his thoughts of that time in his life were no longer thoughts anymore. They were like visions that started to appear in his mind day and night. He was so used to them that he didn't think they were thoughts or visions anymore. They felt as if they were part his life. So he kept gathering them in his mind as they surfaced in his memory. His first encounter was in 1968, and now, in 2014, he was still seeing these visions. He had no idea how long they would go on or if they would ever stop.

THE PICTURE: *THE DEFFINITION OF HUMANKIND*—1982

In 1982, Saad bought a new computer called the Macintosh 128KB, with a floppy drive—the first Mac by Steve Jobs. He was doodling around to learn the different aspects of the new computer, and he drew an exact replica of the picture he had drawn on the wall of Maharaja restaurant in South Sea, Portsmouth, in 1968. Later, when he bought a more sophisticated colour Mac computer, he managed to add colour to it. He called the picture *The Definition of Humankind*. This turned out to be a perfect rendition of one of his visions. He realized then the meaning of Mrs. Griffiths's stories and why she could see the brown-suited man. It became clear to him, just like mathematics.

Image 1. Definition of Humankind.

Assume that everything in the universe, including human beings, is made of two energies, negative and positive. When those two energies converge somewhere in the cosmos, the quantum particles slow down and begin to solidify, and as a result, solid entities such as humans are formed. For a human, the equation is the balance of the two energies at fifty-fifty, negative and positive. This isn't necessarily bad or good. It's just two energies. The religions call those two energies devils and angels. Each of them consists of pure, single energy. As a single energy, its molecules vibrate so fast that it is invisible to the human eye. Our physical eyes cannot perceive the higher vibration of devils or angels. But how is it that we humans can see one another, hear one another, and speak to one another? Because we are in the same frequency.

When the atoms slow down as a result of the reciprocal reaction between two energies, matter is formed to give humans physical bodies. These bodies still contain the two energies in the ratio of fifty-fifty. When the atoms of the particles slow down further, they become lifeless (lower-frequency) objects such as stones and earth. As a matter of fact, there is nothing lifeless in the universe. Or nothing ever gets destroyed. They are in the different frequencies or in different forms, the same way the whole universe is constantly forming into planets, stars, galaxies, and so on, and then constantly transforming into nothingness through the process called black holes (destructive energy). So the nothingness in space is not really nothing, per se. We just cannot perceive it with our limited human senses.

This also means that other intelligent beings of higher vibration are around us, even though we can't see or hear them or communicate with them. But can they see us or hear us? Maybe one day when humans evolve into more advanced beings, we will be able to communicate with other spirits or other intelligence.

In the meantime, since humans consist of two equal energies at a fifty-fifty ratio, our life cannot be just positive or just negative all the time. It cannot always be good, even if we desire that. For that reason, it fluctuates from good to bad and bad to good, according to the feelings we have. Furthermore, we have to make choices constantly to fulfill our desires. According to our choices, our feelings change, and according to our feelings, our energies fluctuate. And when our energies fluctuate, our experiences in life vary. That is to say, there is no good without bad, no negative without positive, no up without down, no darkness without light, no big without small, no far without near, and so on.

But how could Mrs. Griffiths see the spirits of dead people?

Chapter 4

CAN WE SHIFT OUR OWN ENERGIES?

He had no reason to disbelieve or doubt Mrs. Griffiths, and he could not find a reason to disregard her stories. To start with, why would an eighty-four-year-old lady make up stories like these? From the day he met her, she seemed very trustworthy, kind, and giving. On many occasions she reminded him of his own grandmother.

During the time off from his hospital duties, Saad's grandfather, a surgeon and herbalist, would treat approximately fifty to a hundred people every weekend free of charge at his home. These people could not afford to go to a hospital. At the same time, his grandmother would open her kitchen for them and feed them after they had been treated by his grandfather. Remembering his grandparents being so benevolent in nature, he started to think, could it be possible that when we make our purpose of life doing positive things, we can raise the level of our positive vibration to 25/75 or 10/90, so that we could develop the ability to perceive the spirits of higher frequencies? When we are normal human beings at 50/50, we can only use our limited physical eyes and other four limited physical senses. At the level of 10/90— either negative 10 percent and positive 90 percent, or the other way around—can one use his or her sixth sense to perceive spirits in the higher frequencies? That could explain how Mrs. Griffiths could see the spirits of deceased people.

When the two energies, negative and positive, are converged, the atoms slow down and form solid entities such as humans, animals, water, earth, stones, trees, and so on. That also means higher-frequency beings have no definite shape or body. Human spirits are also higher in frequencies when they're temporarily living in the human body. This was the conclusion that inspired him to create the picture called *Definition of Humankind* to illustrate the equation and the mathematics of energies.

That explains why Mrs. Griffiths could possibly see the brown-suited man and his lady friend when they were both deceased. That was the question in his mind that had haunted him since the time he had heard the story from her. He felt a compulsion to continue wondering why, how, and what it all meant. It almost became an obsession for him. At the same time, he continued with his career in the restaurants.

Now it became clear as daylight to him. Mrs. Griffiths's ability to see the spirits, even though she seemed like a normal human being, puzzled him for the longest time. Although her frequency was higher than 50/50, she was not quite 100 percent positive or 100 percent negative. But if she was 10/90 either way, she could remain as a human and at the same time perceive the higher spirits and perform superhuman abilities. She was able to do only positive things, because her energy was 10/90 in favor of the positive. As he came to this understanding he decided to call her Maaculla. *Maa* means "mother," and *culla* means "everyone's," or "the whole world" in Sylheti colloquial. It meant "mother of the world." Because if anything, she was positive—the exact opposite of the devilish Dracula. Incidentally, this might shed some light on why Dracula could remain human while at the same time be able to perform superhuman feats. The nature of the negative energy is destructive. That was why Dracula continued his destruction. At the same time, he was craving love—because of his 10 percent positivity, which created human tendencies inside his mind.

Saad never found out, though, whether Maaculla, a.k.a. Mrs. Griffiths, had deliberately developed this ability or not. Nevertheless, he felt a compulsion to just move along, especially after that encounter in Portsmouth. You might have noticed that he just left the restaurant to his headwaiter and went back to London. He didn't take any money for his investment of over £50,000. In today's value, it is close to a million dollars. Now it feels strange to think that. But at that time, he thought nothing of it. He could not explain his action there.

Can anyone deliberately develop this ability? And then what?

HOW DOES ONE KNOW ONE'S ENERGY HAS SHIFTED?

Every time Saad went to visit Mrs. Griffiths, a.k.a. Maaculla, she was surprised to see him, as if she was not expecting him. She told him later it was because she wanted him to come of his own free will and not because she asked him to come or was even expecting him to come. Then, one day, Saad asked her, when she spoke about the fluctuation of energy and vibration, how does one know that one has transcended to higher energy? She explained that, for instance, during meditation your mind will still remain active. But you will see unfamiliar faces, places, objects, and so on. Then you will know that you have transcended from this limited, familiar material world to and unlimited, unknown world of possibilities. On the other hand, if everything looks familiar, then you know you are still here in the known world. That's how you know if you are here or there. She laughed.

She also mentioned that people often make mistakes by trying to experience higher beings, or God, for instance, with their physical senses. Needless to say, one has to transcend to higher frequency to perceive higher beings. That's why scientists sometimes disregard God—because they cannot touch, feel, or see God with their physical senses. In science everything has to be physically proven or perceived. Many scientists, on the other hand, can perceive God all the same because they can transcend into a higher frequency—the source, nirvana, vortex, or gap, whatever you want to call it.

On the other hand, human experience works best at 50/50. To reach nirvana and stay in touch with human experiences at the same time can send your body into a convulsion. That's why a process of meditation is so important. You gradually transcend into nirvana. The reason why a human experience works best at 50/50 is that it's the perfect balance of the material human world and the spiritual world. You have 50 percent positive (nirvana) energy to receive things and 50 percent negative (material) energy to spend those things. All the material things are descended from the virtual world.

This brings us to the question, who Mrs. Griffiths really is?

Chapter 5

HOW MAACULLA AQUIRED THIS ABILITY

Mrs. Griffiths was doing all the talking. Saad was listening most of the time. But sometimes he couldn't help being curious, and he asked Mrs. Griffiths, "How come you can see the spirits while no one else can? And how did you develop this ability?"

She said, "I'm glad you're asking the right questions, Saad. That's why I like you so much. It shows that you're thinking and not just listening." Then she explained, "I've always had that ability because it runs in our family. Once someone acquires this amazing ability, it continues in the family for generations until one becomes childless. The following history will explain how all this began."

WHO IS MRS. GRIFFITHS, A.K.A. MAACULLA?

It all began in 1369. One of her ancestors, Richard Earl of Arundel, was appointed lieutenant governor of Portsmouth. Her home was at Albert Road (Saad's restaurant was at 16 Albert Road), South Sea (a subsection of Portsmouth), which used to be called Wish Lane. King Edward III was the king of England then. England had been at war with France for years. France had burned down Portsmouth in 1338, before Richard Earl was appointed as the lieutenant governor, or caretaker of Portsmouth. During his time, it happened three more times—in 1369, 1377, and 1380. After these horrible experiences, Richard feared the French king, Phillip IV, and his reprisal. He was also under pressure by his own king to find a solution to protect Portsmouth from this cruel French king's attacks. Fearing the French and his own king, he resorted to some supernatural power for help.

RICHARD MEETS THE PINK WITCH

Richard secretly found out about a powerful witch called the Pink Witch of Portsmouth, who lived on top of a mountain in one of the remotest areas of Portsmouth. One side of this mountain was facing the sea, with a ninety-degree elevation. The other side was more approachable from the land but was still a very treacherous climb. One had to be extremely strong and fit. Although he never had any training as a mountain climber, he was a fit, strong twenty-six-year old and a trained soldier. He had only two options: either this or face the fate of continued reprisal by the French king. Early one Sunday morning, he decided to set out on the long, arduous journey to meet the Pink Witch on the top of the mountain. Eventually, when he set his eyes on her, he thought that she was the ugliest person he could ever imagine. John Merrick, the Elephant Man, was handsome compared to her. Pieces of flesh kept falling as she moved. Her hair was almost nonexistent. Her eyes were closed in, and she could barely see through them. Her nose was elongated like a beak, with a constant drip. One ear was larger than the other. Blisters constantly appeared on her face and popped on their own, discharging a greenish-yellow mist and pus, along with an awful smell. She looked as if someone had boiled her alive. No one could invent ugliness like this, even if they tried. The smell that surrounded her was so bad that it was difficult to breathe inside the cave. But Richard was desperate for help. He wrapped a thick scarf around his face to prevent the unpleasant odor from over powering him. She was extremely conscious of her own appearance, and during his visit she remained behind a screen, as she usually did.

The rueful Pink Witch explained that once she had been a beautiful witch. She had been the most beautiful witch of all. She used to smell like rose petals. But her beauty became her curse. One of the warlocks, Adonai, fell in love with her when he first laid his eyes on her. Unfortunately, he was the lover of the jealous Green Witch of the Isle of Wight. She was also one of the most powerful witches of all. When she found out about his affection for the Pink Witch, she became outraged. She blamed her for encouraging his affection. She confronted her lover, but he was madly in love with the Pink Witch. In that part of the world, unlike female witches, the warlocks came in only two colors, white or black. They were very mild mannered, kind, and gentle. He happened to be a black warlock and was famous for his kindness and mild character. Black warlocks were also very passionate lovers. The warlocks didn't do any work in the witches' world. It was the women witches who did all the work and had all the power. Adonai could not do anything to help the Pink Witch. The Green Witch was much more powerful than he was. But he refused to let the Pink Witch go from his mind. Then the Green Witch put a curse on all the beautiful young witches within a thousand-mile radius to be ugly and smelly so that no warlocks would ever desire them or even go near them. The Pink Witch also felt responsible for the fate of the rest of the young witches within a thousand square miles. They didn't deserve to suffer for her own unfortunate circumstance.

THE PINK WITCH'S ADVICE

The Pink Witch agreed to help Richard on one condition. It turned out that she also needed Richard's help. If she could travel a thousand miles from there, her curse would dissipate. She would turn into a beautiful woman again. This also could be the salvation for rest of the young witches too. Because once Pink's curse was over, it would also be the salvation for witches within a thousand square miles. Richard was desperate, and he was also a good-hearted person, so he agreed to help her, not knowing what he was getting involved with.

The Pink Witch of Portsmouth's advice didn't come without a challenge. She advised him that he needed to be born again of a virgin to acquire certain power to be able to beat the French king's army. The virgin would have to conceive him with his own sperm. But she needed to remain a virgin during conception and during the period of the pregnancy, similar to the Virgin Mary. Only this would be in the absence of divine intervention. The virgin pregnancy was needed because the energy transfer would take place during the birth of the baby. Instead of the normal 50/50, the virgin would retain 90 percent of the positive energy, and the baby would consist of 90 percent of the negative energy. The 10/90 ratio would allow him to remain human and at the same time able to perform superhuman tasks, similar to Dracula. Although the baby would be born with a separate body, it would be like an extension of Richard himself in every which way. Also, because the sperm would be Richard's, the baby would grow up to be always under his control. The baby's virgin mother would also share this connection to him with the same invisible umbilical cord. In other words, all three of them would always remain very close to one another, with their superhuman abilities. They would always be loyal to one another in every sense, and they would be able to communicate with one another telepathically.

She informed him that the only people in the world who had knowledge of this sort were the practitioners of Tantric Kama Sutra in

India. This place was situated a few thousand miles away in the province of Ajanta, India. He was exhilarated to know of this possibility for a moment. But his enthusiasm became subdued in the same breath with the prospect of travelling to India. In those days, travelling that distance was extremely hard, if not impossible. Richard knew India lay in the east. The only transportation was by sea, and it would take a long time to travel there and back.

Chapter 6

RICHARD MUST FIND A WAY TO GO TO INDIA

Richard was desperate. He agreed to take the ugly, smelly Pink Witch with him to India. She didn't look pink in any sense. At this moment, he himself had no clue how he was going to go to India. On the flip side, Richard was quite spiritual with a winning mentality, and he accepted every moment as it occurred. He also believed that however impossible the journey ahead seemed, he could set his own course by changing the feeling to good deep inside his gap (mind). Every problem was an opportunity in disguise. The universe would find a way for him. Right now he would put 50 percent of his energy (faith) on the prospect of success. For a human, a 50/50 ratio is the best way to achieve one's goal. It is not wise to involve ego in this equation by being overly optimistic—50 percent keeps the balance.

It was in the Pink Witch's best interests to go as far away as possible from there because if she was able to reach a distance of thousand miles, her curse would be over and she would turn back into a beautiful woman and would look and smell like delicate rose petals again, thereby also helping the other young witches within a thousand miles who were suffering the same fate. India would be a good distance for that purpose. So this was an ideal opportunity for Richard and the Pink Witch equally. It was mysterious, to say the least, how the universe put people in need together to solve all of their problems in one single event. In order for that event to be realized, one needed to allow the universe to act accordingly.

OPPORTUNITY COMES IN THE DISGUISE OF ADVERSITY

In the meantime, King Phillip's cousin Robert Artois of France, who was his enemy, escaped from France and was harbored by King Edward III of England. He stayed in Portsmouth at the request of the king to advise Richard Earl and to witness the damage that the French had done to Portsmouth. Robert was advising Richard on how to protect Portsmouth from such future attacks. Both Richard and Robert were the same age, twenty-six. They became close friends in no time.

Fortunately, Robert was also an inventor, a hot-air balloonist, and an expert navigator. He refused King Phillip's order to train the prisoners for this kamikaze mission of attacking Portsmouth. He was using Robert's invention, the hot air balloons, to burn down Portsmouth. The pilot of each balloon would crash the balloon over houses and buildings in Portsmouth, thus setting fire to them. He was deliberately sending death-row prisoners on these suicide missions. The prisoners were asked to volunteer for this kind of suicide mission or face the guillotine. Many of them would volunteer because it was better than the guillotine; also, there was a slim prospect of escaping. Incidentally, all of a sudden there was an increase of death-row prisoners in France. Robert believed this was an act of inhumane cruelty because the king was deliberately sentencing more prisoners to the guillotine to serve his purpose. Robert had invented this hot-air balloon for future transportation for the people of the world to travel to distant countries. He refused to help the king to use his balloons for this purpose anymore. The king was furious and imprisoned Robert.

One day, Robert disguised himself as one of the kamikaze pilots and escaped to England via Portsmouth. He landed the balloon instead of firebombing Portsmouth and met Richard. He surrendered to Richard, who was the lieutenant governor of Portsmouth. King Edward III was pleased with Richard for capturing Robert. After talking to the prisoner, they realized that he was the cousin of King Phillip IV of France, an enemy of his. He had just escaped from jail, in disguise as a kamikaze balloonist.

With this knowledge, Robert became a royal guest instead of a prisoner. He also disclosed many of Phillip's secret plans, which made him very valuable and popular with King Edward III. He swore to beat the crazy King Phillip one day and vowed to bring peace between France and England. He intended to do that without any bloodshed, by raising the people's awareness. He believed there was much more to gain by having peace between countries than wasting resources and lives in wars and conflicts. King Edward was thoroughly impressed by this young man and his visionary beliefs. Robert earned the king's trust in no time. He was free to roam around England anywhere and anytime he desired. Robert took advantage of this freedom to study the English culture and meet English people. He was an advocate of new cultures, new people, new inventions, and so on.

Richard came back from seeing the witch with mixed feelings. At the same time, he felt a tiny flame of hope deep in his heart. When that happened, he always left the possibilities to the unknown, meaning the universe. He was trying to figure out a quicker way to travel to India. The universe already knew the answer. Also, he needed to be back from the journey before King Edward discovered his absence. At the same time, he was worried that King Phillip of France would find another way of attacking Portsmouth soon. So he couldn't be away from Portsmouth too long. Going by ship was out of the question. It would take too long to go there and back.

Phillip's incursions on Portsmouth were due to the fact that it was one of the most lucrative and popular ports at the time in the whole of Europe. It was Richard's job to protect Portsmouth and its people from this mayhem. Even though Robert was advising him and they had been somewhat successful in protecting Portsmouth, he needed to find a way to permanently stop this aggression. The only way he could do it was by using a devilish power the Pink Witch had suggested to destroy another devil. So far, he had never shared his secret plan with anyone.

Richard and Robert sat down to eat their dinner that night.

Richard said, hesitantly, "Robert, we have not known each other for a long time, but I feel that I can trust you as a friend."

"Sure, Richard. I trusted you with my life when I landed my balloon in Portsmouth, and you've never let me down."

"In that case, I need your advice on this. I have an incredible plan to stop Phillip's aggression for good. It would require that I travel to India to fulfill it."

Richard explained to Robert the whole plan that had been laid out by the Pink Witch. He also mentioned that right then, the only way he could go there was by ship, and it would require some travel on land as well. It would take too long. King Edward might find out about his absence, and he didn't want to make the king angry by being absent in this time of imminent attacks.

Robert thought for a few minutes. Then he got up from his chair, bowed, and said, "I am at your service, Sir Richard." He had a big smirk on his face.

31

Richard watched his gesture and smiled back. "Whatever do you mean, Robert?"

"What did Phillip use to attack Portsmouth?"

Richard grew excited. "Do you mean to use a balloon for our transportation to India?"

"Yes. Originally I invented it to travel to distant lands. My cousin, King Phillip IV, decided to use it as a weapon. Let us use his own weapon against him. The only alternative to travelling by ship and land is to travel by hot-air balloon. I have the ideal balloon for it, too. I used King Phillip's largest balloon for my escape. And we have it here in Portsmouth. It also has enough fuel to go to India and back. I can train you to fly and navigate. He did us a favor by sending his biggest balloon to commit arson on Portsmouth."

"That's a great idea," Richard said. "Funny how the universe plans the future by putting two people together through adversity. We can't comprehend its plan. But are you sure it will fly that far?"

"I'm sure. I invented it for transportation for everyone. To prove it, I made many trips to Bulgaria, near the border of Turkey, and back. It's only a few stops more to India. Yes, I'm sure it can be done, and fast. When Phillip wanted to use it for his evil plan, that's where our disagreement began."

Richard was excited. "I knew the universe would never let me down." He got up and hugged Robert.

Robert said, "Richard, I must warn you, though. It's not as simple as it sounds. I have to make a map, plan a route, and study the weather. You have to learn all that too."

"Let's start tomorrow."

Chapter 7

ROBERT TRAINS RICHARD TO FLY THE BALLOON

The next day Robert started to train Richard in how to operate the balloon and to navigate. During training, he realized that it would be advantageous for him to go far away from King Phillip IV, because there had already been a couple of attempts on his life. Robert was quite a flamboyant character. He liked his drink and was a womanizer. King Phillip IV knew that. That was why he had sent a beautiful woman agent. But Robert was way ahead of his game. He had a good time with the woman, and in the morning, he handed her over to the guards hogtied. The woman was pleading for mercy and swore to be loyal to him. But Robert was no fool. He didn't want to leave an enemy lurking around, especially when she had been apprehended with her vindictive plans. Searching her, they discovered weapons and poison in her possession. The English guards took her away, and she was awaiting execution the next morning. In England, they used public hanging for death sentences, unlike the guillotine in France.

King Phillip was famous for his cruelty, and he continued attacks on Portsmouth, simply because he could and at the same time with the hope of capturing Portsmouth, the busiest port in Europe. It could be quite lucrative. Robert had never supported King Phillip for his unnecessary warfare, greed, and killing. He had been very vocal about it. He believed making friends with neighboring countries and cultural exchange was better for trade and prosperity. This was the way to the future. He was a strong advocate of peace. The majority of French people agreed with him but were afraid to oppose King Phillip IV.

At that moment, he had nothing to do in England other than just be a royal guest in the palace. Occasionally he would advise the English against the recurring attacks of his cousin. Any chance to see and explore a new country, their culture, and their women was tempting for him. He proposed accompanying Richard on his secret adventure to India. If anything, it was advantageous for Richard too. First of all, they wouldn't have to waste time in training. He could learn as they travelled. It would also be good to have an expert navigator and an expert pilot on board the balloon. Richard was no fool. He agreed instantaneously.

So now there were three people on the gondola of the balloon, including the Pink Witch. This was not a problem because the balloon could easily lift up to ten people. The other advantage of this particular balloon was that King Phillip had originally ordered it sent because it was the biggest balloon—the purpose being that when they crashed the balloon in Portsmouth, there would be enough fuel to set fire to entire town centre. Previously, the small balloons had done minimal damage. The plan was to send the largest balloon to attack Portsmouth in order to do maximum damage to the town. At that time the dwellings in Portsmouth were wooden structures with thatched roofs. They burned very easily. On the other hand, it was easy to replace them. But little did Phillip know that his biggest weapon would help his enemies rather than destroy them as he intended. The large balloon would travel far, with enough fuel to go to India and back. The big balloon also travelled faster in the wind than the smaller ones. They needed to be back before King Edward III found out that they were missing. At the same time, they needed to stay in Ajanta, India, long enough to be trained in Tantric Kama Sutra. So time was of the essence.

Robert explained to Richard that the best time to leave would be on the first of January, when the wind current was easterly, towards India. In three months, in March, they would have to catch the westerly wind to bring them back to Portsmouth. It was also very good timing because King Edward always visited Bristol during Christmas and the New Year.

Now all the plans were ready. They loaded the fuel on the gondola, along with enough water and food for three people to last the journey. Lieutenant Governor Richard had appointed guards to protect the balloon twenty-four hours a day until their departure, in case of any unexpected dangers while they were waiting to leave. Only a handful of people were involved and had knowledge of this project. It was important to keep it a secret. Most of the king's armies in Portsmouth had no knowledge of this adventure. In those days, everything was done secretly and on a need-to-know basis. One never knew who was going to betray whom and when.

There were only seven days left before the January 1 departure. Richard had to secure the whole of Portsmouth in case of attack by the French while they were away. He was making sure that the man in charge was the right person and capable of handling and protecting Portsmouth. With Robert's advice, several watchtowers had been built to watch for any such attack from land, sea or air. They were on guard twenty-four hours a day. Only a handful of Richard's trusty commanders were aware of his journey to India. The safety of Portsmouth lay in their hands.

Robert was a very clever navigator. He had already drawn a map of the route to India. They would have to avoid flying over France, for obvious reasons. Instead they would travel over Germany. Then the Czech Republic, Hungary, Romania, Bulgaria, Turkey, Armenia, Iran, Afghanistan, Sindh province (Pakistan), and then to their final destination in India. Ajanta was near Bombay, or Mumbai, in the province of Maharastra. (Recent names are used here so that the reader can relate to the route, as many names have been changed since the fourteenth century.) The distance they would have to travel was about 4,500 miles. Robert was already familiar with the route up to Turkey, which was only one more stop from Bulgaria. He had never travelled as far India before. He was always interested in knowing and exploring new lands, new cultures, and new people. He was a very modern and forward thinker for his time. He believed in exchanging knowledge and cultures rather than weapons. That was the fundamental difference between him and his cousin King Phillip IV.

Chapter 8

THE BALLOON TAKES OFF LIKE A BIRD IN THE SKY

On the first day of January, everything was ready to go. They had the fuel, water, and food loaded on the gondola. The only problem was the smell. The Pink Witch's odor was like a rotten dead body. She wrapped herself up with their help with many layers of clothes, but the smell was still quite strong. The French were famous for their perfumes. Robert used some of his strong perfumed oil on a couple of silk scarves and wrapped them over their own faces, covering their noses. This way they could only smell the perfume, thus defusing the bad smell up to 90 percent. He offered one scarf to Pink. But she said she had become used to the smell. She used some perfumed oil over her outer wrap, thereby further reducing the bad smell so that they wouldn't get hit by it so badly. Yet another problem was solved with Robert's ingenuity.

Early in the morning of January 1, they planned to take off before anybody woke up. They deliberately picked that time to fly for secrecy reasons. They kept the balloon in a large barn, out of sight of onlookers. This area was also very private. There were only a few people around at any given time of the day. The night before, they brought the Pink Witch into the barn so that early in the morning they could fly off without being noticed. Also, the sight of the balloon in the sky might stir up panic among the people of Portsmouth. They might assume that they were being attacked by the French again.

The huge balloon covered the skies of Portsmouth momentarily as it filled with hot air from the furnace. The ground crew untied the balloon from the anchor simultaneously. This had been rehearsed many times during the training sessions with Robert. It was one of the crucial moments when the balloon lifted off. It must maintain its equilibrium. Otherwise everyone and everything would be thrown from the gondola. Robert used sandbags as weights for balancing the gondola and special knots that could be unhitched simultaneously. It took off like a bird in the sky and reached the altitude of thousand feet in no time. This was what he had been hoping to achieve. They didn't want to hover over Portsmouth too long, in case it drew too much attention.

Robert was very busy navigating towards the northeast, to avoid France. Their first stop would be Germany. They planned to travel through the daylight time and go as far as they could before nightfall. They estimated that if they travelled eight hours per day, they should reach Ajanta, India, in ten to fifteen days, give or take a couple of days, depending on the wind speed. They had to take into consideration the possibility of facing stormy weather on the way, which might delay their journey a day or two. Also, some parts of Europe might have some snow or rain at this time of the year. When they reached Asia, they calculated that the weather should be pretty good until the summer monsoon began there in May. They would have plenty of time to get back before the winter season in Europe. Prior to leaving Ajanta, they would have intense training of Tantric Kama Sutra for twenty-eight days. They didn't have a day to waste lazing around. Robert might not have time to explore any other parts of India.

THE TRANSFORMATION OF PINK

They arrived at the border of Romania after passing through Germany, the Czech Republic, and Hungary. All of a sudden, they noticed a strong but delicate smell of roses overpowering the atmosphere. They assumed that they must be approaching a large rose-growing field. It was getting dark, so they decided to land on an open field. They would camp there until the next morning. Then they would continue on their journey early the next morning. They were busy preparing to eat dinner. The smell of roses was still very potent. It was a pleasant break from the smell they had been carrying with them all this time.

Robert said, "There must be a rose-growing field very close to here."

Richard said, "Good. I wish it would be like this for the rest of the way."

"But I don't remember smelling it the last few times I came this way."

"Whatever! We don't have to wear the scarf over our noses, at least for now."

They sat down for dinner. They would normally take some food to the Pink Witch. She was huddled in a corner of the gondola and had wrapped herself with many layers of blankets so that her bad body odor would not affect Robert and Richard. They made a plate of food ready for her. It was Richard's turn to take the food to Pink. Robert was putting some extra perfume on Richard's silk scarf. Then they heard some footsteps, and they both turned around to see who was coming. Their jaws dropped with sheer amazement. A beautiful young girl was standing there in front of them. She was about sixteen or seventeen years old.

Their first thought was, how did she get in the gondola?

She was wearing a beautiful rose-pink chiffon dress and was smiling graciously as she looked at them.

Wow! They were both totally lost for words.

Richard said, under his breath, "Robert, were you expecting anyone?"

Robert whispered back, "No. Are you?"

"Better still, can you see what I see?"

"I see a beautiful girl standing in the middle of our gondola. Who is she?"

"Yes," Richard said, "but can you see how beautiful she is? You can see her, right? I want to make sure I'm not dreaming."

"I must be dreaming. Otherwise, how could this be possible? Let's make sure and pinch each other."

Both were rubbing their eyes. They were trying to make sure that what they were observing was for real.

Richard said, "I can feel your pinch, Robert. She's for real!"

"I know. Let's find out. Who are you, and how did you get in the gondola?"

The gondola's walls were quite high. No one could get inside without a ladder. She just kept smiling broadly. Her overpowering beauty hypnotized them both. Could a girl be so beautiful? Her soft, pink, delicate skin was so radiant, it was glowing in the dusk light. Her shapely waistline and her belly, exposed up to her breasts, was as smooth as pink rose petals. The matching delicate rose-pink chiffon dress she wore looked like the floating wings of an angel blowing gently in the breeze. Her luscious, darker-pink lips contrasted with her pearly white teeth every time she smiled. Her periwinkle-blue eyes resembled two twinkling stars in the sky. It seemed as though the entire blue sky was captured and concentrated into her eyes.

They couldn't believe what they were witnessing. They kept staring at her with utter amazement. Also, the smell of roses was even more potent now. They had no doubt then that she must be the source of that delicate rose fragrance.

She stood there in the dusk light as a fuzzy, dreamy, delicate glow of light in half transparency and half reality. Dare not disturb the wind, in case it blows it away. They were dumbfounded by her presence. The girl realized that they were in shock.

Then she gently asked, "Don't you recognize me, Richard?"

They both shook their heads. "No."

As she spoke, it sounded like music coming out of her mouth. It didn't sound like the ugly witch's voice, which had been croaky and unpleasant. It was more like the enchanting, gentle, breathy sound of the ancient Japanese flute shakuhachi, soothing and magical.

She asked, "May I sit down? I'm really hungry. I hope you got some food for me."

They both stood up simultaneously to make room for her and nodded. "Yes."

As they sat again, they bumped into each other. They immediately composed themselves and pointed at her to sit down. They were both still lost for words. They forgot to take the food to Pink. They handed over the plate they made for her, and she started eating. Both of them kept staring at her as if they had never seen anyone eating before. "Do angels eat food?"

After she swallowed a couple of bites, she spoke again. "Your cooking is getting better; it's delicious! You know, I used to get this kind of reaction before the Green Witch made me ugly and smelly."

They couldn't believe what they were seeing and hearing. Their eyes almost popped out of their sockets. That couldn't be the same ugly, smelly person they had been carrying as their passenger. They almost forgot the word "ugly." Also, what had happened to her horrible, croaky voice?

"OK, OK, I give up. I'm the Pink Witch, your passenger."

They found it hard to get their heads around the fact that she was the same person. They made grunting sounds of disbelief at the same time.

Pink said, "Sooner or later you will have to actually speak to me. I am the Pink Witch of Portsmouth, gentlemen. We must have passed a thousand miles. I changed into my normal appearance as soon as we were a thousand miles away from Portsmouth. The curse is no longer affecting me."

They said at the same time, "Normal appearance! But you're so beautiful!"

"That's a good start. For a minute I thought both of you had lost your tongues. Now let's finish eating, and then we'll talk. I'm still hungry. You must be hungry too. I know it's a big shock to see me like this."

She continued eating. They slowly and cautiously and silently started to eat.

After they finished, Pink announced: "We need to take a rest. I'm going to throw away those smelly old clothes." She made a gesture. "I won't be needing them anymore. My curse is over for good. Thank you for the delicious dinner. Good night, gentlemen."

She went to her side of the gondola. They put all the rest of the food away. Richard took a glass of water to her.

Pink said, "Thank you, Richard, and thank you for bringing me along with you. I owe you my life." She tossed the smelly bundle of clothes over the side of the gondola—she was unusually strong for a girl.

Richard quietly said, "You're welcome. It was our pleasure to bring you. Thank you for coming." He had never thought he would say that to the smelly witch.

"She must be tired," Robert said. "Let's all go to bed. We have a big day ahead."

"Thank you, Robert, for making this journey possible," Pink said. "Otherwise, I would still be a smelly witch. I couldn't have imagined anybody would even take me aboard, let alone bring me this far. Good night."

She lay down on her bed and covered herself with a blanket. She blinked her big periwinkle lotus eyes a couple of times, and then she closed them. It seemed as if someone had turned off the light and magically all the blues had been restored back to the sky, because the blue in her eyes was so intense that one couldn't notice any other blues when her eyes were open.

Then she said, "We'll speak tomorrow if I still look like this." She giggled without opening her eyes.

They looked worried. Richard said, "We could stay here and make sure everything is all right."

Pink opened her eyes again and looked at their worried faces. "Don't worry. I'm never going to change again. The curse works only once. I am immune to it now. This is the first time I am going to sleep on a fresh bed without any smell after a long time. You know what I mean. You have a lot of questions, and I have a lot to say. We will have plenty of time from tomorrow. Good night, loves. Thank you again."

They said in unison, "Good night, Pink. We love you too."

They went back to their side of the gondola. They both lay on their backs, speechless. Was she for real? As they gazed at the twinkling stars in the background of the dark-blue sky, their entire perspective changed. Everything looked so beautiful all of a sudden. The air smelled so fresh and good. They still could not believe their own eyes—or noses, for that matter. All the stress and anxiety of the journey had disappeared suddenly. What had just happened? It must had been a miracle.

Both were saying, silently in their minds, "Thank you, Pink, for giving the sky back the blue. The stars are smiling in gratitude."

They must had fallen asleep at some point, but quite late. They woke up to the gentle sound of someone moving around the gondola. They both sat up abruptly. It was Pink. She was wearing a deep-periwinkle-blue dress that matched her blue eyes. Again they were speechless and paralyzed by her beauty. It hadn't been a dream last night, then? She couldn't be a witch. Not even a human. She must be an angel. Only angels could be that beautiful.

"Good morning, gentlemen," she said. "You know, I can hear your thoughts." Then she said, in a hurt tone, "No, I am not an angel. I'm a witch. Witches are beautiful creatures too, until..." She choked up. "Well, some of them."

41

She insisted on making breakfast for them. They all sat down for breakfast after a quick wash.

Richard said, "You needn't bother making breakfast for us. We could make it for you."

"You've been taking care of me all this time when I really needed it. I owe you both. You took care of me when I was ugly and smelly without any hesitation, prejudice, or judgment. I'm really grateful to you both. Please allow me to pay my debt a little. Let me do my share of work now that I can. Really, I owe you both for my life."

"Thank you, Pink," Robert said. "You'll probably make a better breakfast than we would, anyway."

Richard said, "I can cook because I had training in the army."

"I'm French," Robert said. "We all cook, but you cook better. I can tell from the smell."

Pink said, "Thank you, Robert. French people are good at smelling food, wine, and perfumes. I apologize for my smell before. It must have been agonizing for both of you."

"It's nothing that we couldn't handle," Richard said. "But thank you. You know what they say: there is a purpose for everything that happens to us."

Robert said, "You're a very sensitive person."

Pink let them know that she also had recovered all of her witch's powers. She could forecast the weather and foresee any danger approaching with her higher vibration. She told them that some farmers were coming. They might not be very nice people. After all, this was their land they had landed on.

They ate their breakfast quickly and took off. They could see some men on horseback arriving as soon as they were out of reach. The men were curious about the bundle of clothes Pink had left behind. As soon as they went near that, they started to react to the smell. Even the horses went out of control because they could sense the presence of a witch in her clothes. That was exactly what Pink had intended, in case they were delayed in taking off.

They could also see from a distance that the men were running away from the smelly clothes she had left behind. They laughed.

Pink said, "Aren't you glad you don't have to put up with those anymore? It's their turn now. Poor men."

They all laughed again.

Pink said, "Thank you, gentlemen, for putting up with me all this time."

"It wasn't that bad," Richard said. "The universe never gives us something we can't handle."

"It's certainly worth it," Robert said. "The truth is, I would have done this just for your sake, Pink."

"So would I," Richard said. "Yes, it is definitely worth it."

They both looked at her with admiration.

"We'll celebrate at the next stop, Bulgaria, with a glass of wine," Richard said. "I hear that their wine is almost as good as French wine."

"Almost as good, but that will do," Robert said.

They were heading towards Bulgaria, bearing with the southeasterly wind. The good thing was, they had Pink with them in full force. Before, she had to hide in a bundle of clothes because of her odor. And her appearance was just as unpleasant. They could not land anywhere without fearing that her smell might bother people there. Now she could actively participate in every chore of the journey and use her powers to help out.

There was a beautiful blue sky, and the balloon was travelling at full speed on the southeasterly wind. It looked like a red lantern in the dawn light. It matched the crimson colour of the eastern sky at dawn. The sun was breaking out slowly. It was observing the balloon with admiration—the possibilities were endless only if the intelligence of men was utilized positively. It turned the whole eastern sky a crimson red, matching the color of the balloon, as if to say welcome.

Pink was standing at the edge, holding the eastern wall of the gondola, against the background of the sky, where the sky was separated from blue to a gradually deeper crimson below. Thus creating a gradient effect in the sky. Her blue dress, blue eyes, pink skin, and deep-pink luscious lips resembled all the colours of the sky at that moment. It was difficult to say who was emulating whose beauty. Both Pink and the sky looked equally and naturally beautiful since Pink had transformed herself from the ugliest, smelliest being on earth to the most beautiful woman they ever could lay their eyes upon. Only one word can describe her beauty: *heavenly*. Heaven was certainly complimenting her by imitating her beauty.

Saad's grandfather once told him that you can even find a lotus blossom in a pile of cow dung. What he meant was that the way you look at things changes the way you are looking at it. You can observe the possibility either way. In other words, you can find beauty in everything you look at or vice versa. This lotus had blossomed for Richard and Robert from the most horrible atrocity committed by the Green Witch. They were glad to be a part of it. Their kindness was certainly appreciated by Pink. She would do anything in her power to fulfill their dreams. The universe had designed this world in a way that we can fulfill our dreams for one another only if we accept one another without prejudice or judgment, with love. It was like natural symbiosis.

At the end of the day, they landed in Bulgaria, at the border of Turkey. They landed on a beautiful green field near a winery. It was dusk, and a few of the winery workers were on their way back home from their daily tasks at the vineyard. They were curious to see what had landed in the field. In Europe, almost everyone spoke and understood French. Robert introduced Pink, Richard, and himself to the owner of the winery, Ivan Draganova, and his young wife, Aneliya. Robert presented a bottle of French wine to them. The owner saw the royal seal on the bottle and immediately bowed to Robert. He told Robert that some years when they got exceptionally good vintage grapes, they sold the wine to the French royal family. But now, because of the war, he was afraid to travel to France. Robert informed him that he was on a secret mission and would rather keep this between themselves. But he would be happy to accept his hospitality for the night. They enjoyed a delicious Bulgarian dinner prepared by the owner's wife—banitsa and yogurt. They drank a couple of bottles of fine Bulgarian wine between them and went to bed. They planned to leave very early at dawn.

THE BALLOON LANDS IN AJANTA, INDIA

At the break of dawn, after a typical Bulgarian breakfast consisting of fruits, yogurt, fresh farm eggs, and cheese, they lifted off from Bulgaria. A southeasterly wind took them towards Turkey, and then to Iran. Their next stops were Afghanistan, Sind province (Pakistan), and then Ajanta, India. In ancient times, this was all undivided India. These were friendly countries, whose cultures had

44

existed for centuries. Robert knew that. He used diplomacy to get cooperation from these highly cultured countries. He told them they were on a historical mission, in search of different advanced cultures. With his diplomacy, Richard's cautiousness, and Pink's power, they safely arrived at their destination, Ajanta. An entire horseshoe-shaped mountainside had been carved to create a series of temples from a single rock. From afar they resembled caves. They landed their balloon on a clearing just above the Ajanta temples. From there it was only a few hundred feet down the hill to the main temple.

These temples were made by cutting the hard granite rock on the mountainside. Even with today's technologies and tools, it would take many thousands of years to complete a project like that. Some theorize about the intervention of some alien technology unknown to man that made it possible to build buildings with such precision and exquisite architecture and detailed with paintings and carvings. It would be impossible to cut granite with their primitive, unsophisticated tools, let alone the carving of the artwork with fine details on the walls of each temple. The caves covered an entire mountainside. It is difficult to believe that they carved out thirty full-size temples from one single mountain of rock. To add even more infiniteness to the subject, these temples were carved out starting from the top of the building downward.

Although it's just speculation, some historians believe the Buddhist monks began to build these caves in the second century, during the Satavahana dynasty, and it took over seven centuries to complete fifteen temples out of thirty.

Image 2. Horseshoe Mountain in Ajanta.

Thirty temples were carved altogether, out of which fifteen were not finished. Some caves were used for the monks' living quarters; they were called viharas (monasteries) and were furnished with stone beds and stone pillows. The others were Buddhist cathedrals called the Chaityas (caves 9, 10, 19, 26, and 29), and they were used for worship. All of the finished caves were decorated with intricate sculptures and murals depicting the many incarnations of Buddha.

They met with the high priest in the centre main temple. Richard offered him some gold coins as a donation to the temple. Donations were always welcome, but they taught all the knowledge of the Kama Sutra and the Yoga Sutra for free. This love-awakening art was taught to the serious students only. The high priest was very pleased. He was an unusually tall man with a close-shaved head. He wore nothing but an orange dhoti (cloth). His muscular, athletic body was the result of many years of yoga practice—a perfect model of a men for Leonardo da Vinci's art. It was obvious that he took his practice very seriously.

They were taken to their rooms in one of the Viharas temples. These rooms had no furniture, only stone walls. There were statues and statuettes carved on the walls. There were no doors or windows. Three wooden khat (beds) were brought in. They were similar to

46

futons, but without mattresses. They looked more uncomfortable than they actually were. There were two choices: either that or the stone beds and stone pillows. After the long journey, they fell asleep as soon as they hit the khats. Amazingly, they forgot about how hard and uncomfortable the wooden khat beds were.

The high priest planned to meet them in the main centre temple at dawn.

Image 3. Ajanta Temples by the Waghora River.

Chapter 9

THE TEACHINGS OF THE HIGH PRIEST (Maha Guru)
Early at dawn the high priest himself came to wake them up. After a quick bathroom trip, he took them to the Waghora River for sun salutation and bathing. After that, their training would start at the main temple. Then they would be taken to the first cave temple for further instructions. The lessons were carved into the walls of each temple as figures and statuettes depicting different sexual positions. That began with kellie (teasing), a means of foreplay, but there was a difference. Unlike normal foreplay confined to the bedroom, kellie could begin in any place, such as in a garden, in a restaurant, during shopping, at a party, in a living room, or in any other place. Couples can discretely hint to each other. Only they would know their secret signs. That could start with singing, dancing, or just playing around, gradually touching each other's entire body, thus arousing the whole body for sexuality. To an onlooker it may seem a normal act of playing around.

There were no written instructions there. They were done with action figures and drawings so that no one would have to translate it—it was an international language. Each temple depicted a different lesson (or suggestion). Every day they would be trained in a different temple until twenty-eight temples were visited, depicting twenty-eight pages of a book. This was a whole month of training. It was similar to today's videos, only without moving pictures. The Maha Guru would act out the actual positions. They must have been very visual, skillful, and knowledgeable people who created these instructions with carvings and drawings. They knew that one day people would come from all over the world to study these. A written language can be limiting and inhibiting in that sense. Even today's digital recordings might not have lasted this long. They were visionaries.

On the other hand, the sexual urge is not just meant for pleasure and propagation. More on that later. Maaculla had already explained to Saad that transgender people were not freaks of nature; they could be the future rendering of human evolution. Everything happens for a purpose and a plan. That is to say that the universe does not make any mistakes. Maybe in the distant future, a couple will decide who will conceive and bear their babies. It was unfair to think that only the female or just one partner had the responsibility for carrying out this major act of propagation. This would make her the weaker partner. Maybe nature was slowly introducing another alternative—that is to say, the man should equally share this responsibility too. For that reason, she mentioned that in the future, we may see more and more transgender, or rather bi-gender, people born for that purpose. Both of the partners will share the responsibility for carrying their babies.

That brought them to the other aspects of their journey. Now Richard strived to acquire superhuman powers. He needed to be able to end the attacks by defeating Phillip IV of France. He planned to do that without any bloodshed. There had been enough suffering and loss on both sides. It would defeat the whole purpose if he were to continue the same barbaric acts of war. Robert also believed in the same principles of peace without bloodshed.

According to Pink's advice, Richard would have to impregnate a virgin without destroying her hymen—similar to the Virgin Mary, only in this instance without the intervention of divine power. She would remain a virgin during the length of her pregnancy. As a result, the energy transfer would take place during the birth, and the baby would be born with 90/10 ratio of energy. That would give him extraordinary human ability, as opposed to normal human beings, who had a 50/50 ratio of negative and positive energy. This energy transfer would not be possible without the presence of hymen. For Richard's requirements, it was also important to have an energy ratio of 10/90 in favor of the negative. That power would remain with the boy until the age of twelve. Richard would have access to his son's superhuman power, and they would have plenty of time to achieve their goals. Also, during the energy transfer, the mother would receive the remaining 90/10 in favor of positive energy so that the energy equation would remain balanced. The mother, though, would permanently retain her 90/10 ratio in favor of positive. She would have extraordinary power to do only positive things in her life. Thus the first Maaculla would be born.

One needs to meditate silently for one minute for each year of one's age. For instance, Richard and Robert were twenty-six, so they needed to do silent meditation for a minimum of twenty-six minutes each day to recharge their bodies, preferably between four and five in the morning. The technique of meditation was simple. They sat comfortably with their eyes closed, concentrating on their breath, following the breath as it came in and out of their bodies naturally (not forcibly). Their own breath would be their guru. That would guide them to the nirvana, the field of all possibility. Incidentally, in the future, as life got more demanding, they would need more and more meditation. One needs to understand that all things needed to live in this material world were actually brought forth in our world through the field of all possibilities, or the nirvana. Once they lost that contact with the source, their lives would face turmoil.

The purpose of meditation is to charge one's body with cosmic energy. The human body is like a battery. It loses its charge through daily use, such as thinking, working, talking, and so on. During sleep it gets charged, but that is not always enough. That's why it feels tired and inadequate. With meditation it receives maximum cosmic energy, which enters through the head and get distributed throughout the body by naries (nerves). These naries are like the roots of a tree spread throughout every inch of the human body. The body needs to be fully charged for high performance or even to perform the highly demanding daily activities of modern life.

Maha Guru excused Pink from doing meditation if she wished, because he recognized that she was already enlightened with higher vibration. But she insisted on continuing with everyone. She was too humble to receive any special treatment.

The high priest would read the carvings and drawings on each wall and explained the procedure and meaning of each Yoga and Kama Sutra position by acting it out. He himself performed the poses with a partner, but only as pretend.

DANCE OF THE VIRGINS

After meditation, everyone gathered around the main centre temple. The lessons began with the Dance of the Virgins, and about 150 people were attending. They had no idea that many people were attending the course. When they first arrived, it seemed as though they were the only ones there. Now they wondered, where had all these people come from all of a sudden? It seemed as if they had all been hiding somewhere in a secret temple. People came from all over the world—China, Africa, Europe, Japan. The entire main temple was filled with gorgeous girls and boys. The dancers formed a circle around the centre podium of the hall. The maha guru (the high priest) was in the centre of the circle on a slightly raised pedestal. The dance depicted twenty-eight tantric Kama Sutra positions out of sixty-seven. One by one, the dance of the kellie was performed, and then each female partner practiced each position being taught that day with the maha guru. Then each of them practiced with her own partner. That way they learned firsthand from the expert how to properly perform it. The maha guru himself went around to each couple to examine and instruct each of them individually. As he touched each of the boys or the girls, energy magically ran through each of their bodies, transforming him or her to sexually aroused. Their entire bodies were immediately transformed into sexual organs. The purpose of that was to involve the entire body in the sexual act. These acts were for a purpose higher than just sexual pleasure.

Image 4. One of the gifts to Richard from high priest of Ajanta.

Each girl ended her dance with the maha guru as he picked her up and brought her down into an explicit Kama Sutra position. Then he did a different position with her the next day, until twenty-eight positions were completed. As he released her, her original partner picked her up simultaneously and practiced the same position with her. There was no dominant partner in these positions. Each of them had to perform his or her position explicitly in order to be successful.

The high priest explained that these were not meaningless sexual positions and procedures. In ancient times, they were used regularly to transport souls (birth) to this material world. Our bodies were used as vehicles—or portals, as it were—from the higher dimensions. These were not regular births. These procedures were meant for energy transfers for a higher specific purpose. Sometimes assistance was required for following certain procedures correctly and explicitly—twosomes, threesomes, foursomes, and so on. These acts weren't regarded as perversion, as they are in today's ignorant society. In the same way today, we do not regard the birth of a child in a hospital as a perversion or a shameful act. Somewhere along the material journey, we humans lost contact with reality and the possibility of the spirit world. A great deal of knowledge from ancient times has been lost. Because our modern society regards the sexual act as a taboo subject that not to be discussed or practiced openly, the pressures of the modern world have become somewhat of an unbearable burden to modern men and women. Many men and women are too tired to have the greatest pleasure of all, regardless of their choices of partners. But in fact, our bodies were designed to put up with a thousand times more pressure than that of today's living. In the next century or two, if we are to explore interstellar worlds, we need to charge our bodies to their peak performance level. In order to do that, we need to understand our energy and how it can be used to achieve our peak performance level effortlessly. To start with we need to change our derogatory attitude towards sex.

Image 5. The second gift to Richard from the high priest of Ajanta.

For similar reasons, Saad felt ashamed and embarrassed for displaying these paintings of Kama Sutra positions on the walls of his restaurant, Maharaja. At the time, he had no idea what had motivated him to display them. Mrs. Griffiths, a.k.a. Maaculla, explained it to Saad when he felt ashamed of these paintings (which he referred to as rude) of Kama Sutra positions. She explained that these primitive, natural (not perverted) urges still exist in our memories in the akash (our virtual storage). That's the same reason some people act abnormally in sexual acts. In ancient times, they knew these weren't meaningless sexual positions, similar to the way the high priest explained. It pops up in our memory, although we may not realize at the time where this is coming from. Some people also paint or draw pictures similar to these paintings. Other people try to act that way in reality with their sexual partners or wives and husbands. Our modern society regards this as the imagination of erotic perversions and hence taboo. She also explained that there is no such thing as imagination. No one can imagine or invent anything, however exceptional, odd, or outrageous it may seem. It exists somewhere in the universe for a purpose. We sometimes inadvertently tap into this knowledge. Similarly, for the same reason, sometimes you will notice that a deaf and blind person can compose a classical piece of music from virtual memory although he or she is incapable of hearing or seeing.

Image 6. Saad felt embarrassed for these paintings.

Then Mrs. Griffiths asked him, "For instance, what about you, Saad? Had you ever seen any art like this or had any training before you painted *Definition of Humankind*?"

53

Saad admitted that he had never even seen paintings like this in his life, let alone having been trained to paint. He also admitted that he might not be able repeat the same thing again.

She explained to Saad that modern society has moved away from this real knowledge. All the knowledge we have now, so far, and all the knowledge we will have in our lives in the future, is stored in the virtual storage called akash (the sky). The concept of this exceptional knowledge has been neglected. For instance, the Ajanta caves were discovered accidentally. They were totally abandoned and forgotten to the extent that for centuries no one had any idea that these caves ever existed or what they meant to our human existence. Accidentally, in 1819, Ajanta was rediscovered by a mad dog, an Englishman called John Smith, during a tiger-hunting trip. Then Robert Gill visited there 1844 and stayed there until his death. He made life-size copies of the carvings and sent them to England. Unfortunately they were destroyed in a strange and mysterious fire in the Victoria and Albert Museum in London. Some say it was cursed. On the other hand, some say it was a malicious effort to suppress this knowledge.

Chapter 10

WHAT RICHARD NEEDED TO LEARN FROM ALL THIS

What Richard needed to learn there was how to impregnate a female without spoiling her virginity. The right Kama Sutra knowledge was required for that purpose. In other words, her hymen would still be intact after intercourse. This had been done many times over the centuries. On the other hand, many people had acquired this training and had failed to achieve their ambition. It not only required the knowledge of one's own organ (length, angle, and size); one also had to have knowledge of his partner's vagina—most importantly, the size, shape, and placement of the hymen—and the use of Kama Sutra techniques. In the near future, when our science is more advanced, this procedure might be replaced by in vitro fertilization and still keep the hymen intact that way.

Maaculla told Saad, "Incidentally, many other organs in our body, such as appendices, men's prostate glands, and women's hymens, are believed to have no purpose—or at least no one knows what their functions are. The ancients believed that the hymen was a kind of sensor. It is instrumental in energy transfer. That's why when a woman loses her virginity, only then can she fully transcend into her physical womanhood—meaning she embraces carnal pleasure by relinquishing her angelic innocence or purity. In that case, her energy equation will now be 50/50. That also explains the existence and purpose of the hymen in a female body in the first place. Maybe because of this knowledge, the ancients were so insistent on the importance of virginity. To forcefully take someone's virginity was a serious crime in ancient time."

She went on to say, "Moreover, only the female has the responsibility of giving birth to a life and nurturing it. Yet the only variation between the male and female genders is the second sex chromosome XY, male, and XX, female. Think about it. Maybe the time will come when couples will need to decide who will bear the offspring in a relationship. In that case, maybe the bi-gender XXXY are the future rendering of human evolution to come and not a freak of nature, as commonly and ignorantly believed today. In that case, both partners will take turns bearing their offspring. That is to say, everything that we experience in life is happening for a purpose, however odd it may seem to us. The universe is infallible."

That was the main purpose of the existence of the hymen from the pragmatic point of view. During intercourse and throughout the course of pregnancy, the woman would remain pure and virginal from the scientific and physiological point of view. During birth, however, her hymen would be destroyed and the energy transferred. She would absorb 90 percent of the positive energy, and the baby would be born with 90 percent negative energy. This would result in her having angelic (constructive) powers, and the offspring would have devilish (destructive) powers, exactly opposite to each other, and both would remain as humans (Maaculla and Dracula).That was exactly what Richard intended to accomplish. He could then use the baby's destructive strengths to beat the evil king of France, thereby saving Portsmouth and its people from his reprisals. At the same time, he would save the people of France by removing the tyrant from their life. That is to say, the devil fears only devilish powers that are equal to or more powerful than his own—fighting fire with fire. We will learn more about this later on.

SELECTING THE RIGHT PARTNER

Maaculla said, "Females are all different, according to their size and structure. For example, a well-rounded posterior is different from an elongated one. In that case, the placement and size of the vagina and hymen will be different. On the other hand, men also come in different shapes, angles, and sizes. That means one will have to choose a partner according to one's own anatomy. This is a combination of tantric Yoga Sutra and Kama Sutra knowledge, which teaches us to allow our minds to make a natural selection, simply because our inner mind already knows who is the right partner for this purpose. This happens naturally and automatically if only we allow our inner minds to select spontaneously. On the other hand, when we use our outer, ego-based mind, this selection becomes biased with social, religious, and family pressure, or aesthetic dogmas. You will notice when men and women make a natural selection for each other, it might even look odd to onlookers. But this selection might be exactly the right one, satisfying each other's sexual and physiological needs. In other words, beauty is in the eyes of beholder from the scientific point of view, rather than from the social and aesthetic point of view. That is to say, a physical beauty that is proportionate and pleasing to the eyes may not provide satisfaction in sexuality or may not even meet the criteria for one's arousal."

Incidentally, we all know about how the blue-blood disease was manifested in many societies that resisted natural selection and succumbed to family, social, and religious pressures. Then again, animal breeders around the world, especially horse breeders, found out that when they bred their horses from different gene pools, the offspring were healthier, stronger, more resilient to disease, and more intelligent. This has been proven with humans too. A combination of two races breeds more intelligent and healthier offspring. Does this mean that indirectly the universe is coaxing us to mix our DNA with different races? Consequently, we should be seeing more and more mixed marriages among different races in the near future. But first we need to abolish the social stigmas associated with racial prejudices from our minds.

After training, finding the right virgin was another task for Richard. But he was not worried about that for the time being. Right then he had to finish his training and arrive back in Portsmouth before the king found out that he and Robert were missing. That might not be a good situation for them.

Image 7. The centre main temple, carved out of a single rock.

Chapter 11

RICHARD AND ROBERT ARRIVE BACK IN PORTSMOUTH

After four weeks of intense training, they came back to Portsmouth, at the beginning of April. Although the wind was not quite westerly, Robert steered on the right path to Portsmouth with his ingenuity. They were also lucky that King Edward III didn't enquire after them while they were away. Apparently he had been too busy with Easter celebrations in England. They attributed that to Pink. With her magical witch's powers, she had somehow kept him occupied with other business. She decided to stay in Portsmouth and help find the right partner for Richard.

Another phenomenon nobody expected was that hundreds of young girl witches started to come and visit Pink in Portsmouth. Normally witches stayed away from humans. They were all so grateful to her for rescuing them from the bondage of the Green Witch. One by one they also met Richard and Robert. From Robert's point of view, the more girls the better, especially when they were young and beautiful.

The next day Richard and Robert joined a few friends to celebrate the safe journey back to Portsmouth. Naturally, Pink joined them too. Within an hour the entire pub was filled with people. They came from all over Portsmouth. About two hundred young witches came to join Pink. There was no room left inside or outside the pub.

All the young witches expressed their gratitude. At the same time, they all swore to be loyal and helpful to all three of them forever. Richard and Robert now had an army increased to three thousand beautiful young witches at their disposal. During their absence, they were already guarding Portsmouth from any possible attacks or intruders from France. Needless to say, with the witches' power, Portsmouth became a literally impenetrable fortress. A bird couldn't fly in without being detected by the witches, let alone any balloon from King Phillip IV. Consequently, there wasn't one attack by the French while they were away. They both hugged Pink with gratitude.

Richard said, "We want to thank you and all your friends for keeping Portsmouth safe while we were away."

"If I had known all the girls were going to be here, I would have stayed back here," Robert said jokingly. "But thank you, Pink, and all your friends. We're lucky to have you on our side."

"No, no. Thank you for saving all of us from bondage," Pink said.

"That's the law of the universe: symbiosis," Richard said. "We're supposed to depend on one another instead of destroying one another." To the bartender, he said, "We need one more round of ale here."

The bartender announced, "You can have as many rounds as you like. The king is paying for it all."

The whole pub shouted, "Hooray for the king!"

The drinkers were shouting, "Barkeeper, this calls for some singing. You don't have any musicians. What kind of celebration is this?"

Another shouted, "No music? What kind of pub is this?"

Everyone started chanting, "We want music. We want music."

Richard quickly went outside. That morning he had met Alex Spittle on the way to work. He had been singing a song he really liked called "Rain or Shine." Richard saw him on the way back, still panhandling by the roadside, about fifty feet from the pub. Alex was only eighteen years old, and he was from a good family. His mum and dad had gotten killed in the last French attack when their house burned down. Now he was homeless. Pub keepers didn't like panhandlers. So Alex kept his distance from the pub. Richard promised to help him after learning his sad story. He brought Alex to the pub and told everyone he had gotten a musician. He took Alex to the toilet and cleaned him up. He gave his own jacket to him to wear. He looked quite handsome after getting cleaned up, combing his hair, and putting on Richard's jacket.

Richard said, "Now you're ready. Don't get nervous. I'll be over there."

Alex knew who Richard was and thanked him profusely.

Richard said, "Now's your chance. Remember to sing some happy songs."

Alex said, "Yes, sir." He picked up his guitar and followed Richard.

Richard moved some people from one side of the room so everyone could see Alex, making just enough room for him to stand with his guitar.

Richard said, "Listen up, everyone. I've gotten a musician for you. You have to keep quiet." Then he turned to Alex. "Good luck, Alex."

He went back to his seat, joining Robert and Pink.

Alex was a very talented musician. He had written hundreds of songs. He wasn't nervous, because when he performed, he focused on his music and not on the crowd around him, big or small, almost as if he were in meditation. He had had enough practice on the roadside performing. It seemed as if he himself was enjoying the music coming out of his voice and fingers. Everyone was impressed with his singing. Richard went back and picked up the old hat Alex was using for panhandling, placed it by his side, and put some money in it. Soon the whole hat was overflowing with money. Everyone walked by and gave some money to him and thanked him for entertaining them. The barkeeper was also very impressed with his performance. He hired him to play there every night from then on.

"I didn't know you had it in you, young man," the barkeeper said. "You're welcome to play here every night. I'll pay you."

"Thank you, sir. It will be my pleasure to play here every night."

"Alex," Richard said, "you're coming home with me."

"Sorry sir," Alex said, "I can't impose on you anymore."

"It's going to be a cold night. Where are you going to sleep? I have plenty of rooms. This is an order."

Pink and Robert nodded their heads.

Alex said, "Thank you, sir."

FRIENDS FOR LIFE

Later that night, they were still in the pub.

Robert had also been trained by the high priest in Ajanta. He might not use this knowledge for the same purpose. Nevertheless, he felt privileged to have the opportunity to learn this extraordinary knowledge.

He got up with his beer in hand. They had already had a few beers, and their voices were slurring a little. It was time for the truth to be known.

Robert said, "Thank you, Richard, for taking me with you to Ajanta and giving me this opportunity to learn something extraordinary. I had no idea anything like this existed, let alone that I might learn it. I will certainly think before I have sex next time."

Richard said, smiling, "You're welcome. But look at it this way. We're meant to be friends. Pink, you, and I—these events are just excuses to bring us all together. I never had any close friends before. Now I have two I could die for."

Robert said, "Neither did I. We are meant to be friends for life; that's for sure."

Richard said, "I'm grateful to have you as a friend."

"No, no, thank you. I thought I would never say that. I might even get married someday. It is you and Pink who have changed my life around. Thank you."

They both got up and hugged. Smiling, Pink joined them. All three hugged lovingly.

"Thank you, Pink," Richard said. "If we have to remain friends for life, we have to love and trust one another. I couldn't find better friends. Thank you, Pink. Thank you, Robert."

"I feel the same way about you," Robert said. "Isn't it ironic? Only a few months ago, we were considered enemies. We've known each other only for a short while, and now we're best friends. Love you." Their speech was getting slurred even more.

Pink said, "Thank you, Robert and Richard. Now I have a family."

"I love you both," Richard said. "The universe moves in a mysterious way."

Robert said, loudly, to the whole pub, "You're right, Richard. The universe wants us to be friends. In fact, all the French people can be friends with all the English people." He pointed at Pink.

Richard said, "Let us set an example for all the people—that we can be friends if we only choose to. It is mysterious how the universe brings good fortune in the disguise of adversity. It is certainly challenging for our faith."

They all raised their beer glasses. "Here's to friendship."

Everyone in the pub raised his or her glass. "Here's to friendship."

Robert normally drank wine, but he was drinking English ale as a gesture of friendship to Richard and all the English people. The people of Portsmouth were really grateful to Robert. Since he had arrived, there had been peace in Portsmouth. For the first time in many years, people were coming out to pubs and shops without fear. They raised their glasses to Richard, Pink, and especially to Robert, singing, "For he's a jolly good fella."

Robert said, affectionately, "I think there's something in the English beer. You can't help liking it and the people who drink it. Love you all."

He stood up and raised his beer mug.

The whole pub raised their glasses again. "Here's to friendship."

There were lots of beers to come—the elixir of truth and friendship, meaning it's hard to lie when you're drinking English ales. Your true nature comes out.

The whole pub joined in to sing, "Friends forever…forever friends."

As the chanting died down, they noticed that all the girl witches had suddenly disappeared. Pink was still standing by them.

Richard asked, "What happened? Where are all the girls, Pink?"

Robert said, "Maybe they didn't like our singing."

They all laughed.

Pink said, "I don't know. But I'm going find out. Something's up for sure."

Pink borrowed Richard's horse and went after the girls. She found them by the watchtowers along the seashore.

One of them said, "We noticed that all the guards from the watchtowers have gone to the pub to celebrate with Richard. The whole shoreline is left unguarded. Apparently someone came and told them to join Richard in the pub. This is Green Witch's trick."

Another girl said, "We've already found a couple of ships that are advancing towards Portsmouth. They're unknown. No way to tell who they are from this distance. But for sure they're hostile."

Pink asked, "Who knows all the guards?"

A couple of girls stepped forward. "We do. We were posted with them."

Pink said, "Go and get them from the pub. Do it discretely. Don't tell Richard or Robert anything. The people must not know. They're enjoying a peaceful moment after a long time. Let them be. Just bring the guards. We'll handle this."

Pink had just gotten back from seeing the girls. She had made sure all the guards were on duty. She had told them never to listen to anyone other than Richard, Robert, or her.

Robert asked, "What happened? Did you find the girls?"

"The girls are OK," Pink said. "They're at the guard posts. They thought they could sense something. They got used to guarding Portsmouth. But it's a false alarm. Nothing to worry about."

Richard said, "Thank you for checking everything, Pink. You're a darling. Now, Alex, are you OK so far?"

Alex said, "Yes, sir. Thank you for your kindness."

Richard said, "No, no. Thank you. I want to hear more songs. Especially the one you sang this morning, 'Rain or Shine.' Only if you're not too tired."

"I'm surprised that you remember this song, sir."

"Of course I remember that song," Richard said. "Everyone will remember this song when they hear it. It was too sad to play in the pub tonight. But I want my friends to hear it. It's also romantic."

Then Richard said to Pink and Robert, "Wait till you hear this song. It's so real."

Alex said, "It is real. I wrote that song when I lost my girlfriend. I met her when I was in school. Then I lost my mum and dad, along with our house, in the French attack. Her father didn't want her to marry a panhandler. They went away to Bristol to live. I haven't heard from her since..." His voice was breaking up. "They offered me a job there. But I wanted to stay in Portsmouth. I'm a musician, not a businessman."

Pink said, "I can't wait to hear the song."

"Yes, me too," Robert said.

Richard asked, "Alex, are you sure you're up to it?"

"It's the least I can do to return your kindness."

Richard said, "OK, then. Let's get some more beer."

Alex started to play his guitar and sing.

Rain or shine, rain or shine, nightfall;
Rain or shine, rain or shine, sunrise.
Sun

Never stop rising,
Moon
Never stop shining.
Then why
You have stop calling,
Keep my love stalling.
All over my life,
I've been
Waiting
For a girl like you
To come to
Make my
Dreams come true.
I've never met a girl like you;
Never had a feeling so strong;
Never knew loving was so wrong;
Loving you would be so wrong;
That will make you be gone.
Didn't know you'd be gone.
Didn't know loving can be wrong.
Girl,
I'll go out of my mind,
If you don't hold me now.

    After Alex finished his song,
Richard said, "Thank you, Alex. I can see how much you loved her."

    "I envy you there, Alex," Robert said. "Not many of us go through life experiencing true love."

    "I totally agree with Robert," Pink said. "Thank you, Alex, for sharing your song with us. You are a true artist."

    "Thank you all for your kindness," Alex said.

    "Alex, come with me," Richard said. "I shall show you your room."

    "Please don't bother for me," Alex said. "I can sleep in here."

    "Don't be silly," Richard said. "We have plenty of rooms here. You always have a room here from now on. Let's go, Alex. And call me Richard."

"Thank you, Richard. I will clean your jacket before I give it to you tomorrow."

"It's yours now," Richard said. "You can do whatever you want with it."

"Thank you for your generosity. Thank you, thank you. Good night."

UNEXPECTED THREAT

The next day, unbeknownst to everyone, there was a hidden threat lurking around them. The Green Witch of the Isle of Wight was trying to sabotage Richard's plan simply because she had found out that Richard had helped Pink and the other witches get out of her curse. She couldn't do anything to them anymore because the curse would work only once.

She was trying to lure Richard into marrying someone other than who he had planned for. She might look suitable to Richard, but, in fact, she was totally wrong for his purpose. That was how she planned revenge on Pink—by ruining Richard's plan. Once he married someone unsuitable, his plans would not work anymore.

Pink noticed that all of a sudden, there were many new girls in Richard's vicinity. Each of them was flirting with him and trying to hit on him. They were making any excuse to be close to him. It looked like innocent flirting, but there was a vindictive plan behind it.

Richard was being naturally kind and extremely helpful. The girls would pretend to have an accident, falling off a horse or into the water. Their plan was to get close enough to Richard to puncture his skin to deliver a witch's potion into his body. But Pink was always on guard. She suspected the Green Witch might try something like that, especially when she could not do anything to Pink. Green would try to hurt Pink any way she could.

On one occasion Richard and Robert were riding their horses by the beach. They were just making a routine visit to make sure all the watch posts were still in operation. Someone was always supposed to be there, twenty-four hours a day, on guard. Also, there was supposed to be at least one volunteer witch in each post to help out with her witch's power. They could sense an intruder from a long distance. Since Richard had been away, there had been one or two incidents of spies from France trying to infiltrate. The guards were armed with bows and arrows. But with the help of the witches, they were able intercept intruders beyond the shores of Portsmouth. Since they had come back from Ajanta, only a handful of incidents had been reported. But it was always good to be prepared. They were making a routine visit at each watch post and making sure they were on alert.

Suddenly, a horse raced past them. A young girl was on it. She was screaming for help. Obviously, the horse was out of control. Robert and Richard both started to chase after it. The girl was thrown off the horse, and she was lying facedown on the beach. Richard continued chasing the horse. Robert stopped to help the girl. He dismounted his horse and approached her.

He asked, "Are you OK? Can you hear me?"

He leaned over her to see if she was breathing.

The girl suddenly turned around from her prostrate position, grabbed his extended arm, and punctured his skin with a sharp needle. Robert immediately fell unconscious. He was lying on the sand. The girl took his horse and disappeared in the opposite direction.

Then Richard came back with her runaway horse. He found Robert lying on the sand unconscious. There was no sign of his horse or the girl.

He managed to put Robert on the girl's horse sideways, with the help of a guard from the nearby watchtower. He took him to Pink. His suspicion was right. Pink explained that the potion had been meant for Richard. The girl had made a mistake, assuming it was Richard she was delivering it to. However, it wouldn't work if it was delivered to the wrong person. All witches' potions had to be delivered to the right person to be effective. Instead of making Robert fall in love with her, it knocked him unconscious temporarily. Realizing her mistake, she ran away with his horse. Pink would be able to track her down easily because she had Robert's horse. She quickly administered an antidote to Robert and left with two other girls to look for the runaway girl.

They finally tracked her down in a remote village in a remote corner of Isle of Wight. She wasn't a young girl at all. She was over fifty years old, way past her childbearing age. That was the Green Witch's plan—to make Richard fall in love with an older woman without any hope of bearing a child for him, contrary to the purpose of their journey to Ajanta. Richard would be infatuated by an older woman, thereby jeopardizing the entire plan. Thus she would take revenge on Pink. She had the same mentality as King Phillip IV of France, who used his intelligence in evil ways.

Chapter 12

RICHARD MEETS THE GIRL OF HIS DREAMS

The following Saturday the church was holding its annual Easter fair. That had been a tradition before the war began, but they could not hold the fair for a long time because of the fear of attack by France. That was exactly what king Phillip wanted. He wanted to instill fear into people and disrupt the normalcy of people's lives in Portsmouth. That was one of the popular fear tactics used by many war mongers. It was also Richard's responsibility to restore normalcy and tranquility among the citizens of Portsmouth. Since they had managed to keep Portsmouth safe from attack for a whole year, they decided to allow the fair to go on as usual. It would also bring people's confidence back. For this purpose alone, this fair would be worth it.

Holding a fair at Easter time would bring tranquility and confidence to the minds of the people of Portsmouth. The message was clear that slowly but surely life was becoming normal again. Richard, Robert, and Pink arrived in the fair. They were making sure that their presence was known to everyone. They also posted a large number of army personnel in strategic places. The army presence would make the population feel safer.

Pink said, "I sent two hundred girls to the seashore to guard the port. They will know way ahead of the guards on the watch posts if there is a suspicious balloon or if a ship approaches."

Richard said, "Phillip knows if he can jeopardize events like this, he can break people's confidence and morale. He wants to drive people out of Portsmouth. I also invited people from nearby towns to join the Easter fair, especially those who moved from Portsmouth to these areas out of fear."

Robert said, "I agree. We're ready for him. We're using his own tricks on his soldiers. These witches are slowly creating fear in them."

Richard said, "This is the biggest event in Portsmouth. People are already arriving from Arundel, my home town; Brighton; London; Surry; Kent; and as far away as Bristol and Cardiff."

Robert said, "I hope your mum and dad can come too."

Richard said, "My mum, dad, and sister should be here soon. I sent a carriage for them. I hope they arrive before the opening ceremony."

Pink said, "They're here already, Richard. They're inside the church talking to Father Reynolds. They're asking for you."

Richard said, "Let's go in. Father Reynolds is going to present all of us to the people at the opening."

They all rushed inside the church. Richard's niece, Monica, came running to him as soon as she saw him.

"Uncle Richard!" she said as he hugged her. He picked her up and twirled her around.

His mum and dad turned towards them and walked to them.

Richard hugged them both. He introduced Pink and Robert to them. "Mum, Dad, this is Robert Artoire, and this is Pink."

Then he turned to Pink and Robert. "This is my mum and dad, and this is my sister, Louise, and her husband, Dennis, and their daughter, Monica."

They all shook hands.

Robert said, "It's a pleasure to meet you all."

Pink: "It is a great pleasure to meet you finally. We've heard so much about you."

They heard the gong. It was time to open the fair. Father Reynolds and his family were on the first-floor balcony so that everyone could hear and see them. Richard, Robert, and Pink joined them.

The gong went off again.

After the gong, the crowds became quiet and looked up to the balcony. Father Reynolds raised his arms to signal the crowd to listen.

He said, "Ladies and gentlemen, may I have your attention, please. It is a great pleasure to open our Easter fair again after a long, long time. As you all know, our last fair was held here over a hundred years ago. So this is a historic day for us all. We welcome all the visitors from all over England. I would like to say a small prayer and thank the Lord for granting us peace at last. Everyone please stand still to join me in prayer.

"Dear Lord, we thank thee for your kindness to grant us peace at last. We are eternally grateful to you, Lord. Amen.

"And before I announce the opening of this great, historic fair, may I present to you the man responsible for finally bringing peace to our beloved town of Portsmouth. He and his friends have been instruments of God to make it happen. Richard Earl, our beloved lieutenant governor." He pointed at Richard. "At the same time, I would like to introduce to you his and our friends, Robert and Pink. It is due to their joint effort that we have been enjoying peace in our beloved Portsmouth for last year. May God grant us a long-lasting peace, and may almighty God grant them a healthy and happy life. Amen!"

There was a crowd of about two thousand people cheering Richard, Robert, and Pink. They were waving back at them.

Father Reynolds raised his arms again in the air. "May I have your attention for a few more moments, please. I know you all are eager to start enjoying your favorite fair. Let us not forget to thank those who are responsible for making it possible. We thank God the almighty for sending them to us. Today, we are also witnessing another history being created in the sense that today, for the first time in the history of human civilization, we can live side by side with the witches. There are good and bad among all races. The goodness in all of us only can enhance our existence. The Lord has also brought Robert to us to prove that we can all live together in peace and harmony. This entirely depends our intentions. Together we can enhance one another's happiness. So let us raise our voices to our Lord for granting us this invaluable friendship now and in the future. Let the Lord almighty decide who lives and who perishes. Let us all welcome Pink and Robert as gifts from our almighty God. Amen!"

The whole crowd shouted, "Welcome, Pink!" and "Welcome, Robert!"

Robert and Pink came forward, waved their hands, and threw kisses to the crowds.

Father Reynolds stood in the middle and raised Pink's and Robert's arms in the air. "Welcome, our friends."

Robert said, "Thank you for accepting me. I've always believed in peace between countries. That's why my cousin, King Phillip, wanted to punish me. Pink is also in a similar situation in her society."

He pointed at Pink to speak.

She said, "As you all know by now, the Green Witch of the Isle of Wight cursed me for life for a similar reason. It was Richard and Robert who saved me and the rest of the girls from the lifelong bondage of curse. They went beyond any expectations to save us all from this atrocity. As Father Reynolds said, there is good and bad in every race. Today I speak to you for all good witches of the world. We swear friendship between us forever. And only Lord Almighty decides who perishes and who lives in this beautiful world."

She pointed at Richard to speak.

Richard said, "Let us separate good from the bad. Together we can defend ourselves from the bad. Let us set an example to everyone, good and bad, that we can be all friends and live together beautifully. Let us maintain this peace forever. And last but not least, keep your watch all the time. If you notice any suspicious activities, please report it to us immediately. With your constant help, we can keep Portsmouth safe all the time. Enjoy!"

He pointed at Father Reynolds to speak.

"Without further ado, let us enjoy this moment God has granted us. I declare this fair open, and many more to come. Enjoy!"

A band started playing music, led by Alex.

After the opening ceremony, they all came down to the main entrance of the church. Father Reynolds introduced his family to Richard, Robert, and Pink. "Sorry, we didn't have time before to introduce my family to you. This is my wife, Emily. As you can see, we are expecting our second child after sixteen years."

They all shook hands with Emily.

"So nice to meet you all," Emily said.

Pink said, "And the little one inside." She waved at him.

"Thank you," Emily said. She could feel the baby waving back to Pink from inside.

Pink said, "Have you decided on a name for him?"

"How interesting you said that," Emily said. "We don't know whether it's a boy or a girl. We could only decide on a boy's name so far, Steven."

Pink said, "That's right. He likes the name Steven."

Emily gave her a stunned look. She could feel Steven moving more since Pink had started to talk to them.

Pink said, "That's OK." She noticed Emily was not feeling comfortable. "Here, sit down in this chair. I will get you a glass of water." Pink walked away.

Father Reynolds said, "And this is the love of our life, our daughter, Stella Rose."

Stella was sixteen, a redhead, following her father. But she also was tall, like her mother. She was dressed very tastefully, wearing a beautiful silvery floral summer dress and a white hat with a bunch of colourful freesias to match the occasion. She had a attractive and shapely body, like a dancer bursting with youthful life. She greeted them with broad smile.

Father Reynolds said, "Why don't you go with these good young people and enjoy the fair. I shall feel safer if you stay with them. I shall stay with your mum."

Stella said, "OK, Daddy."

Father Reynolds said, "That way you can get to know them better, too."

Stella had been waiting for that moment. She walked forward and held Richard's arm as they walked away. Pink was holding Robert's arm.

Stella's mum and dad exchanged looks, smiling.

Emily said, "Rennie, I swear Steven was waving back to Pink from inside."

Father Reynolds said, "Of course. She's a witch." He smiled. "Also, you're in an advance stage. He or she is moving a lot now."

"I hope she's right that it's a boy. We won't have to find a name for a girl then."

"Let's leave that to God Almighty."

RICHARD MEETS ALEX'S GIRLFRIEND

Richard, Stella, Pink, and Robert visited many stalls, games, and rides—the usual events in a fair. But it felt new to Portsmouth after a hundred years. They were all excited.

"Thank you for bringing me with you," Stella said. "I haven't had this much fun in a long time. Actually, never." She giggled. "Daddy said you made this fair possible. I've never been to a fair in Portsmouth. Thank you, Richard."

"You're welcome," Richard said. "With the help of my friends, of course. Oh, look. The band has stopped playing. Let's go and say hello to Alex."

"That's a good idea," Pink said. "Poor Alex—working so hard."

"He needs a break," Robert said. "He's been playing all morning."

"Who's Alex?" Stella asked.

"He's the band leader," Richard said.

"You know him?" Stella asked. "I like his music."

"Yes," Richard said. "He lives with us."

They walked to the stage. Alex was sitting down with a glass of lemonade. He stood up as he saw them coming.

Richard said, "Stella, this is Alex."

Stella, still holding on to Richard's arm, said, "Nice to meet you, Alex. I like your music."

"Nice to meet you, ma'am," Alex said.

"Just call me Stella."

At that moment, they heard some voices from the crowd behind them.

A young girl said, "Mum, Dad, can I just go and say hello to Alex?"

Her father said, "Are you sure this is Alex?"

Her mum said, "It sure doesn't look like him, all dressed up and all. Looks familiar, though."

"Yes, Mum, it is Alex. Please let me. Please, please."

A young boy ran through the crowd and got on the stage. He went and stood by Alex.

Alex tried to pick him up. "I didn't know you were here, David. You've grown a lot in couple of years. How old are you now?"

"Twelve."

They all turned around to look. Alex's face was flushed.

A few feet away from the stage there was a family standing there. Mum, Dad, a young girl, and the young boy David was already standing by Alex. They look like a well-to-do family. They were all dressed well for the occasion.

Richard said, "Alex, don't be shy. Go and say hello. I think I know who they are."

He whispered in Alex's ear, "Is this the girl you wrote 'Rain or Shine' about? She is exquisite."

Alex nodded. "Debbie," he whispered back, and then he walked forward to greet them.

Richard, Stella, Pink, and Robert followed him.

Debbie's father, John Smith, instantly recognized Richard. "Thank you for making Portsmouth safe again, Mr. Earl. We're thinking of coming back to live here again."

"Please call me Richard. I had help from my friends, Pink and Robert here. It's a great pleasure to hear that, though."

"The pleasure is ours, Richard," Mrs. Smith said. "We miss Portsmouth. It is our home after all."

"How rude of me," Mr. Smith said. "I am John Smith, and this is my wife, Liz; my daughter, Debbie; and our son, David. We live in Bristol now."

Mrs. Smith said, "We have so many friends here. We feel safe being back for the first time."

"It's nice to know that," Richard said. "May I introduce, Pink, Robert, and Stella. And I see you already know my cousin Alex." He put his right hand on Alex's shoulder. Alex turned to Richard with a look of surprise.   They all shook hands.

Richard said, "Alex, why don't you take a break and take Debbie and David around the fair. Let me get some refreshments for our new friends."

They all went and sat down by the lemonade and biscuit stand.

Richard bought some lemonade and biscuits and put them on the table for all.

Liz said, "We didn't know Alex had any cousins—I mean relations."

Richard said, "We didn't know either. We lived in Arundel. He's my mum's cousin—Uncle Jim's son. Distant, nevertheless my cousin."

Mrs. Smith said, "That's not so distant."

John said, "Disasters happened to his family. We were fearful of our lives. That's why we left Portsmouth."

Richard: "Don't blame yourself. Many people left Portsmouth out of fear, and rightfully so. I'm glad people are feeling confident to come back. It's my job to make sure they do."

Liz said, "We asked him to come with us to Bristol. John could use him in the business. But he was not ready to leave Portsmouth, especially since his whole family just got buried here. He was only fourteen years old."

Richard said, "I'm lucky he didn't go. Otherwise I wouldn't have met him."

Robert said, "He's a very talented musician."

Pink and Stella said, "We love his music." They were smiling.

"Let me know when you plan to come back to live here," Richard said. "We are encouraging people to come back to Portsmouth, and we have a special incentive program." He pointed at Pink and Robert. "We're making sure that neither King Phillip nor anybody else ever attacks Portsmouth again."

Mr. Smith said, "Yes, we read about all of you in the papers. We're grateful to you all."

They all spent a couple of hours at the fair. Richard and Robert needed to go back for some official business. At Stella's request, Pink stayed back with her for the rest of the afternoon. They were both the same age. It was no fun for Stella hanging out with her parents at the fair. They never participated in any games or rides. Dad sometimes joined in with horseshoes or ball throwing, but that was all. Teenagers needed to do their own things. Pink was the right partner for that purpose.

Richard said to Mr. and Mrs. Smith, "Sorry; we have to rush back. Would you like to come for dinner at our house tonight—that is, if you don't have any other plans?"

Mrs. Smith said, "That would be lovely. But I hope it's not too much bother."

Richard said, "Not at all. We have to eat dinner ourselves. It will be good to know you better. Sorry; we have to rush. Alex will show you where we live. See you tonight, then. Good-bye for now."

RICHARD'S MANSION THAT NIGHT

Richard lived in the governor's mansion, called Wish Villa, on south side of Portsmouth (now known as South Sea) at the north end of Wish Lane (now Albert Road). He had a full live-in staff there. So having eight guests for dinner on short notice was not a problem at all. All he had to do was inform his butler, Charles. He sent a messenger with a note to Charles informing him of the guests.

Richard and Robert were running quite late. They arrived a few minutes before dinnertime, which was 8:00 p.m. They quickly went upstairs to change. About ten minutes later, they both came down and apologized profusely for being late. Their guests had been well taken care of by Charles and his team. They had been served predinner aperitifs, sherries, mead, and so on. David was the youngest guest there. But he thought he was old enough to hang out with Debbie and Alex. They were served nonalcoholic beverages.

Exactly at 8:30, the butler announced that dinner was served. Pink was seated to the left of Robert. Stella was with Richard.

Richard said, "Mr. and Mrs. Smith, how long are you staying in Portsmouth?"

Mr. Smith said, "Just this weekend, I'm afraid. Monday we will have to be back in Bristol."

"Are you still maintaining your house in Portsmouth? You're welcome to stay here."

"Thank you for your offer," Mr. Smith said, "but we're OK. We have the house already opened this morning."

"We're glad Alex is staying with you," Mrs. Smith said. "We asked him to stay at our house. It's empty except for the lady who takes care of it. But he's very proud and independent. He wouldn't impose on us."

Father Reynolds said, "We miss you in Portsmouth. I hope you will come more often."

"Oh, yes," Mr. Smith said. "We were telling Richard that we might even come back to live here. We still have to do business here from the port. Although Bristol is nice, we miss Portsmouth and our friends."

Father Reynolds said, "Thanks to Richard, Pink, and Robert, finally we have some peaceful moments in Portsmouth. We feel safe holding the Easter fair. God willing, we will have lasting peace in Portsmouth."

Robert said, "I personally apologize for all of France, for my cousin's behavior. The majority of French people don't want wars. They are absolutely fed up with it. France is not friends with any country now because of him. I'm sorry for his outlandish behavior. He's a crazy man."

Richard said, "Don't take it so hard on yourself."

Robert said, "You know if you have to make others run, you have to run with them. Same condition in France. People have lost lives, property, friends, children, parents, and loved ones, just like here. King Edward III was asking me to see what they've done to Portsmouth. I told him I witnessed the same things in France. Absolutely crazy. I apologize for my outburst. Please enjoy your dinner. I thank everyone for accepting me as a friend. One day we will have peace between our countries and an exchange of culture, trade, wines, knowledge, and so on, and of course my favorite English beer, instead of this barbaric war."

Richard said, jokingly, "What else can we do with you?" Everyone laughed. "Look at it this way. You're helping to establish peace for England and the French people. By golly, we're going to do it."

"Hear, hear!" Mr. Smith raised his wine glass. "Peace and friendship—and business, of course—for both our countries."

"You were meant to be here," Pink said. "You're an ambassador of peace. Look how you made my rescue possible."

"Pink was telling me all about it," Stella said. "How brave, and what an adventure. I wish I had gone with you."

"We still have the balloon," Robert said. "We'll do the trip again when we have peace everywhere. I'm going to improve the balloon more. I've already redesigned it. One day everyone will travel through the air just like we travel through the sea, only faster and safer."

"That's a great idea," Stella said. "That's a great idea. I like it."

"The French people are not going to take it anymore," Robert said. "They're going to revolt soon. We will have peace. We will land our balloon there as friends."

"I'm sure," Richard said. He looked at Stella. "You already have a following. But we will have to take care of few things before that. Right now, I want to officially thank you from the people of Portsmouth and the people of England." He raised his glass. "Thank you, Robert. And especially, thank you for making the journey to India possible."

Pink stood up with Richard. "Without you, I would be still in the bondage of the Green Witch. Thank you, Robert."

Everyone stood and raised their glasses. "Thank you, Robert. God bless you."

Robert stood up. "Thank you for having me. My cousin doesn't know what he is missing—your friendship. I love you all."

Stella said, "Let us also not forget Pink and her girls for their contribution to this event." She got up again and raised her glass.

Everyone stood again. "Hear, hear. Here's to Pink and the wonderful ladies."

Richard looked at Stella with admiration. Could this be the girl he was looking for? She was beautiful, she was forward thinking, she was virtuous, and, for sure, she was still a virgin.

Moments like this reveal a person's true nature. Within a few short hours, they came close, as if they had known each other for a while. The universe certainly knows how to put jigsaw puzzle pieces into the right place. Richard and Stella were the perfect match for each other. But did they know that? Would they make a move towards each other?

Chapter 13

THE GREEN WITCH'S HIDEOUT

Pink was not worried, because the Green Witch could not harm her and the girls anymore. She found out that since Richard had helped Pink, the Green Witch was sworn to destroy Richard and his plans. She also didn't like the idea of witches being close friends with humans. She was losing control over the witches. Some religious leaders and politicians around the world used a similar tactic. If they were divided, the Green Witch could control them. Pink knew that she was hiding in the mountains of the Isle of Wight. She was also secretly collaborating with the French king, Phillip IV. Green was of a mentality similar to that of the French king. They believed that it was easy to manipulate and control the people when there were conflicts between them. Pink was also concerned for the Black Witch, Adonai, who had fallen in love with Pink before. She hadn't heard from him since her curse was lifted. She had never had any feeling for him romantically. But she was concerned that the Green Witch might have done something horrible to him since the news of her transformation.

Maaculla said, "Just to let you know, Saad, like Richard, Pink, and Robert, even as recently as nineteen sixteen—many people felt the same way about wars. There was graffiti by many soldier prisoners—conscientious objectors—on the walls of the Richmond Castle. They were held prisoner in Richmond Castle for refusing to go to war in World War I. The graffiti speaks for itself."

The only war which is worth
fighting is the Class War.
The Working Class of this
Country have no quarrel with
the Working Class of Germany
or any other Country. Socialism stands
for Internationalism. If the workers
of all countries united & refused
to fight, there would be no war.

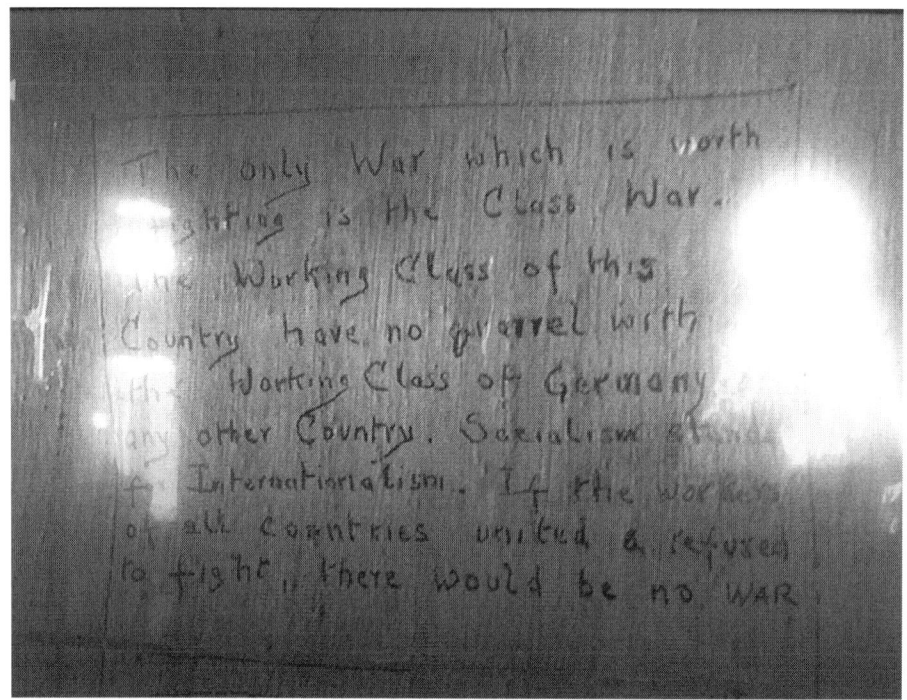

Image 8: Graffiti on a wall of Richmond Castle, N. Yorkshire, by a prisoner.

Violet was the oldest of the young witches. She had become the assistant in charge under Pink. She reported to Pink that many of the Green Witch's followers were deserting her and joining Pink's team. They didn't believe in her anymore. They didn't agree with the Green Witch's cruelty and punishments. They didn't like the way she had punished Pink and other young girls unjustifiably. Also, they themselves had been living in fear of reprisal all this time. Similarly, many French people were deserting France for the same reasons, following Robert's example. They were becoming refugees in neighboring countries, such as Germany, Belgium, Italy, Switzerland, Luxemburg, and so on. They were being welcomed in these countries as guests.

Violet said, "Pink, we have some good news. So far, fifty more witches have joined us from the Isle of Wight."

81

"This is really good," Pink said. "We can now find out where her hideout is. They must know where she is operating from."

"I agree," Violet said. "We have to move quickly, because when she finds out they've deserted her, she'll change her hideout location."

"But we'll have to wait for the full moon. That's the time when we good witches derive maximum power and the bad witches are weakest. We must attack with maximum power. We may get only one chance. She's extremely cunning."

"We have only two more days before the full moon. Do you think we'll be ready by then?"

"We'll be ready, but keep this a secret—only to yourself. It's only on a need-to-know basis. You never know. Just keep them together and on alert."

"I've already told them to stay together for safety reasons."

"Good," Pink said. "I'll talk to the girls from Isle of Wight. We need to calculate the distance and pinpoint her hideout. But they must not find out that we're planning an attack—just in case there's a spy among them. Just like Phillip IV of France, Green uses fear to manipulate others. Also, we need to keep at a safe distance when we launch the attack on her hideout. The closer we get, the better the chances of her sensing our threat. Right now she thinks she's the only one on the offensive. Let's keep it that way. There's nothing better than surprising your enemy in an attack."

"I'm thinking of sending one of them back to her as a double agent. What do you think, Pink?"

"Let's not be too hasty on that. We need to know if we can trust them first."

"You're right. I'll keep my eyes on them."

RICHARD AND STELLA ARE BOTH IN LOVE, BUT…

The universe was working in their favor. Finally, Richard had met a girl who was exactly right for him in her body and spirit. She was beautiful, and she had an adorable personality. Her body type was perfect for Richard's purpose as she fit into his plans according to the Kama Sutra. She was a perfect match for the requirements of the energy transfer. Pink also checked her out to make sure she was the right one. All these things happened as soon as Richard had let go of trying too hard to find a partner. The Maaculla (Mrs. Griffiths) always said that as soon as you let go of trying to remember something, it will come to you. Similarly, when we try too hard to achieve something, we block it and hence inhibit the desired forthcoming. Instead, take an action and then rely on the unknown to deliver it. In other words, do your part and leave the rest to the unknown because the universe already knows your desires. That's exactly what Richard did.

After meeting Stella he realized that the requirements for his original plan, to be born again through a virgin and achieving superpowers, seemed insignificant. He could easily spend rest of his life with her even if he did not succeed with his extraordinary plans. Three months had gone by, and Richard and Stella had been seeing each other casually almost every week. It was customary for a boy to ask the girl's parents for formal permission when they intended to become serious in their relationship. She was only sixteen years old, and Richard was twenty-six years old. In those days, older men married younger girls all the time. But her father might object to the fact that he was in the army. A military life was not safe, especially in wartime. Any father would prefer to have a son-in-law with a normal profession of some kind. The war had been going on in Portsmouth for over a hundred years. There was some kind of threat almost every day. How long the present peace was going to last, no one knew.

Obviously the universe had other plans for them. Richard went to meet Stella's parents. Naturally, Pink went with him. They had already met Pink. She was like a sister to him. There was no doubt that as the lieutenant governor, he had the top job. The king himself had appointed him.

Her father said, "Richard—if I may call you by your first name."

"Of course."

"May I be frank with you? I'm not at all comfortable with your present position as an army person. Not only that, you are the lieutenant governor. You are the target of all our enemies, especially King Phillip IV."

"I can't give you any assurance about that. But gradually we're winning. We have *not* had any attacks for last year or so, for the first time in over a hundred years."

"Richard, I'm well aware of all that, but this war has been going on for over so many years, even before you and I were born."

"I totally understand your feelings," Richard said. "But without disclosing any secrets, I plan to stop this war for good."

"My concern is—God forbid—suppose something happens to you."

"I understand your concerns. I cannot give you any assurance about this, either. At the same time, I can say that this plan is to make Portsmouth and France safe places to live—for now and in the future."

"I can tell you are a good boy Richard, and you mean well."

"I would like to do things amicably, without causing any concerns on your part—rather, with your blessing."

They talked for a few more minutes, and then Stella's mother brought some refreshments.

After that, they talked for a few more minutes.

As Richard was leaving, he said, "Thank you for the tea and delicious refreshments."

Stella's father said, "Let me discuss this with my family. We will definitely give it our full consideration. This is a matter of heart. I want both of you to be happy."

"Thank you for seeing me," Richard said.

"Thank you," Pink said. "Good-bye."

However, Pink agreed to negotiate with the father on Richard's behalf. She could not use her witch's magic for this purpose because the girl had to willingly give herself to Richard. Otherwise the energy transfer would not take place. It was a good thing that Stella had already fallen for Richard. Finally, after a long month of convincing by Pink, they agreed to give their daughter's hand to Richard, especially when they realized that Stella had already fallen for him. They wanted to leave the final decision to her.

That night at the dinner table at the Reynold's house, Mrs. Reynolds said, "Stella, you know that we never make a decision without prior discussion with you. This is a very serious matter. We have to think it through from every angle. After all, your happiness depends on this. Mummy and Daddy want to know your true feelings about Richard."

"I like him a lot," Stella said. "But as you said, he has a very risky career. But—"

Her father said, "In his defense, he has been very truthful about it. He seems to think a lot of you, and at the same time, he has respect for our concerns."

Stella said, "I was going to say, he takes his responsibility very seriously. He knows that the safety and happiness of the people is his first priority. He has really worked hard to come this far. He's confident he can make this peace permanent. He reminds me of you, Daddy, in many ways. You could have left Portsmouth long ago. But you stayed with St. Mary's and with the people of Portsmouth. Richard says people draw strength from you to stay here. He wants to make this a permanent reality."

"I agree with Richard," her mum said. "He has Pink and Robert with him, but he needs your strength to keep people's confidence. What Phillip IV wants to do is to drive people like Mr. and Mrs. Smith away with fear."

"He is saying how much he admires your courage," Stella said. "No matter what happens between us, he will still need your courage, Daddy and Mum, of course."

Mr. Reynolds said, "It may be the divine wish to put our family together. I couldn't just leave Portsmouth in the face of all these atrocities. I shall pray on that."

Chapter 14

IN SEARCH OF THE GREEN WITCH

In Richard's office, Pink, Robert, and Richard were discussing plans for making Portsmouth safe for everyone once and for all.

Pink wanted to concentrate on finding the hideout of the Green Witch. "
Richard, I can take care of Green by myself. Besides, you have many things to take care of here."

"There is no way I am going allow you to face her on your own," Richard said. "I know you have your full power now. Also, Green is just as much as a threat to Portsmouth as to you."

"I agree with Richard," Robert said. "We are all for one another. We have camaraderie between us. We all stand together to face our nemesis."

"OK," Pink said. "You know Green is not going to give up that easily. She's like Phillip. They believe in a very different philosophy than we do—or, rather, that's her nature."

"That's more of a reason for us all to combine our energies together to beat these notorious enemies," Richard said. "I know they need to be stopped permanently. I will be risking my son's life for that reason, although he'll be involved temporarily and indirectly."

"Yes, of course," Pink said. "After the age of twelve, he will be like a normal human being, with a little extra power he can always borrow from his mother. She will have the positive power which is permanent and non-consuming, to herself. I think we need to stop Green Witch immediately because she has started to collaborate with Phillip."

"Maybe there's some way we can destroy her hideout in England for good," Robert said. "She can go live with Phillip as far as I'm concerned."

"Our shoreline and ports are safe now," Richard said. "I don't think Phillip will be able to attack with his balloons anymore, especially when his balloon expert is here with us."

"If she's helping Phillip, that's not good for the people of France," Robert said. "I have an idea. We can use balloons to search for Green's hideout."

"That's a great idea, Robert," Pink said. "She won't suspect anything about a balloon in the sky."

"Once we find out," Richard said, "we can advance by land and sea to destroy her hideout for good."

Pink said, "I wasn't planning for you and Robert to get involved in this witch's war."

"This is not my or your war," Richard said. "This is our war against negative energy. There are good and bad people everywhere. These negatives are joining forces now."

"I totally concur with Richard," Robert said. "This is good against bad and not yours or mine. Besides, you and your girls are involved in our affairs, protecting us and fighting for us. As Richard said, we are all in it. We need to join forces against these villains."

"OK," Pink said. "How long will it take to get the balloon ready? We have two days before the full moon. That's the time the good witches' power is at its extreme."

"The balloon is ready," Robert said. "I just have to double-check it."

Richard said, "We have to make it look like someone having a joy ride, to avoid their suspicion."

"That's why we should go during the day," Robert said. "This is good for visibility. Once we spot something, we will drop a harmless marker. Nobody will suspect anything."

"You should take Pink with you," Richard said. "She will recognize them better than we can. Violet and I will follow the balloon on land with the rest of the girls."

"We will land somewhere safe once we've dropped the marker," Robert said. "We will join you by the marker at exactly midnight on the full moon."

CAPTURE OF GREEN'S HIDEOUT

They had only two days before the full moon. The next day, Robert made the balloon ready. Richard, Violet, and the girls left on a boat for the Isle of Wight. Richard took two hundred of his specially trained soldiers for this kind of reconnaissance operation. Their job was to search for and rescue Adonai and other innocent victims of the Green Witch first, and then destroy the enemy hideout. The Isle of

Wight is an island on the English Channel, approximately four miles south of Portsmouth by the sea. It would take only a few minutes by boat. The plan was to go there before the balloon arrived and be ready to follow the balloon by ground.

Early in the morning, Richard and Violet left by boat for the Isle of Wight. Robert would follow with his balloon in two hours. This would give Richard and his group enough time to land on the Isle of Wight and be ready for the balloon to show up. From there they would follow the balloon on horseback. The balloon would need to follow a southwesterly wind to pass over their destination. The Isle of Wight was pretty much deserted land. There were no roads there, only some pathways through the woods. It was totally isolated otherwise—an ideal location for a hideout for the likes of the Green Witch. It was close to the mainland of Portsmouth yet secluded and separated by the waters of English Channel.

The balloon lifted off as usual into the skies of Portsmouth exactly two hours after Richard and Violet left, as they had planned. The people of Portsmouth had gotten used to the sight of the balloon by then. They only had to travel a very short distance—about four miles or so over the English Channel—before they reached the northern shore of the Isle of Wight. They would need to go another few miles to reach the remotest part of the island. Most likely it was there that they would find the Green Witch's hideout, according to the descriptions of one the girls who had deserted her. She wasn't sure whether Green was back from her trip to France. Green's followers were very unhappy with her. They couldn't take Green's constant threats anymore. They lived in fear. That was how she controlled everyone in her group. A group of fifty girls had taken advantage of her absence to escape to Portsmouth.

Richard's two hundred specially trained soldiers plus Pink's girls made the number about three hundred, including Pink, Robert, and Richard. That should be enough to make a surprise attack on the hideout. According to the guide, there were no more than fifty girls left there to guard the hideout. They planned to give them a chance to surrender before they launched the attack. Fifty against three hundred had very little chance of winning, or even of defending their hideout, especially when their leader, Green, was absent. Rumor had it that she had abandoned them and had gone to live in France for good. She had sought sanctuary with King Phillip IV in exchange for information that might be valuable for attack on Portsmouth.

Richard and his group had had enough time to get ready for Robert and Pink to show up in the balloon. They were all ready and raring to go. As soon as they spotted the balloon, they would start following its path. Pink took one of Green's girls to guide them to the hideout. Robert was keeping the balloon low so that they could spot them from the ground.

Richard was waiting in a little open field with a red flag. The rest of his soldiers were on horseback. They were all keeping out of sight. Anticipation was growing in everyone. One hour had passed. Richard was looking towards north sky in the direction of Portsmouth, hoping to get a glance of the balloon. Ten minutes later they could see a red dot in the sky. This red dot was slowly but surely getting bigger as they kept their constant focus on it. Richard was sure now that the balloon was on the way. But he doubted that Pink and Robert could see them yet. They started waving their red flags. Richard also alerted everyone to get ready to follow the balloon's path. Robert would drop a marker for Richard. They were going to land the balloon in the nearest convenient place when they spotted the hideout.

It took another seven or eight minutes for the balloon to reach Richard. Before he knew it, it had whizzed past them. Robert waved back at Richard to let him know that they have seen them.

All the soldiers and the girls started to follow Richard. There were many trees and boulders of different sizes in their path. They had to be extremely careful to avoid accidents. The speed of the balloon was about ten miles per hour. It was easy to keep up with it. But they got slowed down by obstacles on the ground. There were also some ditches, which can be treacherous. There also could be some traps set up by Green.

Richard had sent a group of half a dozen soldiers about a hundred yards ahead of them. They were scouting and evaluating the path ahead. They were crisscrossing one another to make sure the path was clear for the rest of the group. Then the alternating group of scouts would go forward so that they could spot obstacles and dangers ahead and warn Richard and the others. It was early in the morning, and the fog had not yet lifted all the way. The balloon was visible to them through the trees and bushes. But they couldn't see them from the balloon. This was not a problem. As long as those on the ground could see the balloon, they could follow it. At the same time, they would have to look out for Robert's marker. What Robert and Pink were looking for was an old, abandoned fortress, according to the guide.

They flew about twenty more miles inside the Isle of Wight. Visibility was much clearer by then, by morning light. Finally they spotted the fortress. Robert got ready to throw a firebomb at the building.

"No," Pink said. "Please wait. There might be some prisoners there, including the black witch Adonai. They won't be able to escape when the fire engulfs the fortress."

"Quickly, what shall I do?" Robert asked. "I have to drop a marker for Richard."

"Drop a small, harmless marker." She pointed at an opening near the building. "Drop it there. They'll see the fire from any direction."

Robert quickly dropped a marker, but it missed the exact spot and hit the outside wall of the fortress. The fire rose about twenty feet high as fuel spread across the wall. The balloon whizzed past the building. They had to find a big enough open space to land the balloon now. About mile from the fortress, they found a space.

Richard had already spotted the fire and arrived at the location. He quickly sent three horses to Pink, Robert, and the guide a little farther from the fire where they landed the balloon. In the meantime they were met by a group about twenty girls who already wanted to surrender and join Pink. One of Green's girls knew them. She welcomed them. The soldiers immediately surrounded them. They told them that the leader of the group, Val, and about thirty girls were still defending the hideout. She let them go. She didn't want to fight her own people. Richard quickly got one of Green's girls and sent her inside the fortress to ask the leader to come out and talk to him.

About ten minutes later, the girl returned with the leader.

Richard said, "My name is Richard Earl. I am the lieutenant governor of Portsmouth."

"I am Val. I know who you are, Sir Richard."

"Val, we don't have to fight and kill each other."

"I made a promise to Green that I would protect our home."

"Where is Green?"

"She is in France. She was due back three weeks ago.

Until I hear from her, I will protect the fort with my life."

Richard said, "I admire your courage. But it doesn't make any sense. You have thirty people against more than three hundred highly trained soldiers."

By then Pink, Robert, and the guide had joined them.

The guide said, "Val, I'm Flo. Remember me? Look, nobody has to die here today. I have joined them willingly. Green has abandoned us all. She's not coming back. It's not worth dying for. They're here for Adonai and other prisoners. Come on, Val. We were friends once. I still think you're my friend."

Val looked around at all the soldiers. "Where am I going to live?"

All the girls cheered, thinking she had changed her mind.

Flo said, "Val, you are a brave witch. But you can be so daft sometimes. Why, you can come and live with us in Portsmouth instead of this dirty old building. There's no life here."

"Do you mean I'm not a prisoner anymore?"

Richard said, "You were never a prisoner, Val. I really admire your courage. We could be good friends like everyone here."

Pink said, "Let's go and get Adonai and the other prisoners before the fire gets to them. It's good that we don't have to wait for the full moon to attack any more. "

Val said, "He still loves you, you know."

"Well, I don't, and I never did. I just don't want to see any harm come to him or anyone else. No one has to be punished just because he or she loves someone."

Val said, "He's in the dungeon. We weren't supposed to go there. Also, there are others there too."

Robert said, "That was close. I hate wars and killing."

Richard said, "I hope we got rid of two enemies for good—your cousin Phillip and the Green Witch."

Robert said, "As far as I'm concerned, let them live together or kill each other. I don't care. But we have to rescue France from them."

Richard said, "That will be a big operation. We'll have some peace for a change. It's been over a hundred years."

Everyone cheered.

They rescued thirteen prisoners, including Adonai. They were grateful to Pink, Richard, and Robert.

"Let's destroy all the evidence here," Richard said. "Robert, we'll need one of your firebombs big enough to destroy the whole structure."

"Richard, we don't have enough fuel to destroy the whole structure," Robert said. "Is that necessary? I think we should leave things as they are."

"Yes, Robert. If she ever comes back, she won't look for them, thinking everyone was destroyed with the building. That way it's safer for them."

"I agree with Robert," Pink said. "Leave things as they are. I think it was meant to be this way. Green is very persistent. She'll come back someday. Maybe we can set up a trap for her. This way we can capture her. But if we destroy it, she will never come back."

"I think this is a better idea," Robert said. "When she comes back, we'll be waiting for her. I mean, our people will be waiting for her."

"I know," Richard said. "You're right. It will also discourage her from coming back here again if we destroy the hideout."

"That's right, Richard," Robert said. "We want her to come back so that we can capture her. Right now she's always a threat even if she is in France."

"You've got a point there," Richard said. "Let's not waste our energy here. We can use that fuel for more constructive work. Take Adonai and the other prisoners with you, Robert. They're very weak. Looks like they haven't been feeding the prisoners. They need water immediately."

"I think she abandoned them all and left the prisoners to die," Pink said. "That's why the others weren't allowed in the dungeon."

"This is getting weirder," Robert said. "What a mentality. We call my cousin Phillip a monster; even he feeds his prisoners."

Chapter 15

THE DAY BEFORE THE WEDDING

At Richard's mansion on the day before the wedding, Robert and Richard were having breakfast. Pink had just joined them. Richard wanted to have a meeting with them before the wedding. Someone trustworthy had to take care of the safety of Portsmouth while he was busy with his wedding.

"Thank you both for coming," Richard said. "I can only trust you two for sure. While we're all getting involved in the wedding, our enemies may take advantage of this event. I know this is supposed to be a happy occasion. But we have enemies lurking all around us. We have come this far without any attack. Now Green has joined Phillip. So we have double trouble."

"Richard," Pink said, "I'll take care of Green. My girls are also keeping an eye on her girls. You never know. So far so good, but it will take time to develop trust with them."

"When I was in France, I used to think, why do we even need an army?" Robert said. "All this expense to train them, uniform them, arm them, feed them, and barrack them costs nearly 70 percent to 80 percent of our budget. Is that worth it, especially if we don't provoke anybody to war? Now I can see from this perspective. If you don't provoke them, they will provoke you. So, to defend your home and country, you need to maintain an army all the time."

"Unfortunately," Richard said, "that's how the whole world is. We have to protect ourselves. It's not so much a question of being aggressive. It's a question of being defensive. There are many like Phillip around the world."

"I agree," Pink said. "Green is one of them. You don't have to provoke them. They will do that to you for no bona fide reason other than greed, jealousy, envy, or whatever. They're just bullies."

"Sorry to get sidetracked," Robert said. "Just thinking. If no country ever had any reason to have an army and weapons, we could save 80 percent of our budget. We could spend all this money and resources for better lives for the people. Sorry, never mind me, Richard. Please continue what you were saying."

"No harm in dreaming a positive dream," Richard said. "Utopia is a myth in all respects. Who knows? One day it might come to fruition. Every event begins with wishful thinking. That's why I respect you so much. You're a visionary, Robert. Unfortunately, right now we have to deal with the present reality."

"You are quite right," Robert said. "Sorry to distract you, Richard. Please tell us what you need us to do."

"First of all," Richard said, "when we all get involved in the wedding, our enemies might take advantage of this moment. We always have to be alert."

"Especially now that our enemies have joined forces," Pink said.

"At least she's not here in England," Robert said. "We have to be vigilant. But don't worry. I know my cousin Phillip. As soon as he finishes using her, he will destroy her. I was valuable to him when he could use me."

"Or she will destroy him," Richard said. "Two of a kind. Two negatives repel and destroy each other. They will consume each other. That's the nature of negative energy."

"We just have to be careful she doesn't come back here when things get hot over there," Pink said. "But don't worry. I can sense her presence if she comes close enough. I also left a watch post in the Isle of Wight. Val and Flo are best friends again."

"That's a great idea," Richard said. "I'll send a convoy of soldiers to the Isle of Wight. If she enters England, it'll be most likely through the Isle of Wight. Well, you already know what needs to be done. I really appreciate your help and ideas. Together we will keep Portsmouth safe. The mistake they made previously in this war was that after every attack, they would let down their guard, assuming that was final assault. I can't believe this war went on for over a hundred years. Now we have to be vigilant. That way we will always be ready for any event."

"Our plan should work if we carefully execute it," Pink said. "Your baby should have superpowers. That's the only way we'll be able to penetrate Phillip's army and destroy it for good, from the inside out."

"We have no reason to doubt your plans," Robert said. "So far, you have never let us down."

"Hear, hear," Richard said. "Sometimes we have to rely on power beyond human abilities." He stood up and raised his glass. "Here's to our plan. Also, I want to remind you that power is not in the knowledge; it's in the execution of it. We have to be vigilant in the execution of all our knowledge."

All three of them stood up to drink the toast.

THE WEDDING

The wedding ceremony took place at St. Mary's church (now it's Portsmouth Cathedral). The entire church compound was decorated. Many tents had been hoisted. Fresh plants and flowers were used to decorate all the tents. Each tent had several candle chandeliers. The tents were lined up on both sides of the main path of the church. The church entrance had been decorated with palms and fresh flowers. Colourful lanterns were hung from the ceiling all the way to the main podium of the church. Seaforthia palms, flowers, and lanterns had been imported from different parts of the world—China, Japan, India, Italy, Greece, and so on. Fireworks had been also imported from China and Japan.

All of Portsmouth had suddenly come alive. People's spirits were uplifted. Every house had been decorated, and during the night, hundreds of candles had been lit. Many families had moved back to Portsmouth since the Easter fair. Many new people and businesses had also moved there. New businesses were popping up every month. People were extremely inspired.

Another six months had passed without any major incidence of war. It would not be an absolute truth to say that there hasn't been any incident at all. A few spies and infiltrators had been caught from time to time. They were executed publicly to discourage any such incidents from happening again. The vigilance of Pink and her battalion of witches with their special powers, Robert's ingenuity, and Richard's leadership had been extremely effective against this kind of flare-up. People's confidence had been restored. Portsmouth was no longer a deserted town. It was bustling with people, new businesses, and new visitors.

The king himself made the proclamation that Richard would be knighted on his wedding day. Although it was highly unusual, King

95

Edward also proclaimed that he would make Robert and Pink both MBE for their parts in restoring peace in Portsmouth. The king and the people of England and especially the people of Portsmouth were extremely grateful to them because of their hard work, courage, and dedication to restoring peace in the whole of England.

This wedding was going to be a political statement for England, similar to their Easter fair. It was to show to the world that England was not fearful of any threat nor incapable of protecting its people and territories. The invited representatives from each friendly country in Europe were there except for France. Everybody was invited. It was the biggest wedding ceremony in Portsmouth in a long time. This was one of the ways of sending a message to everyone that finally life was back to normal again in Portsmouth after years of war. They had never seen such a lavish and elaborate wedding ceremony ever. Dignitaries came from all over England, Scotland, and Ireland. Guests came from India, Europe, and Asia.

Once again Portsmouth was a major trading port for the whole world. This was one of the main reasons King Phillip of France was jealous. He wanted to discourage other countries from doing business through Portsmouth. His jealousy was well known all over the world. He was driving people away from Portsmouth. Now, also by this wedding, they were sending a message to king Phillip that Portsmouth was once again back to normal and that the people of Portsmouth were no longer intimidated by his rivalry. In fact, Portsmouth was doing better than ever in business, the economy, and, most of all, peacefulness.

Richard, with help from Pink and Robert, doubled up security, especially by the seashores. Extra watchtowers were built in case of balloon arson attacks. Many young witches were helping Pink for that purpose. They were grateful to her; when she disabled the curse for herself, it freed all the young witches within a thousand square miles of the Green Witch's curse.

Many guests from faraway countries came just to show their support for Richard and Portsmouth. Richard was extremely happy to see that the high priest of Ajanta himself had come. He brought a couple of handcrafted artifacts of the Kama Sutra as a wedding gift. The maharaja of Rajasthan could not come himself, but he sent a couple of elephants as a gift. He sent one of his ships with the high priest and a group of dancers. Needless to say, the elephants would be extremely useful in guarding the seashores and in warfare. Elephants were also used in India to fight small fires. They could carry a huge amount of water and spray it into the fire. These two elephants were fully trained for this purpose. Wine came from Bulgaria, beer from Germany, famous muslin and silk cloths from India, and so on. Gifts from Romania, Serbia, Turkey, Armenia, and Iran arrived—all the countries they had visited during their journey to Ajanta. Portsmouth turned into a colourful international cosmopolitan city during their wedding. King Edward III was surprised at Richard's popularity in all these countries. He was especially pleased to have allies in those countries that were bordering France. This was part of Robert's dream—to make friends with all the countries rather than war.

After the elaborate wedding, Richard and Stella thanked all their guests for coming to their wedding, especially those who came from faraway lands. They also showed their special gratitude to King Edward III. As a wedding gift, he gave Richard ten thousand acres of land in his own hometown of Arundel, by the bank of the Arun River. This land was the most valuable gift because it eventually became the playground for their son, Richtella. More about that later.

Chapter 16

PHILLIP IV OF FRANCE TEAMS UP WITH THE GREEN WITCH

With the news of Richard and Stella's wedding, King Phillip was burning up with rage. He would do anything in his power to disrupt life in Portsmouth again. Especially a majestic wedding like this. This would further disrupt his plan to drive people out of Portsmouth. Out of frustration he had accepted the Green Witch's offer and teamed up with her. He hoped to use her knowledge and her witch's power for his evil ambitions. Now that the Green Witch had joined him, he had regained his confidence to attack Portsmouth again. Especially after Robert left, he had no one to train or organize the balloon attacks anymore which, was his main source of reprisals. With Green by his side now, he had new ideas to continue with his assaults. The Green Witch knew Portsmouth like the back of her own hands. The only difference between her and Robert was that he had carried out his destructive orders unwillingly and with regrets.

As soon as the opportunity arrived, he risked his life to escape to England. He thought that even if he died in the process, that would be better than organizing reprisals on the innocent people of Portsmouth. Out of that adversity came an opportunity that was now knocking at his door to defeat King Phillip IV permanently and bring peace between these two great nations. You will notice that since the beginning of time, in any war situation, it has always been the leader of one side beginning a war out of bullying, jealousy, greed, or just the power to instigate the war. It has never been the population of either country that had any say about it. The defending country always ended up forced to defend themselves. More on that later.

The Green Witch was sitting down with King Phillip.

"My cousin Robert has betrayed me," King Phillip said. "With his help they have made the Portsmouth shoreline impenetrable. We also don't have any more balloon experts in France. He is the inventor of balloons. We used up all of the experts trained by Robert in our last attacks over a year ago."

"Don't worry, King Phillip," Green. "There are many different ways to skin a cat, as we say in England."

"Are they eating cats now? Have they run out of food in Portsmouth? Ha, Ha, Ha."

Green looked at him with disbelief. "Never mind! They've secured the Portsmouth shoreline. So what? First we have to find Robert's family. You have to attack their weak point."

"Oh, Green," Phillip said, "I like your fresh new ideas. But all his family has left France. They're traitors. They're living with my enemies, just like Robert. How could they leave France at a time like this? His father was my commander in chief."

"That's a shame," Green said. "This tactic always works. Break them down with their loved ones."

"Someone told me there is a girl who fell in love with Robert," Phillip said. "But he didn't care about her that much. She's too religious and virtuous for him."

Green's face lit up. "In that case there's no harm in finding out how much he really cared for her. This will be a good beginning. What is her name?"

"I don't know, but I can find out."

He called one of his men. "Where is that girl now who fell in love with Robert? What's her name?"

"She has become a nun, my beloved king," the man said. "Her name is Brigit."

"That's not good news," Green said. "My power doesn't work with nuns. I am a negative witch. But find her anyway, and we will send a message to Robert."

"But she lives in Notre Dame," the man said. "No soldiers are allowed there for this purpose."

"Doesn't she ever come out?" Green asked. "I see the nuns on the streets all the time. Oh, my skin crawls with their purity."

"We also don't know which one she is," the man said.

"These men have no brain," Green said. "Take me near the gate. Not too close, because my skin burns and comes out with spots of maculae. I will call her name when I see a group of them. When she turns around, you'll know which one to grab. But don't bring her too close to me. I'm allergic to too much positive energy." She turned to Phillip. "I'm glad I'm not allergic to you." She smiled wickedly.

"Thank you," Phillip said. "I can't stand those goody-goody people either. Robert is one of them. He wants to make friends with all the people, all the countries. He wants to use his balloon for transportation and export them and give away our power to them. He makes me sick."

Green had a smirk on her face as she opened up a map of England. "There are many different ways 'we' can attack."

King Phillip looked at her with the word "we."

"You see, I left my witches in my hideout on the Isle of Wight. They're waiting for my signal. We can send a ship with soldiers to the north shore. Don't worry, King Phillip. Our time—I mean *your* time—is coming. They will crawl in front of you. I know their weaknesses."

Phillip just looked at her blankly.

A TRAP FOR THE GREEN WITCH

Pink, Richard, and Robert were in the Isle of Wight.

Unbeknownst to Green, Val, and rest of the witches, including the black witch Adonai (still alive) had now joined forces with Pink, Richard, and Robert. With Pink's intuition, she knew that one day Green might try to come back and penetrate Portsmouth.

"I have a feeling that Green left Val and the others here not just to imprison Adonai and others," Pink said. "They would die in the dungeon with no food or water anyway. She wanted them to suffer before they died. I think she's also planning to come back one day when these prisoners are long dead and buried. Otherwise she wouldn't have left Val and the others to guard the place."

"I know for sure Phillip will try something different now that he can't use balloons to attack Portsmouth," Robert said.

"You are both right," Richard said. "She might come back with a vengeance. She might also bring Phillip's soldiers with her. If they take over the Isle of Wight, it will be easy to launch attacks on Portsmouth from there."

"Phillip would try to use her this way," Robert said. "Probably he has run out of ideas, and Green will provide him with new ones. He used to get ideas from people and claim they were his own, especially if that idea was a success."

"We cannot ignore any possibilities," Richard said. "Prevention is better than cure. Pink has already spoken to Val, Black, and the girls about staying there. I think it will be a great idea to leave enough soldiers there also, just in case."

"I brought about a dozen signaling balloons," Robert said.

"What are they, Robert?" Richard asked.

"Well, they're brightly coloured small balloons," Robert said. "They're fired by a smaller fire. They're highly visible, day and night. They're also colour coded. Green means they spotted some activities. Yellow means the enemy is approaching. Red means they're under attack. White means all is well now. I brought three of each colour. They're bright and big enough for our guards in the watchtowers in Portsmouth to see them. That's how we'll get the message."

"This is ingenious," Richard said. "This will be really useful. You are truly an inventor. I can't believe Phillip wanted to use you for warfare."

Adonai said, "I want to help. Besides, I haven't had a chance to pay my gratitude to you all. I don't even know you, and you are all helping me. I owe you my life. Now I understand there is good and bad everywhere. I want to help eliminate bad from this world."

"It's a good choice," Pink said. "It always pays to be good. If allowed to, the negative energy will destroy this world. It doesn't matter who instigates it."

"She left us to die without food or water," Adonai said. "The others haven't done anything wrong. They were just standing up for me."

"It will be good if you stay and help," Pink said. "But make sure you're up to it. The time will come when she will fool you with deception. You have to be strong."

"She can't fool me anymore," Adonai said. "I fell for her when she was young and then she slowly changed into a monster. Then I realized her true nature. She used to talk of killing and torturing all the time. At that time I was looking for a way out. Sorry I used you for that purpose. I was devastated when I heard what she did to you and the others. I am truly sorry for what you went through. I really tried to do something about it, but I was not strong enough. No, she can't fool me anymore. I want to see the look in her eyes when she sees me alive and well."

"At least I know I can trust you," Pink said. "So that she doesn't become suspicious, we need to leave Val here as well."

"That's a good point," Richard said. "If she doesn't see Val, she may not enter the compound. Can we trust Val, though?"

"I think she's a good person," Adonai said. "It is she who saved our lives. She betrayed Green to save us all. Green gave her strict instructions not to even allow anyone to visit us. No food or water. Her own words were 'They can eat each other if they're hungry. I don't want anyone go near the dungeon.' She locked the dungeon herself. Even Val didn't have the key."

Robert said, "That sounds like my cousin Phillip—pure evil. How did you get out of there?"

"Val secretly broke the lock and gave us food and water every day without others knowing. She couldn't even bring enough food for us. Just enough to survive. She risked her life for us. We didn't even know her until she came to our rescue one day. She is a good person at heart. I think you can trust her."

"Thank you, Adonai," Richard said. "Don't say anything to her yet."

"Yah, thank you, Adonai," Pink said. "You've been a great help already."

They left Green's hideout intact, as if nothing had happened. They covered up the fire damage with bushes and shrubs. The black witch Adonai insisted on staying there with Val and the others. He personally wanted to help capture the evil Green Witch. In this way they had created an ideal trap for her when she came back. They also left highly trained soldiers there. They would be waiting for any French soldiers trying to enter Portsmouth via the Isle of Wight. Fortunately, Robert had some connections left in France. He received updated information about Phillip's movements and plans regarding reprisal on Portsmouth regularly.

"I have left very specific instructions with my men not to just blatantly trust everyone," Richard said. "I want to know every move anyone makes."

"I told my girls the same thing and to blend in with Green's girls," Pink said. "Your men can tell the girls to telepath a message to me as soon as they notice any suspicious activities."

Richard said, "Robert's balloon signals should be used only in extremely urgent cases because we have a limited supply of them. You can use them only once. I don't want them to run out of them."

Robert said, "One of my men just arrived with some more good news. The morale of the French soldiers is very low. If Phillip continues pressuring them for wars, there is a chance of total collapse. This is good news for us. If Phillip pushes them further, there may be a revolution again."

"As much as I hate bloodshed," Richard said, "this may be the only way Phillip can be stopped from his aggression."

"I don't feel sorry for him," Robert said. "This is a madman. He needs to be stopped, for the sake of France and England."

Chapter 17

RICHARD HAS SECOND THOUGHTS ABOUT THE BABY

They continued talking about different plans for defending and protecting Portsmouth. So far they had been successful. But it would be an ongoing job. Whether there is war or not, one has to be vigilant about protecting one's territories. Once neighboring countries see you are flourishing, they get greedy or jealous. So instead of competing with their trade and commerce, they try to destroy your economy or acquire it through war. The ideal way of doing things was to develop better technologies, better products, and better service to compete with others. That was healthy competition. Robert wanted to encourage France to follow the latter way. But king Phillip IV had different ideas.

"Don't forget we are almost there, with our other plan with the baby," Pink said. "Once we get our superpower on our side, Phillip's entire army is no match for it."

"I hope we can stop Phillip before any revolution and bloodshed begin," Richard said. "Anyway, defeating Phillip won't be the end of aggression. We have to have an ongoing defense system from now on."

"Are you having second thoughts about your plan?" Pink asked.

Robert said, "I'm not putting pressure on you, Richard, but remember what we went through to get this far."

"This is not just to win a war with Phillip or use this energy just for war," Pink said. "The universe is sending us a clear message that we can access the superpower for many other purposes. We have a lot of work to do here at home. For starters, separate the good from the bad. The negative people are ganging up on us. For example, look how the Green Witch joined Phillip. This is not just about Green and Phillip. It is about positive and negative. If we allow it to, the negative will grow and take over the world. The nature of negative energy is to destroy. They don't care if they destroy themselves and the whole world with it during that process. That's why they will never change. We have the choice of either destroying them or being destroyed. We have to stand up for ourselves. Phillip and Green will never change. It's like asking water to be dry or fire to be wet. There are also people like Adonai and Val, who are confused and brainwashed into believing the negative ways. They need to be educated and given a choice."

"Wow, Pink," Robert said, "you've never spoken to us like this before. This is democracy. People have their own free will to make choices. But you're right. Before that, they need to be educated."

"Thank you, Pink, for explaining it this way," Richard said. "I fully intend to go through with our plan. I'm just afraid to reveal it to Stella. I don't know how she's going to react if I ask her to use the Kama Sutra knowledge from Ajanta and have a baby while she remains a virgin and then use the baby's powers for our purpose."

"Don't worry, Richard," Pink said. "Everyone is born with a purpose. It will be her and his purpose. And she is destined to be a superpower too, and she knows it. She also knows about the baby with his power. She will be lending him her power temporarily until he is of age and until all the enemies are defeated. Then he goes back to normal again, like you and Robert. She's waiting for you to make a move. You need to get rid of your own fear. As Robert said, she will use her own free will democratically. She already knows about using the superpower for a bigger purpose."

Richard got up and hugged Pink. "Thank you, Pink. I was so worried that I might lose Stella if I mentioned the plan and baby's power."

"Thank you, Pink," Robert said. "I was also a little concerned about this. Are you sure Stella is OK with all this?"

"Yes, I am sure. That's why I'm a witch. You people have to give us witches some credit. Like you two, she knows the sacrifice she has to make for Portsmouth to become a safe and a peaceful place. Like all of us, she is part of the plan. She is destined for that purpose. Stella is the beginning of a superpower generation. Her daughter will inherit her powers, and so on."

Richard was stunned to hear his daughter Rose's name because their son was not even born yet.

RICHARD USES HIS KAMA SUTRA KNOWLEDGE

Richard had been worried about how to explain his plan to Stella. Now that Pink had given him assurances that Stella would be understanding about it, he was feeling a lot more confident. He had gone this far with the plan, and it would be a waste to just let it go. First of all, he had found and rescued Pink from the evil Green Witch's atrocity. Then he met Robert and went for a risky journey to India for the education in the Kama Sutra. Lastly, he found Stella, the right partner for that purpose, and married her. After all that, how was he thinking that Stella would take it the wrong way? He couldn't afford to lose her over this. She had become the most important person in his life. He was madly and passionately in love with her, and she was with him. He could spend rest of his life with her, with or without that plan. He had gone through all that because he ardently felt that something extraordinary and bigger than normal life had to happen to stop this aggression. Was it worth taking the risk of losing her over this? He was torn. His recent discussion with Pink and Robert gave him a renewed courage to mention the plan to Stella.

One night they were at home but hadn't consummated their marriage yet.

"There's something very important I need to discuss with you, Stella," Richard said.

"What is it, Richard? You seem like you've seen a ghost."

"I apologize for not discussing this with you before. By 'before,' I mean even before we got serious and got married."

"Honey, you can talk to me about anything. I'm your wife. And I love you. There's nothing in the world I wouldn't do for you."

"Forgive me for doubting you. But I had a definite purpose and plan for marrying you. The safety of Portsmouth depends on this plan. It also includes our unborn baby boy. I don't know what I was thinking. But now, since I've met you and fallen in love with you, the plan doesn't seem that important anymore. Now I think that even if you don't go ahead with this plan, I can't lose you."

"What is it, honey? Do you plan to go to war again?"

"In a way it is, but not the way you think. Whatever happens, I won't be able to live without you. I don't want to lose you, no matter what."

"Richard, you will never lose me. I'm your wife, and I always will stand by you. I love you too much, and nothing can stop me loving you."

"Thank you, Stella. Let me explain from the beginning."

He explained to Stella, right from the beginning, how and why he met Pink. Then he told her about their journey to India and learning the Kama Sutra knowledge. And now it was time to put all that into action.

He was pleasantly surprised with Stella's attitude towards all that. As Pink had explained, Stella was well aware of the whole plan about the baby and his power. She herself was destined to be a superpower. In other words, she would have power through the energy transfer during the birth of the baby. Two superpowers would be born at the same time, although the baby's power would be temporary—until he reached the age of twelve. Then he would go back to a normal human being. The purpose was to use him—or, rather, use his negative energy—to destroy an evil power for good. Otherwise, it would be almost impossible to stop this aggression.

In fact, we all have that negative energy, but we cannot use it to the extent we need to for a purpose such as this. It would depend upon Richard whether or not he could apply his Kama Sutra knowledge successfully to impregnate Stella without destroying her virginity. He was grateful to Pink and a couple of her friends for assisting. They needed to follow the particular Kama Sutra position and procedure meticulously for that purpose. The high priest hadn't given Richard a certificate for the course, but he had given him a statuette depicting the Kama Sutra position he needed as a wedding present. That way he would never forget his lesson. All his training was worthwhile.

IS STELLA STILL A VIRGIN AFTER CONSUMMATION?

Richard used all the knowledge he had learnt in Ajanta on their first night of consummation. They were careful to follow every move, from kellie, the foreplay to arouse sexuality in the entire body, to actual intercourse. After consummation, Stella was virtually and physically still a virgin. With Pink's advice, Richard had to stay away from Stella until the baby was born. Pink also advised Stella that it was important for her not to have intimacy until the baby was born. She believed and respected Pink's advice. She had become her best friend since they met at the Easter fair.

Stella was at home having a cup of tea with Pink.

Pink said, "It is a good idea to keep this knowledge limited to us four and those two friends who helped out."

"Of course," Stella said. "Especially from my parents. I can't wait till we move into our new home in Arundel. It's not that far, but I'll still have more privacy there. It won't be finished for another few months—almost in time for the baby to be born."

"Isn't that Richard's hometown?"

"I know what you mean. No, it's not too close to his parents. It was very generous of the king to give us this land as a wedding gift by the Arun River. Richard and I went there many times when we visited his parents. It's one of the most beautiful spots in the whole of Hampshire. Who would have known we would have a house built there? It's like a dream come true."

"You'd better get used to it," Pink said. "You're enlightened. That means whatever you think with deep feeling in your gap will manifest into reality."

"Thank you, Pink, for explaining things to me. I've noticed that some unusual things are happening around us."

"You were born this way, Stella—with a purpose. The universe chose you to be this way. For a normal person, becoming enlightened requires years of meditation. Only a handful of people are born this way over the centuries. You are one of those chosen ones."

"It's amazing how the universe put us all together. I love you all—Richard, Robert, and you."

"We are all instruments," Pink said. "The universe uses all of us to help one another. This is the symbiotic plan of the universe."

"Just as the Bible says, we are all instruments of God. Sometimes I wish those bad people like Phillip and Green Witch didn't exist."

"Oh, but they serve a purpose too. For instance, they helped us to be together. The negative energy propels us to take action when we allow it. If they hadn't threatened us, we wouldn't be combining our energies to work together. One day we all will forget our differences and combine all our energy for a bigger purpose. Who knows the universe's plan?"

"You are so knowledgeable," Stella said.

Pink said, "So are you. Let me put it this way: I'm just channeling what the universe wants you to know. One day soon you will be tapping into the knowledge of the akash—the sky. All the knowledge of the past, present, and future is stored there. There is no such thing as past, present, and future there. Just being. You can't even imagine anything because there is no such thing as imagination. Whatever weird thing you imagine, it exists somewhere in the universe."

"These things sound so interesting. I hope I can remember all of this."

Pink smiled. "Don't worry, Stella. When the time comes, you will remember all this and more. You will use it for a purpose."

Chapter 18

A couple of days later, Robert and Richard were sitting in the office.

"How are things at home with Stella?" Robert asked.

"I didn't see this coming. Pink told us to stay away from each other until the baby comes.

"I don't envy you. Women are like honey, especially the one you love. You go after it like a honey bee, again and again. You want to keep tasting it. Every time it feels like the first time."

"Nine whole months," Richard said. "I'm sure it's hard for the girls too."

"If it's true, they can hide it very well. I've always had to initiate it myself. They're like, take it or leave it. To tell you the truth, Richard, I wish I hadn't slept with many girls and had saved myself for someone special, like you and Stella did. Especially after our education in the Kama Sutra with the high priest."

"Do you regret it? You're still the same Robert. You were doing what the universe wanted to you do. We each have a purpose in life."

"No, not so much regret. Now I look at sex with a different perspective. That's why I'm waiting for that special person too. I want to experience the spiritual journey with her. The science of transporting a soul into this world. I asked the high priest about it. It's never is too late for men, he said. He also said the only thing to do is to clear your conscience. Nothing physically alters in the man, like the woman's hymen. Knowing all this makes me feel I should wait for the right person and right moment."

"Thanks, Robert. It helps me a lot too. I never thought I would get addicted after making love once. It will be worth waiting for."

"Sex is an addiction. Especially where I grew up—French palaces are very promiscuous. It's normal for us in France. I never thought I would look at sex differently. Thanks to you, Richard. If you hadn't taken me to India, I wouldn't have known any difference. I am grateful to you."

"I hope you find her soon," Richard said. "I told you there's a purpose for everything."

"Oh, but I've already found her. Unfortunately, she's in France. We're in love, but she's still a virgin. I never thought I would be worthy of her because of my upbringing and promiscuity. She's the main reason I asked the maha guru if it was too late for me to experience all this. That's another reason I hate war. I would rather have an exchange of culture and knowledge like we did in India."

"This is more of a reason we have to defeat Phillip," Richard said.

"The only way she can save herself from people like him is by becoming a Catholic nun."

"So you know where she is? In a convent? That's great. What's her name?"

"Her name is Brigit. She's so beautiful and pure. She looks similar to Pink and Stella mixed. I was keeping away from her, because I didn't think I was worthy of her. Now, after speaking to maha guru, I desire her. I would marry her. I want to have children with her. I want to spend rest of my life with her. Thank you, my friend. Without you, I could not have found the truth." He got up and hugged Richard, tears rolling down his face.

"No, no, Robert. Thank and be grateful to the universe. Observe how the universe brought us all together. It's a mystery. We found a common need and purpose. Somehow we found one another—Pink, me, you, and Stella. And next is Brigit, I'm sure."

"I hope so, Richard. Finding you, I thought was my ultimate destiny, and now my dream is about to become a reality. When the universe delivers, it pours down."

"That's right. The universe is unlimited. You can have everything and more. When the universe is moving, nothing can stand in its way. It doesn't know any boundaries. Look how it put you and me together. We are presumably from enemy countries. Now we are the greatest of friends. We are ready to die for each other. I have no doubt, we are going to meet Brigit soon. We will look for a sign from above. Robert, we have nine months before the baby comes. Maybe the universe is planning it this way. We will rescue Brigit and capture Green by then. What do you say?"

"Let's go."

111

"OK. But first, let's go to the pub and have some beer and listen to Alex's music. We both need cheering up."

"That's a great idea." said Robert.

RICHARD AND ROBERT IN THE PUB LISTEN TO ALEX'S NEW SONG

Alex was there already, playing music as usual.

"Hello, Alex," Richard said. "Can you play some romantic music?"

"Yes," Robert said. "We both need cheering up."

"It will be my pleasure."

Alex started playing a few notes on his guitar.

Richard said, "Sounds new, Alex."

"Yes. It's a new one I wrote since you got married."

"It sounds really good and romantic," Robert said. "Just the job, Alex."

Alex just nodded and concentrated on playing.

Booo oohoo oohoo, booo oohoo, oohoo.
Booo oohoo oohoo, booo oohoo, oohoo.
Now that I've met you, after all,
Wish I hadn't met you at all.
Booo oohoo bohoo, oooo bohoo, oohoo.
Booo oohoo bohoo, oooo bohoo, oohoo.
Now that I've met you after all,
Wish I hadn't met you at all.
Circumstance is going wild.
My love is out of control.
Oh, what am I to do?
Booo oohoo bohoo, oooo bohoo, oohoo.
Booo oohoo bohoo, oooo bohoo, oohoo.
Wishing you one thing; seeing you another;
Holding you one thing; hugging you another.
I don't know why—having you near me, making me cry.
How can you ask the bees not to eat honey and birds not to fly?
I don't know why—ask the moon not to glow and river not to flow.
Oh, how can you ask the sun not to rise? I don't know.

I don't know why having you near me makes me cry—I don't know why.

I don't know why; I don't know why; I don't know why.

Oooo, what am I to do?

Oooo, what am I to do?

Having you one thing; kissing you another;

Holding you one thing; loving you another.

Ooo, I don't why.

Having loving me making more cry

I don't know why.

Booo oohoo Bohoo, oooo Bohoo, oohoo.

Booo oohoo Bohoo, oooo Bohoo, oohoo.

After he finished his song, both Richard and Robert got up and hugged Alex.

Richard and Robert both got teary eyed.

"This is the best song you've written so far," Richard said. "Thank you for playing it for us."

"I agree," Robert said. "That's why you're a musician and a writer. You can feel other people's pain as well as your own. It hit the right spot."

"We'll come back and listen to it again another day," Richard said.

"I'm glad you like it," Alex said.

"Yes of course," Robert said. "Thank you, Alex."

Everyone said good night, and Richard and Robert left.

Chapter 19

One of the messengers who was loyal to Robert came from Paris. He informed Robert that Phillip was looking for Brigit. The king was a madman. If he couldn't get his way with Robert, he would try to harm his family or friends or loved ones. The soldiers were mainly Catholic. They were afraid to go into a convent with the intention of searching. But the king was putting a lot of pressure on them to find Brigit.

Robert offered some money to the messenger. "Here. Please, take it."

"That's not necessary. We do it for the love or you and France."

"Please, you have your expenses. This should cover it."

The man hesitated. "Thank you. Merci, monsieur."

"I want you to take this message to Brigit. I don't want you to write it down. Memorize it."

"Oui. Yes, sir."

"That's better," Robert said. "Remember, you're in England now. Always speak English. Nobody will suspect you. I also want you to take the usual precautions. Go into one house and stay there and send somebody else from there with the message. Stay there until he or she returns with the message back. But don't come back here again. Send another person. Remember, you're always being watched. This is the message to Brigit: 'I want you to leave Notre Dame Cathedral and go to Luxembourg via Metz. I want you to stay at our friend's house. My parents are there with my sister. The vegetable delivery man is our agent. He will take you there. Go with him. It will take three days for us to get there with the balloon via Germany. We will pick you up from there.'"

Richard walked in.

"I'm glad you came on time," Robert said. "I wanted to discuss the plan to rescue Brigit with you. This is one of our friends. He just came from France with some news."

Richard shook his hand. "Nice to meet you."

The man humbly, said, "The pleasure is mine, sir. Nous manquons de Robert. Il n'y a personne pour parler, pour nous a Paris." ("We miss Robert. There is nobody to speak for us in Paris.")

Robert said, "He informs me that Sorciere Madame Vert"—the Green Witch—"is with Phillip. They're looking for Brigit. I'm sending her a message to leave Notre Dame and go to Luxembourg via Metz. My mum and dad and sister and my younger brother are there, in our friend's vineyard. She will wait for us there. I also have a friend in Metz who will help her. He supplies vegetables to Notre Dame and the Versailles palace. He comes with his daughter, who's about the same age as Brigit."

"Are you sure this is safe?" Richard asked. "Maybe we could create a diversion at the same time to distract Phillip's attention."

"What do you suggest?" Robert asked.

"It all depends on your people there. They could start some terror attack—without hurting innocent people, of course. The whole purpose is to keep Phillip's mind off Brigit."

"I have some army connections," Robert said. "They could kidnap some key people and set fires here and there. They're loyal to my father. He was their commander."

"That should do," Richard said. "Keep his mind away from Brigit for a few days. Also, we can start some activities at the border of Calais. Let me talk to Pink also. Yes, I think you should send word to Brigit without delay."

GREEN IS AFTER BRIGIT—PARIS

From that day, every morning Green took a royal coach and waited outside the gate of Notre Dame. She didn't like to be too near the cathedral because she would get a blotchy skin condition called maculae. It was similar to an allergy. But this only happened to the negative people when they were near too much positivity. However, she stayed close enough to be heard near the gate. When she saw a group of nuns come out, she would call out Brigit's name. She also had a group of soldiers waiting nearby. They would grab Brigit when she responded.

On Friday, about nine in the morning, a royal coach was waiting outside the gate of Notre Dame, as planned by Green. The nuns inside were alerted because a royal coach was suddenly waiting outside the gate.

The vegetable man from Metz, as usual, finished his delivery and started to head towards Versailles. He had a young girl by his side, his own daughter. A group of nuns came out and turned left. They went in the opposite direction. A sweet female voice—Green pretending to be nice—called out for Brigit. All the nuns turned around for a moment. Then they carried on walking away. It was difficult to see from this distance who was who. The soldiers immediately obeyed Green's hand signal to follow them. They stopped the nuns very respectfully.

The soldiers said, "Bonjour."

The soldiers were puzzled. One of them scurried to Green's coach.

Which is she? They're all over fifty or sixty years old."

"Let them go," Green said. "No, wait. Ask them, where is Brigit?"

The soldier scurried back to the nuns. "

Which one is Brigit?"

One sixty-year-old came forward. "I am Brigit. What can I do for you, soldier?"

He then started to walk back to Green with her.

Green said, "No, no. Don't bring her here, you fool."

She signaled the coach driver to drive off. Moments later, they heard an explosion. There was a fire nearby at an empty house. This was followed by another five explosions around the city. People were running to hide, screaming everywhere. The soldiers left the nuns and headed towards the Palace of Versailles. Within about ten minutes, there was total chaos in Paris. People and soldiers were running everywhere. The vegetable man came in through the palace's back door for a delivery. He was told he could not enter the palace gate. It was an emergency. He had to leave the vegetables by the door. The man and his daughter unloaded the vegetables, and then they quickly left.

BRIGIT ESCAPES TO LUXEMBURG

The vegetable man went back to Metz. But instead of stopping at their own home, they rode straight to the border of Luxemburg. They headed to the mountainous road, pretending to deliver to a house there. They crossed the border into Luxemburg. About thirty miles inside Luxemburg, he drove into a vineyard. The owner of the vineyard, Mr. Schroider, came out to greet them.

"You're early," Mr. Schroider said. "I wasn't expecting you until tonight."

"I don't know what happened," the vegetable man said. "There were explosions everywhere. Paris was in chaos. I was told to leave the vegetables outside the back door of the palace and leave. I took advantage of the situation. That made me four hours early."

Mr. Schroider said, "It's a good idea. It's not good to wait there. You never know what Phillip is going to do next. I'm glad you got out safely."

"Oh, yes. I got your merchandise with me. My daughter is bringing her out." He said smilingly.

His daughter was helping a young girl out of the lower storage area of the coach. He usually carried oranges there. She had been lying under the oranges. His daughter walked forward with a girl dressed as a nun.

"Here is the beautiful Brigit," the vegetable man said, smiling. "I present you Miss Orange of Metz. She is perfumed with orange."

They all laughed. All her clothes smelled like oranges now.

Mr. Schroider said, "Go inside, Brigit. My daughter will give you a change of clothes. Robert is late. He may be having a problem with the wind for the balloon. But his parents are here. All four of them went to the field to look out for his balloon. We weren't expecting you until tonight. I'm glad you're here, safe and sound. My daughter Claire will show you your room. You can have a bath or wash there."

She thanked the man and his daughter and went inside.

Mr. Schroider tried to give money to the man. But the man wouldn't take it. He wanted to go back before nightfall.

Mr. Schroider said, "You and your daughter can stay the night and leave in the morning."

The vegetable man said, "I think we should go back, in case they come looking for me or suspect something."

"I'm sure he and his parents are grateful to you."

"I think it is my civic duty to do it. I will see you soon," the vegetable man said.

He drove off with his daughter without delay.

Chapter 20

Robert, Richard, and Pink had left Portsmouth two days ago. Robert was hoping to get some northeasterly wind to carry his balloon towards Germany. But as they approached the border of Belgium, a strong current took them inside Belgium instead. And if they were to continue on this southerly wind, it would take them towards Calais, France. That was not a good idea. So Robert decided to land in Belgium for the day instead. The balloon itself had gotten a little old, and there were small holes starting to appear, which made it even harder to steer. So at midday they landed in an open field in Belgium. Robert hoped to repair the holes with some patches. He had come prepared for this kind of emergency.

"I think I'll spend rest of the day repairing these patches," Robert said. "Early in the morning, we'll leave for Germany. Hopefully, the wind will be favourable tomorrow. We also have to find the owner of the land to pay him."

Pink said, "I can sense that early in the morning, it will be a northeasterly wind, and by midday again, it will change back to southeasterly."

"By then we'll be almost in Germany," Robert said. "If it continues like this, we'll have to travel half a day at a time."

"We have quite an audience here," Richard said. "I'm keeping an eye on them. You never know."

"At least we're not in France," Robert said. "Our reception might have been different altogether. But this is the border of France." He got his repair kit out.

"Don't speak too soon," Pink said.

"Why do you say that?" Robert asked.

"Don't look now, but at your two o'clock. A blond man in his twenties is advancing towards us. He seems friendly, though."

"I got him," Richard said.

The man was about ten feet from Robert when Richard interrupted him. He was in between Robert and the blond man. All of a sudden, the man was smiling and looking over his shoulder at Robert. By then Robert had turned around and was smiling back at the man.

"It's OK, Richard," Robert said. "This is a friend of mine, Jean-Pierre. He left France too. I had no idea he was in Belgium. We went to school together."

Jean-Pierre said, "Robert, what are you doing here? I heard you were in England. I was coming to see you one day there."

Robert said, "Jean-Pierre, this is Pink, and this is Richard."

They all shook hands.

Jean-Pierre said, "This may sound funny to you, but for the last seven or eight days, I've been thinking about you a lot."

Robert, Richard, and Pink exchanged a look.

Robert asked, "Do you happen to know who owns this land? We want to pay them for parking here tonight."

Jean-Pierre said, "This is my property, Robert. You can stay as long as you want. We came and bought this land. We didn't want to go too far from France because we hope one day things will get better and we can go back. I have my mum and dad with me. My sister is here too. She married a Belgian boy."

Robert hugged him. "Thank you for your hospitality."

Jean-Pierre said, "You must come and say hello to Mum and Dad. How about you and your friends come to dinner tonight. Our house is round the corner from here."

Robert said, "We have a lot to do before we leave in the morning."

"I'm sure you can find time to eat. It's less than a five-minute walk from here. I can put a guard here, just in case. But believe me, these Belgian people are very honest. They will never touch anything."

Robert looked at Richard and Pink.

"It's up to you Robert," Richard said. "Do you think we can finish the repairs by nightfall?"

"You don't have to do it all by yourself, Robert," Pink said. "We can help too."

"I can help too," Jean-Pierre said. "Tell me what you need."

"That won't be necessary, Jean-Pierre," Robert said. "We'll finish it by nightfall. See you tonight."

"I can't wait to tell Mum and Dad," Jean-Pierre said. "I'm coming back to help anyway." He ran back to his house around the corner.

"That's a stroke of luck," Robert said. "I didn't know what to expect from this foreign land. I haven't seen him for few years. I was worried about going over Belgium because I don't know them at all. I know Germany well. But now the wind has blown us towards Belgium. So we don't need to take a detour through Germany anymore. Actually, it'll be a shortcut. We're already late one whole day trying to steer it against the wind."

Richard said, "Pink, you told me once, 'Every problem is an opportunity in disguise.'"

Pink said, "That's exactly right. The universe works mysteriously."

SURPRISE BELGIAN HOSPITALITY

There were a couple of holes that needed to be patched up. The balloon was quite old, and they needed to inspect it properly. But as Pink had said, without this problem they wouldn't have landed there and met Jean-Pierre and found the shortcut route to Luxemburg. Keep in mind that it wasn't just going there—they also had to go back to England with Brigit. So this worked out to be a blessing in disguise. They just hoped it would be no problem for Brigit to get to Luxemburg.

They finished their repairs and followed Jean-Pierre to his house. He had a Belgian man guard the balloon while they were at his house. His sister Dominique also joined them with her husband. They introduced everyone.

"Do you remember, Robert, how we hated Belgium?" Jean-Pierre asked. "It's only because we didn't know them. There was always some political rhetoric against them. All these are lies—stupid politics to keep people apart to control them."

"That's the same thing I found out about England," Robert said. "You're looking at my best friends from there. They have done nothing but welcome me and help me and give me a home. Now they're helping me to rescue Brigit. The old politics keep people apart, and that way they can control us. The same people, before they met each other, were ready to kill each other. Imagine that two enemies from the past are now ready to die for each other. There is good and bad everywhere. We need to separate good from the bad. That's all. This mad king is driving all the good people out of France."

"You helped us to stop this unnecessary war and killing," Richard said. "Who would have known that one day somebody from your enemy country would come and help restore peace in our own home against his own country?"

"As witches, we always considered people to be our enemy," Pink said. "Richard and Robert rescued me and thousands of other girls from a lifetime curse. If there were no war, we probably wouldn't have come across each other. So again, every problem is an opportunity to learn and grow."

"You did the same thing, Pink," Richard said. "You stood against your worst enemy to help us bring peace to Portsmouth. That's right. We need to separate good from the bad—not by race, country, religion, colour, and so on."

Robert said, "Thank you, Jean-Pierre, and your mum and dad. Thank you for your hospitality. This was an unexpected gift from the universe. Seeing that you all are safe also gives me a wonderful pleasure. If you ever feel like travelling, just get on a boat and come over to Portsmouth. The port is open to all now. It has become the most cosmopolitan city in the world. Everyone is welcome there."

Jean-Pierre eyed Pink. "I think I will soon. I need to travel more and know more people." He smiled pleasantly at her.

Pink was eyeing him and smiling.

Richard and Robert had noticed their attraction for each other too.

Robert said, "You will be most welcome in England."

"Thank you, Robert. If you like you can stay with us tonight. We have plenty of rooms. You can't leave until the morning anyway."

"Thank you, Jean-Pierre," Robert said. "But I will feel better if we go back and check everything first."

"OK, Robert," Jean-Pierre said. "We will make your rooms ready by then. You can leave after breakfast. I can't tell you how happy I am to see you."

"We will keep in touch from now on, mon ami," Robert said. "Don't forget, we're coming this way going back to Portsmouth."

Jean-Pierre said, "In that case, I would like to come with you and show you the way," Jean-Pierre said. "I go to Luxemburg all the time, but not by balloon."

Robert said, "Why not? I'm sure Richard and Pink won't mind. We can catch up with our lost time."

ROBERT UNITES WITH BRIGIT

After breakfast they left for Luxemburg. They didn't need to go through Germany anymore. Jean-Pierre showed them the route through Belgium. They just had to follow the slightly southeastern current of wind, and that would take them directly to their destination. This was actually a shortcut. They arrived in Luxemburg by midafternoon. They were three days late. His mum and dad were a little anxious, but they had confidence in Robert and his balloon. For the last three days, they had come to this same spot and waited for them every day. They were waving a white flag at them. That meant all was well there. Robert saw the white flag and realized it was safe to land there. He came running after they landed safely.

Robert's brother Roger, fourteen, and sister Adele, fifteen, came running to him.

Robert said, "Mum, Dad, you didn't forget the white flag signal." They were hugging each other.

Mum said, "Jean-Pierre, what a nice surprise."

"What about Brigit? Is she here yet?"

"Yes, she came early," his dad said. "There was some kind of problem in Paris. Our friend didn't want to wait. He brought her in directly as soon as he picked her up from Notre Dame. There were explosions and some kind of disturbance in Paris. He thought they would start tightening the security later."

Robert exchanged looks with Richard and Pink. "Good. We were expecting this. We created a diversion so that their attention would be away from Brigit for few days."

His dad, surprised, said, "That's a military tactic!"

"Yes, Dad. By the way, this is Richard, the lieutenant governor of Portsmouth, in charge of the British Army there. And this is Pink. And this is my mum and dad."

His dad, eyeing Richard, said, "They're getting younger and younger every day."

They all shook hands.

Robert's mum said, "Nice to meet you all. Let's go. Brigit is waiting. She's having a wash and rest after the journey."

They got on the two waiting coaches and headed to the vineyard. They left behind a couple of men they had brought with them from the vineyard to guard the balloon. About twenty minutes later, they arrived at the house. His dad was waving the white flag again.

"We all use your signal system from time to time," his dad said. "The world is changing so fast, you can't be too careful. Here are other coloured flags for emergencies. I carry them with me all the time."

Mr. Schroider was waving a white flag at them.

Richard said, "Exactly. Better safe than sorry. We learnt it the hard way in England. After every attack by Phillip, they would think that was the final one, and they would let down their guard. But now we are always prepared."

Robert said, "This is why Phillip couldn't attack Portsmouth for over a year. You should know that, Dad."

"Yes, that is a good military tactic too. Always be prepared."

The coaches arrived at Mr. and Mrs. Schroeder's house.

They all got out of the coaches. Brigit was waiting on the veranda with Mr. and Mrs. Schroeder and their daughter, Clair. Clair was same age as Brigit.

Robert said, "Brigit."

Brigit came running out of the veranda. "Robert." They hugged each other and kissed each other's cheeks. "I thought something went wrong with your balloon."

"Yes, it did. But nothing we couldn't fix. Look who I found in Belgium. You remember Jean-Pierre."

Brigit said, "I thought it was Jean-Pierre. He's grown a lot."

Jean-Pierre said, "Nice to see you again." They hugged and kissed.

Robert said, "Let me introduce you to my bon ami, Richard, and Pink. Pink and Richard, this is my mon amour, Brigit."

They all shook hands.

Richard said, "I'm pleased to meet you. I've heard so much about you. Now I see why Robert spoke about you so much."

Brigit said, "Something good, I hope."

Pink said, "Nice to meet you Brigit."

Mr. Artoire introduced everyone to Mr. and Mrs. Schroeder and Clair.

Mrs. Schroeder said, "Let's go inside. You all must be tired and hungry."

Mr. Schroeder said, "And thirsty, I hope. We have the finest Mosel wine to drink."

They all laughed as they followed Mrs. Schroeder inside.

JOURNEY BACK TO PORTSMOUTH

The next morning at breakfast, Robert said to his mum and dad, "Why don't you both come over to Portsmouth for a visit? You can come with us if you like, or take a boat from Oostende."

"I don't know," his dad said. "We feel quite safe here from all the excitement."

"It's quite safe in Portsmouth now," Richard said, "thanks to Robert and Pink. We intend to keep it that way. We're not taking any chances in any direction. There's plenty of room at Robert's house."

"I don't want to pressure you if you don't feel comfortable," Robert said. "But you're a military tactical expert, so you could advise us too. We're not stopping here. Soon we also plan to stop Phillip for good, for France's sake."

"I know he's a monster that needs to be stopped," his dad said. "He has no friend in any country. Not even in France. People are just afraid him."

Pink said, "If you don't like it after few days, you can always come back."

"Let me think about it and discuss with your Mama," Robert's dad said. "It's quite a sudden decision to make. We're not as young as we were."

"Nothing will change here," Mr. Schroeder said. "You're always welcome. Also, one day maybe we can come and visit you there too. I've always wanted to visit England."

Robert said, "Also, Brigit and I are planning to get married soon."

"Are we?" Brigit said. "This is the first time I've heard about it. It must be Richard's influence. What did you do to him? He's changed."

"That's a long story," Robert said. "I shall tell you soon. Yes, I've changed." He exchanged looks with Richard and Pink. "First we have to go and visit your mum and dad in Switzerland and ask their permission."

"I'm glad they went back to Switzerland," Mrs. Artoire said. "I would worry what Phillip would do to them if they were still in France."

"Yes, Mum," Robert said. "But Brigit stayed back in the convent because of me."

"France is not safe for anybody," Mr. Artoire said. "It's getting worse now. When he put you in jail"—his eyes got tearful—"I was about to tell my men to attack the palace. Then you escaped to England. Thank God for that. That saved a lot of bloodshed. I couldn't imagine attacking my own people. You could have gotten hurt too. Another thing—I have to tell my men before I leave for England. How will I keep in touch with them? They'll be lost without me. From here I communicate with them every day."

"Dad," Robert said, "I also have men coming over to England with news every day from Paris."

"We've secured our shores in Portsmouth," Richard said. "Their men can't get through. But ours can get through easily. Also, we have Pink's girls there. They can sense who's ours and who has negative intentions. We're not letting our guard down for a minute. With your men inside and with your knowledge of wars, we can defeat Phillip for good with minimum or no bloodshed."

"For all I know," Robert said, "French people don't want war. This war has lasted long enough. A generation of people were born in the war and have lived in it through their whole lives, and they're too tired to fight anymore. They want peace. Let us free our people from these warmongers. Phillip and his whole royal family still live in luxury while people are losing lives, arms, and legs and coming home to die— for what? People are losing their husbands, fathers, and brothers every day. And it's the same for England too. This ugly war is killing both sides equally. No one wins in a war. Then people like Phillip provoke wars. They need to be stopped."

126

Mr. Artoire said, "I agree with you, son. I have suffered and seen all this all my life. I just hate to see bloodshed from both sides. We have to find a way to stop Phillip without bloodshed."

Richard said, "We've found a way to do exactly that, with the help our friend Pink. We're not stopping because we haven't had an attack for a year. We intend to eliminate the root of all this permanently."

"Dad," Robert said, "we'll discuss that when you come over. This is a long-term, permanent solution. We don't want to hurry up and make a mistake either. We would appreciate your help, Dad."

"Take your time, Mr. Artoire, to think it over," Richard said. "No hurry. We're going ahead with the plan anyway. If you're with us, we'll be stronger."

"I'm sure you'll be all right without me," Mr. Artoire said. "But I will do everything in my power to stop this madman. I thank you for your confidence in me. I think you should go ahead of us. We'll follow you on a ship from Oostende. It's only a couple days' journey from here."

Robert said, "With a balloon we'll be there in half a day, depending on the wind current."

Brigit said, "I think I'll go with your mum and dad."

"I can drop you in Oostende in eight to ten hours," Robert said. "You can stay with Jean-Pierre and get the boat the next day."

"I like water," Brigit said, "but I'm not good with heights."

Richard said, "One of us can stay back to help."

"I can stay and help," Jean-Pierre said. "I know the route too."

"OK," Mr. Artoire said. "That settles that."

Chapter 21

The next day Robert's mum and dad, with Brigit and Jean-Pierre, left Luxembourg on a stagecoach to Brussels. They changed the stagecoach to go to Oostende from there. That same night, they arrived at Jean-Pierre's mum and dad's house. They stayed there for the night. The next day, early in the morning, all three of them—Mr. and Mrs. Artoire and Brigit—got on the boat to Portsmouth. Everything had gone smoothly so far. They were on the boat to England.

At the Portsmouth dock, Robert and Pink were anxiously waiting for their arrival the next day. This was a straightforward journey by boat to Portsmouth. Every day, mainly cargo ships were arriving. There were passenger ships also docking. There was a separate dock for passenger ships. They waited for three hours. There was no boat from Oostende with Brigit and Mr. and Mrs. Artoire. Midday Richard came to join them. He was wondering what the delay was. The whole day had gone by, and there was no sign of the boat from Oostende.

Robert was angry with himself. "I wish I hadn't suggested that. Now I've lost my whole family and Brigit. Something is dreadfully wrong." He walked up and down the dock looking out at the vast, foggy sea.

"Now, now, Robert," Richard said. "You know better than that. Remember our training? Do not deal with one negative energy with another negative."

"Richard, thank you. I meant to ask you about that, because I wasn't paying attention to that part. I was more interested in how I could rectify my past mistakes."

"Come on," Richard said. "I shall explain while we look out for them. If you fear the fear, you make it stronger. Instead, you push it down your gap."

Pink said, "I can explain the gap while you look out, Richard. The gap is right in the middle of your body. Imagine one side of your body is negative and the other side is positive, because we are made of two energies. Your gap lies in the middle, where all your chakras line up in a straight line, from your crown chakra to your root chakra. That's the

128

doorway to nirvana. That's where we go when we meditate. The place of all positive. The place of all possibilities. The place of limitlessness. The maha guru developed this technique for the normal human being. Because when we get zapped by fear, we start fearing more. Originally that fear attracted that negativity in your experience. We get confused. We don't know which direction to go. So pushing it down to the gap neutralizes that fear instead of getting more negative energy. The result is a positive outcome."

"Thank you Pink," Robert said. "Thank you, Richard. It seems that while I was worried about my past, I missed this important knowledge."

"You know what to do now," Richard said. "Let's concentrate on the search. Believe me, there's nothing to worry about. I can feel it in my gap."

Visibility was no more than half a mile. On a normal, clear day, you could see almost to the shore on the other side, if only it were not hidden by the curvature of the enormous earth. Richard quickly got on one of his navy boats with Pink and Robert and went to search for any boat arriving from Oostende.

"The ship cannot just disappear," Richard said. "There's no storm or anything."

"I think we should look on the Isle of Wight," Pink said. "Sometimes during foggy weather, boats lose their way and turn up there. It's easily done. Besides, I feel something there."

"I hope you're right," Robert said. "I see what you mean. This fog is unusually thick."

"One can lose his way here," Richard said. "It's easily done in this kind of low visibility."

They arrived on the Isle of Wight. Lo and behold, the ship from Oostende was docked there. But they didn't disembark the ship. The captain didn't recognize the port of Portsmouth. He was checking his compass dial. Robert quickly went inside to search for them.

"I don't know how we got here," the captain said. "There was a lot of fog all the way here."

"I think I know what happened," Pink said. "This is Green's work. She created this fog to make them lose their way. Somehow she sensed Brigit's movements from Paris when she saw her there. She can do this kind of cheap trick now that she doesn't have real power anymore."

Val and Adonai joined them on the ship.

"Do you know anything about this?" Pink asked. "What are you doing here?"

Adonai said, "We had no idea what was going on until this girl came from Green. She sent her to tell us to hold everyone as prisoners until she got here."

"Instead we captured her and are holding her for you to talk to," Val said. "We were about to let you know, Pink, but you're already here."

"Who are these people?" Adonai asked. "What does Green want with them?"

Richard said, "Robert's mum and dad and his girlfriend are there. The rest of the people are passengers and ship's crew."

Robert came out of the ship with Brigit and his mum and dad.

"They're OK," Robert said. "Everyone's confused as to why they're here. Looks like my gap is working." He smiled at Pink and Richard.

"That explains everything," Val said. "We had no idea until the girl from Green turned up and told us what to do."

"What do you think we should do now?" Adonai asked.

"Well, we have to let the ship go," Richard said. "But did the girl say if Green is coming here? Robert, why don't you put everyone on our ship and let the captain sail Portsmouth. Tell him to wait there until we speak to him. Pink and I will go and see the girl."

"Look," the girl said, "all I know is Green told me to come and see Val. She wants Val to hold everyone on the ship as prisoners until she gets here."

"Did she say when she's coming?" Pink asked.

"I'm supposed to report back to her," the girl said. "She'll telepath me at midnight tonight."

"This is good, Pink," Richard said. "That means she still doesn't know what happened here, and she may be coming back soon."

"I think she's testing the waters," Pink said. "She's killing two birds with one stone. We have to leave everything as it was and set a trap for her. Let me talk to the girl first. See if I can make her send a

130

message when she calls her. Paris is too far for that. She must be near Dover or in Calais on the other side to reach here."

Pink went to a quiet area with the girl. She told Val to untie her.

"Do you know who I am?" Pink asked.

"No, ma'am," the girl said. Obviously she was nervous.

"I am Pink. What's your name?"

"Oh my God, you're Pink! I've always wanted to meet you. I've heard stories about you. They said you're a legend. You single-handedly beat her curse." She bowed with respect. "My name is Eileen, ma'am."

"Well, Eileen, how do you feel about Green?"

"I'm afraid of her, ma'am. She's the most powerful witch of all."

"She is no longer the powerful witch," Adonai said. "I was afraid of her too. She has no power if you don't fear her."

"What if she punishes me and curses me?" Eileen asked.

Pink said, "As it happens, her curse does not work anymore within a thousand square miles centering on the Isle of Wight. So you're safe here. She's bluffing and trying to live on her old glory."

Eileen said, "If that's true, then I don't care to serve her anymore. What she did to you and the other girls was brutal. I was only following her orders because I was afraid of her, like everyone."

"I'm not afraid of her anymore since I met Pink," Val said. "Do you want to live in fear all your life? She left the Isle of Wight because her power is gone from here."

"What do you want me to do, Miss Pink?" Eileen asked.

"I don't want you to do anything. Just do the right thing. Just tell her you did what she asked you to do. Tell her Val wants to know when she's coming back, and her new prisoners are here."

"I want you to do me a favor," Adonai said. "Tell her that Val said somebody named Adonai is dead. She left me in the dungeon to die, with no food or water. These people saved me because it's the right thing to do. I want to see her face when she sees I've come back from dead."

"No need to be melodramatic now, Adonai," Pink said. "I don't blame you, though."

They all laughed.

Then Pink said to Eileen, "Just remember the instructions, and let me know. There's no need to be afraid. Her power doesn't work here anymore. I will protect you. If you need anything, get in touch with any of us. Also remember, you don't have to do anything you feel you don't want to. You're free to go."

"Thank you, ma'am," Eileen said. "I shall always keep in touch with you, if I may. Nice to meet you, ma'am."

Chapter 22

THE BIRTH OF THE MAACULLA AND THE BABY RICHTELLA—
PORTSMOUTH

Everyone was anxiously waiting for the birth of Richard and Stella's first baby. It was already ten months. Both of their parents were looking forward to their first grandchild. They were just expecting another normal child, like everybody else. But this was not an ordinary birth by any means. Only four people knew that—Richard, Stella, Pink, and Robert. First of all, Stella was virtually still a virgin. A female body gets only one chance at this kind of energy transfer. With evolution and with the rare or lack of usage of the hymen for this purpose, many females are now being born even without a hymen.

In a normal human birth, the baby is always born with a 50/50 negative/positive balance of energies. From the beginning, only a handful of people paid attention to this kind of energy transfer and having superpower. This was due to the lack of knowledge of this sort in today's world. Knowledge of this kind was used in ancient times only. It was lost from lack of use. Maybe that explains why we don't see any prophets born anymore. Neither do we see any villains like Dracula being born with inhuman powers. Over the centuries, only a handful of people have ever used it successfully. This time, the world would witness, though it was rare, an amazing phenomenon. In essence, a baby and a mother would be born at the same time. Each would have an extreme balance of energies. That means there would be two superpowers—one in favour of negative (destructive), the boy, and the other in favour of positive (constructive), the mother. One exactly opposite the other, like, for instance, Dracula and his nemesis, if he had one. She could be called Maaculla.

Pink was very actively present for this amazing event. She assured Richard, Robert, and Stella that it was not unusual for this kind of birth to take ten months instead of nine months. Both the baby and the mother had to be exactly ready for the energy transfer. She learnt all this from her witch's education. But this was the first time she would witness the transfer of energies herself. If everything went well, during the birth the baby would absorb his mum's 40 percent negative energy and relinquish his 40 percent positive energy to her. So he

133

would have 90/10 in favour of negative energy, and his mother would have 10/90 in favour of positive energy. Hence he would have more devilish power, and his mum would have angelic power, so to speak, in religious terms. Thus everyone would be witnessing the birth of two superpowers at the same time, and they would be exactly opposite each other. The rebirth of the mother would be called Maaculla. The baby would be named after Richard and Stella—Richtella (pronounced Rich-stella). Both would possess superhuman powers.

After witnessing this birth, one couldn't refute the fact that humans were not too far from superhuman powers. It was a question of one's energy shifting to one direction, from 50/50 to 10/90. Either way, that 10 percent is necessary for both of them remain human. Otherwise, once they become 100 percent either way, they would become an angel or a devil. As mentioned before, humans can't perceive devils or angels with their limited physical senses.

Pink was staying very close to Stella. She averred that the moment was almost there. All of a sudden, the baby was very active inside the stomach. He was moving around in a very abnormal way. It felt as if he was pushing against the stomach to get out. At the same time, instead of Stella complaining about the baby's excessive movements, she became very talkative. She wanted to get up and walk around. She was also floating a few inches above the bed. She was not even aware of his movements inside. She was not in pain, like a normal birth mother. She was happy and very talkative and smiling. Her energy seemed to be extremely high. It was difficult to keep her lying down. She was laughing and joking uncontrollably, sometimes humming a song. If you witnessed a mother giving birth under hypnosis, the only difference was the floating phenomenon.

All this had been going on for about five minutes now. She was getting more and more agitated. She was singing a song and giggling very loudly, as if someone were tickling her. She was extremely excited. The next moment, she was completely silent and still. At the same moment, a baby's giggling could be heard. He was out, and then he went completely quiet, like his mother. They both were unconscious. This transfer of energy was so anomalous and so powerful that it knocked both mother and the baby unconscious. In a laymen's eyes, they both looked as if their bodies were lifeless, but their pulses were still beating and their body temperatures were still warm and normal.

Richard asked, "What has just happened here?"

Pink said, "Not to worry. Everything is OK."

Richard said, "But they aren't moving."

Pink said, "It's normal in an event like this. They're unconscious but resting. It's a big energy transfer. Without energy, we are all dead. Then again, when we have too much of one energy, it knocks the balance off the human body. Their nervous systems are getting used to this extraordinary balance. I can assure you they're more than alive. They can even hear us."

Richard was extremely concerned. "How am I going to explain all this to my parents? Most importantly, to her parents, if anything drastic happens?"

Pink said, "Look, Richard, I can prove it you. Ask them if they can hear you, and keep your eyes on their right index fingers."

Richard looked at Pink with disbelief. "OK. Can you hear me?"

"Go on," Pink said.

Stella's and the baby's right index fingers rose up at the same time.

Richard smiled. "That's amazing. They can hear us! Shall I tell Mum and Dad everything's OK?"

"Tell them they're resting and not to come straightaway, and Stella's parents too. They'll need couple of days of rest."

"A couple of days! Thanks, Pink."

Pink said, "Just so that you are aware that this is not unusual for this kind of event, it will take a few more days for both of them to recover from it. After all, this is not a normal birth situation."

"I want to believe you, but at the same time, I can't help worrying about Stella and my son. I hope it's worth it. I hope they're not suffering."

"That's understandable," Pink said. Then she said to Robert, "Can you keep Richard occupied for a few more days while the baby and the mother have a chance to recuperate? They need to be left alone from any fears. Any negative energy, such as fear, can delay their recuperation. I'm confident they'll be OK. After all, they're not dead—

just semiconscious from the shock. They're still only human. I can assure you they're not suffering."

"Richard, she's right," Robert said. "We have to trust Pink. We've come this far. She has never let us down once. Let's go and finish those defense plans. After all, this is for the same purpose. Everything will be all right. You saw their fingers moving when you asked."

Richard said, "What am I going to say to her mum and dad if they suddenly turn up? I feel responsible."

"Pink will think of something," Robert said. "She has her full power now. She can create a harmless diversion for them."

"Let's hope so," Richard said. "I'm so worried I don't want to lose them either."

Robert held him close with his right arm. "Richard, everything will be all right. Let's go. We're not helping here. Besides, Pink is staying with them. We really need to trust her. But Richard, I envy you there. I want to feel for Brigit the same way one day. I want to feel that love you're feeling inside. Let's go, Richard, before I too melt down like you. Let's go. Bye, Pink. Bye Stella. Bye, baby Richard."

They both exited the house.

Chapter 23

RICHARD AND ROBERT IN A MILITARY CAMP

Richard and Robert were very busy making plans for defense against possible attack by King Phillip IV. He was not going to give up that easily. Now that Green had joined him, he had renewed confidence. They had double trouble now. So far, with Robert's help, they had managed to deflect his last few attempts. Phillip was more aggressive now that he knew Robert was helping them. He was drawing a renewed strength from the Green Witch. Although Green had lost her witch's power over this area, she could advise him about their weak points, locations, and so on. Like Phillip, she was full of cunning tricks.

They had to be vigilant about guarding their borders. They had secured the Isle of Wight. After the last incident, Green would know for sure that she had lost her grip there. But right now it was good to keep this part as it was so that she wouldn't suspect that all her people had joined Pink. But Green was no fool. She was not going to come until she was sure. That was why she was using others to do her dirty work. Phillip, on the other hand, was fooled by her, because he was not aware that she didn't have any real powers anymore.

Robert said, "I know for sure Phillip is planning something sinister, now that he has stopped sending hot air balloons. Do you remember last time—how he sent a ship with the English flag flying on the mast? He almost fooled us all. That's how cunning he is."

"I know," Richard said. "We're prepared for this kind of deception. We're not going to fall for that again. We have our watch posts all along the shoreline as well. We have our archers on the watch posts to shoot down the balloons before they reach our land. We have Pink's girls there twenty-four hours a day. They keep a presence there in three shifts at the watchtowers."

"I know Phillip," Robert said. "He's very clever. He uses his intelligence in a negative manner. That's how he is. The French people don't like war, but he forces them to go to war."

"He is so different from you. The ironic thing is, Edward and Phillip are related too, and this war is within the family. Rivalry among the family members."

"I know there's room for everyone in this world. It's not necessary to be greedy or invade others. He wastes so much energy and resources in the war and negativity. In his defense, his mentality was born in an *anormal*"—*abnormal* in French—"war environment. If you remember, conflicts between our two countries have always been there. He's just keeping up with the tradition. He believes the French people would think he is a coward if he didn't go to war. Actually, they're tired of his aggressions and this long, drawn-out war. I tried reasoning with him and hoped one day he would change. I'm working for peace and not for destroying Phillip. But I think he can't help being negative. I decided he will never change. We will do him a favor when we put him out of commission."

"I hope we're successful with my son. He'll have inhuman power. The only way to defeat Phillip is by driving his soldiers completely useless with an unusual fear. I fear for my country, my people, and myself. Now I have a family too. I have extra fear. I hope we're successful with our plan. As your father said, he would prefer to win this without any bloodshed."

"I understand," Robert said. "I fear for my life every minute. Do you remember, he sent a couple of women to kill me? That bastard would stop at nothing. My own cousin. Sometimes I think he's the devil himself. But I know his every move. He doesn't care about these people who are dying for him, let alone how many die on the other side. Dad is right. It's painful to see people lose their loved ones and their own lives. It doesn't matter which side it is. Phillip doesn't have any empathy for any side."

Richard asked, "What if he changes his plans and we're unsuccessful with Richtella?"

"Then we will continue doing what we're doing. It's not very likely that he will change his ways, though, because he wants to be always right, and he's told everyone his plans. He's blinded with ego and hatred. It's difficult for him to see any other point of view."

"I hope you're right and things work out as we planned. We need a devilish power to beat another devil. That's all we can do at this moment. We have to be vigilant about guarding our borders."

Robert smiled. "And I will keep my eyes open for any French women."

Richard said, "I thought you didn't want women anymore, Robert." They both laughed.

"Not like the ones my cousin picks for me, beautiful and deadly."

Richard laughed. "Sorry to disappoint you, Robert. We have only beautiful women, but not deadly. Right now that's the best we can do for you."

They both laughed again.

Three days went by. They had not heard from Pink or Stella. That night Richard went to bed unusually early for some reason. He was tired and sleepy. He woke up early at dawn from a dream. In the dream, Stella was with him. She was holding the baby.

She asked him, "When are you coming home? We're waiting for you."

He woke up from the dream thinking, what if that's not true? Then he remembered the maha guru's training, and he immediately pushed his negative thoughts down the gap. His heart told him to go home; they were waiting for him. The dream had been so vivid that he could feel them.

Sure enough, a messenger was waiting for him outside as soon as he got out of bed early at dawn.

The message read, "Your wife and baby are awake and well. Stella is asking for you. Please come home. Pink."

Richard had been waiting for this. He woke Robert up and said, "Robert, I'm going home."

"OK," Robert said groggily. "I'm coming."

"I dreamt it this morning. It felt so real. It felt as if she were here with me. I could smell her and feel her with the baby."

Robert started getting dressed. "Maybe she was. Because Stella has the power now. Pink said that she would be able astro-travel, among many other things."

"I hope you're right. And the baby"—he choked up—"I haven't had a chance to hold him yet."

They quickly had a word with the man in charge and left for home.

They arrived at Richard's home. The door flung open magically. As soon as he came to the door, the baby glided through the air defying the gravity and landed in his arms. Richard and Robert were astonished.

"There you are," Robert said. "You wanted to hold your baby."

Richard said, "Do you think he could hear me?"

Stella whispered, "This baby has some magical power, Richard."

Richard kissed her and whispered back, "I noticed. You will never know what we went through..." He stopped, thinking this was not the right moment. "Honey, I love you so much, and Richtella."

Stella said, "Pink said how anxious you were to hold him. Yes, he has magical powers."

Richard and Robert and Pink exchanged looks.

"You're not so bad yourself, Stella," Pink said. "I noticed you went to visit Richard early this morning."

Stella had a smirk on her face. "Whatever do you mean, Pink? How would you know that anyway?"

They all laughed and exchanged a meaningful look.

Stella said to Richard, "We love you very much too. Sorry you were so worried about us while we were recuperating. And thank you, Pink and Robert, for everything. We love you."

"We love you too," Pink said. "I think we will give you lovers some privacy."

Robert came forward to kiss Stella on her cheek. "Love you all."

Robert and Pink left the room.

Richard said, "Thanks, Pink and Robert." Then, to Stella, he said, "He's such a cute baby. It seems like he understands everything."

"All babies do," Stella said. "Their spirits are ageless, but their bodies are young. Richtella can express himself much better than normal babies because of his power. It will take time for him to speak, but soon. He already knows his name. Call him."

Richard said, "Richtella." He opened his arms.

The baby flew back to his arms again.

Chapter 24

ROBERT SHOWS HIS FAMILY AND BRIGIT AROUND PORTSMOUTH

The next day was Sunday. Robert had taken his mum and dad out on a tour of Portsmouth with his sister Adele, brother Roger, and Brigit. He was very proudly showing them around and introducing them to the people he knew. He took them to St Mary's Church to meet Stella's mum and dad. There was a very big congregation on Sunday, and they were very busy. Mr. and Mrs. Reynolds came over to greet Robert and his mum and dad, Adele, Roger, and Brigit.

"Welcome to our church," Mr. Reynolds said. "We're never too busy for you and your family."

"This is my mum and dad," Robert said, "and this is Brigit, my girlfriend, and this is my younger sister Adele."

"Delighted to meet you all," Mr. Reynolds said. "Oh dear, the service is about to begin. Emily, why don't you stay with our honorable guests. I shall be back as soon as I finish."

"There's no need for any fuss," Robert said. "I'm just showing them around. Please go about your business. We'll see you afterwards. I'm sure you have a few things to do."

"We heard Stella and baby are resting," Emily said. "That's a big relief."

"Yes," Robert said. "Yes, they're resting. They can't wait to see you."

"We can't wait to see them," Emily said. "Thank you, Robert. We'll see you after the service."

Robert found some seats for his family.

"I'm glad we came to church today," his dad said. "This reminds me of our church in Paris."

"Isn't there a church nearby in Luxembourg?" Robert asked.

"Sure there is," his dad said. "Schroeder's home is like a church—so peaceful and green everywhere, with Mosel river running by. Very serene. But I miss seeing those friends. I wonder what they're doing. Are they frightened? With this madman on the throne, no one feels safe, from the labourer to high officials. Let's pray for them."

"I agree," Robert said. "We'll do what we can to end it peacefully. That's why I wanted you here. Thank you for coming."

"We will do what we can," his dad said.

"I think the service is beginning now," his mum said.

"Sorry," Robert said. "Let us pray."

After mass, Father Reynolds came by. "I was looking forward to meeting your family, Robert. In fifteen more minutes. I'll be free. Would you please come by to our humble house? We live in the house behind the church. Emily has gone ahead to prepare some tea for you. I hope this is OK."

"Of course," Robert said. "I know where you live. I was just showing them around Portsmouth. We have no particular plan. Your church is one of the main attractions in Portsmouth. My mum and dad were looking forward to meeting Stella's family."

"Very impressive church," Mr. Artoire said. "I was just telling Robert that it reminds me of our church in Paris."

"Yes," Father Reynolds said. "I must say we're blessed with this beautiful historical church. I'm so happy that you like it too. I can show you round before you go."

"That will be nice." Mr. Artoire said.

"How exciting, Mrs. Artoire said "Are sure you have time? We were planning to look around ourselves."

"It will be my pleasure," Father Reynolds said. "I can also show you the plans to extend this into a cathedral. It may not be as big as Notre Dame. The king has promised the funds already."

Robert said, "My girlfriend, Brigit, used to live in Notre Dame until recently, when she escaped to Luxembourg."

"Oh, how wonderful," Father Reynolds said. "I've always wanted to visit, but the war made it impossible to travel to France."

They all followed Father Reynolds to the main podium in the back of the church.

His assistant, Colin, was standing by.

"Colin, will it be all right?" Father Reynolds asked. "I'm going to be busy for an hour or so. I'm going to show our friends from France around. OK?"

"Yes sir, Father Reynolds. Everything is under control. Nice to meet you all. Welcome."

They walked around the church, and he showed them the plans for the cathedral. The church had a long history. It was built in the twelfth century. Then they followed him to his house behind the church.

They all sat down in the drawing room. Mrs. Reynolds served tea and refreshments.

"We can help," Robert said. "Thank you for your kindness."

"There's no need; thank you," Mrs. Reynolds said. "Everything's under control. Enjoy. You're like family to us, Robert."

"I'm impressed with the plans for the cathedral," Mr. Artoire said, "You definitely have space for it. Looks like you will soon need more room for your mass anyway."

"Unfortunately," Father Reynolds said, "they held the plan to build for a while, waiting for the war to calm down. Now they're talking about it again. Thanks to Robert. With his help, we've had a whole year of peace. People are again gaining confidence to come back to Portsmouth."

"I know he's determined to have peace everywhere," Mr. Artoire said. "I'm sure all of France wants peace, like the people here. But when we have a mad king, no one has any say in the matter. We're all praying for peace, and his sanity."

JEAN-PIERE'S SUDDEN ARRIVAL IN PORTSMOUTH

Pink, Robert, and Richard were sitting in Richard's house. They were discussing a few things about how to continue being on guard and never underestimating the enemy.

Pink got up. "There's someone coming to see you soon. I mean me too."

"Who is this mystery person?" Richard asked.

"You may not believe it," Pink said. "It's your friend from Belgium, Jean-Pierre."

"Jean-Pierre! Why, he hasn't said anything to me about coming here."

"He told me he might be coming soon," Pink said. "But I didn't know it would be this soon."

"What do you mean? He's coming to see you?"

"Do you mean you two are…" Robert said.

"That's nice," Richard said. "He seems like a nice person."

"Good for you," Robert said. "Yes, he's very nice."

"Gentlemen," Pink said, "don't put the cart before the horse. Yes, I like him, but he hasn't asked me out yet. Anyway, his ship is arriving soon. Someone has to meet him at the dock in about an hour."

"We'll all go, unless you want privacy," Richard said.

"Richard," Pink said, "I told you there is no privacy."

Robert and Richard both laughed. "Ha, ha. Pink is in love."

Pink's face was flushed. "OK, that's enough. What are you two doing?"

Richard said, "You're like our sister."

Robert said, "Yes, we can tease you."

"Stop it, you two," Pink said. "Are you coming, or do I have to go on my own? For God's sake, don't say anything to him. I don't want you to put any ideas in his head."

They all left for the dock.

About half an hour later, they arrived at the dock. Jean-Pierre was already there. His ship had arrived about an hour early. He was smiling at them and holding two big bouquets of flowers.

"Pink just told us you were coming," Robert said.

Jean-Pierre handed a bouquet to Pink. "I was thinking of coming for a while. Then I thought, why not now? I was going to drop a line. But Pink said she would sense my coming. I wanted to see how good she is."

"Oh, she is good," Richard said. "Welcome, Jean-Pierre. Welcome to Portsmouth."

Jean-Pierre handed the other bouquet to Richard. "This is for Stella. I heard she's going to have the baby about now. I'm looking forward to meeting both baby and the mother."

"You can give it to them yourself soon," Richard said. "We're going there now. You'll be staying in our guest house, I hope. I would like to return your hospitality."

"Sure," Jean-Pierre said, "if that's OK with everyone."

"Is that OK Pink?" Richard asked.

"Of course," Pink said. "That's very civil of you, Richard."

"I would have him," Robert said, "but my place is quite full with my family right now."

They all got in the coach. Richard and Robert sat next to each other. Pink and Jean-Pierre sat next to each other awkwardly on the opposite seats.

"Actually," Robert said, "I was about to write to you, Jean-Pierre, warning you about an incident that happened to my family, in case you were thinking of coming this way."

"What happened, Robert?"

"Well, everything is OK now. But their ship did got lost in the fog on the way here. But it wasn't natural fog. It was created by our enemy who joined Phillip. We told you about her. It was sorciere Green."

Pink said, "Luckily we had already captured her hideout. She didn't know that, and she sent the ship there, to the Isle of Wight."

"But it was worrisome for all of us for couple of days," Richard said. "Not knowing what had happened to the ship, especially Robert's family. Poor Robert. We didn't know what to say to console him."

"But your mum and dad, Adele, Roger, and Brigit are OK now, right? I should have come with them. I feel bad now."

"Oh, they were unharmed," Robert said. "It was a confusing and challenging time for all of us here. It's more concerning when your loved ones are at stake."

"It was quite confusing," Pink said. "My girls and the soldiers didn't know why the ship was there or who they were. The captain didn't know where he was. And Robert's family and the other passengers didn't know where they were either. So it was more confusing than anything else for all of them."

"While that was going on over there, unknown to us, we were waiting in anticipation for the ship's arrival," Richard said. "We waited for two days, and then we started the search. Of course, Pink found them through her senses."

Pink said, "We're here already."

The coach came to a halt in front of Richard's mansion.

Robert said, "Jean-Pierre, did you bring just this small suitcase?"

"I prefer to travel light."

"I hope you brought enough clothes to stay awhile," Richard said.

"Yes," Jean-Pierre said, "but I can always have them made here. Robert told me the English tailors are excellent. I'm looking forward to staying here. Pink has promised to show me around Portsmouth."

Stella came out to greet him. They all went inside the house.

"Welcome, Jean-Pierre," Stella said. "Pink told me you were coming."

Richard and Robert exchanged looks—this was news to them.

Jean-Pierre handed the bouquet to Stella. "This is for you."

"How very civil of you," Stella said. "Thank you. They're beautiful."

"Pink told me how beautiful you are," Jean-Pierre said. "And the baby must be asleep now."

"Yes, he is," Stella said. "He naps a lot. When he's not napping, he's very active. He's very special, isn't he, Richard?"

Pink whispered to Stella, "They're complaining because I didn't tell them about Jean-Pierre coming."

Stella smiled. "I see. This is girl talk. You don't want to be part of it anyway."

Richard said, "She could have at least mentioned that he was coming."

"Like I said, this is girl talk," Stella said.

"We don't want to know about her private affairs," Robert said.

"We're happy for you, Pink," Richard said.

"Thank you, but let's not jump to conclusions."

"I like her a lot," Jean-Pierre said. "It's up to her. I would be honored if she would consider being my girlfriend."

"It's getting to be a bit too much interfering," Stella said. "Why don't you all sit down and relax. I'm going to go and see how dinner is coming along. You must all be hungry. Richard, maybe you should show Jean-Pierre his room."

Stella left for the kitchen.

"OK," Richard said. "Why don't you follow me, Jean-Pierre. You probably want to have a wash and change before dinner."

"Thank you, Richard," Jean-Pierre said. "Don't mind if I do."

Richard and Jean-Pierre left. One of the boy servants followed them with Jean-Pier's suitcase.

146

"He's a very nice person, Pink," Robert said. "So are you. I think you suit each other very well."

"Thank you, Robert. I like him a lot. He's your friend; that says a lot about his character. Life's been a big rush lately, but they're all good events, mostly. I can see the universe is moving us. Richard got married, and now they have a baby. You're united with the love of your life. My curse is over, and we have peace in Portsmouth. Now Jean-Pierre is in my life. Your mum and dad are here. Alex is united with his girlfriend, Debbie. One good event after another. But if you notice, they all came in as disguise as adversities. Maybe we should welcome adversity in our lives. It always ends up good for us anyway, thank God."

Suddenly there was applause all around the room. "Hear, hear! Well said, Pink!"

Pink didn't realize that Stella, Richard, and Jean-Pierre were already back, and they were listening to her speak.

"Thank you, Pink," Stella said. "That's a very uplifting thought. We'll talk more about it at the dinner table."

Two servers were waiting at the door of the dining room, ready to greet everyone. They all sat down at the dinner table.

"That was quite a speech, Pink," Richard said. "I appreciate your input. I also meant to say sorry for teasing you. We didn't mean any harm."

"There's nothing to say sorry for," Pink said. "And as you remember, this speech is a direct quote from the maha guru of Ajanta. Do you remember that he explained that every adversity is an opportunity in disguise?"

"Yes, Pink," Robert said. "I remember he was giving a hypothetical analogy that in the middle of a typhoon, those who fear get swept away. Their own fear is what originally attracted the adversity to them."

"That's right," Pink said. "But it's difficult to believe that one person could attract something as massive as typhoon."

"Oh, but it's not one person's attraction," Richard said. "Something like this, on a massive scale, can only happen due to the mass awareness of one particular fear. Then again, one person can instigate it by creating mass awareness of that fear—the same way it can also happen with the positive energy."

"Thank you, Richard," Pink said, "for explaining that to me. Now I understand why the maha guru told us to use our gap at a time like this."

"Anyway," Robert said, "I also want to apologize to you, Pink, for those innuendoes. Forgive me."

"Like I said," Pink said, "there's nothing to forgive."

"You're like a sister to us," Richard said. "I guess we became a little possessive of you."

Stella said, "I think that's very sensible and gracious of you, gentlemen." She raised her glass of wine. "Here's to us."

"Here's to us," everyone said.

One of the maids brought the baby down to meet Jean-Pierre. The baby was raring to go to him.

"Open your arms, Jean-Pierre," Richard said.

Jean-Pierre opened his arms. The baby flew from the maid's arms to him.

"Comment astonishing!" Jean-Pierre said. ("How astonishing!")

"Yes," Robert said. "This baby has some astonishing power."

"Do you mean he knew I wanted to meet him?"

Richard said, "Just so you know what you're getting into, yes, he did."

"Pink didn't tell me everything, then," Jean-Pierre said.

"She probably didn't want to frighten you away," Stella said.

They all laughed.

"I shall bid you good night now," Robert said. "It's getting late. My family is waiting for me." He got up and kissed Pink and Stella.

"Next time, bring Brigit with you," Stella said, smiling. "Then you won't have to leave so early."

"Yes," Pink said. "We can get to know her better too."

"I think I shall do that," Robert said. "Thank you. Good night, everyone. Good night, Richtella." He kissed the baby.

Richard came outside with him. Robert got in the coach, and they drove off.

The next morning, Pink and Richard left for work. Pink left a note for Jean-Pierre to meet her at the office when he woke up. He could take one of the coaches there. Pink had promised to show him around Portsmouth. Richard, Robert, and Pink worked from the same office building. They each had a separate office there. The whole office building was heavily guarded.

Jean-Pierre arrived as per Pink's directions. She was in a meeting with the girls. She was listening to yesterday's report about their activities. Each of the group leaders was reading her report to Pink. Jean-Pierre waited another half hour, and then Pink finished giving instructions to the girls. She introduced Jean-Pierre to everyone there. She showed him around Robert's and Richard's offices, and then they left for a tour of the Portsmouth.

The first stop would be Stella's mum and dad's place, and then St. Mary's. The church was one of the major centres of attraction in Portsmouth. It was the main centre for public gatherings. It'd been there since before the town centre was built. Jean-Pierre was looking forward to this tour. He had never visited England before. Actually, the long war prevented all the French people from visiting England, and vice versa. Of course, those who were lucky enough to have escaped from France visited nearby countries such as England, Belgium, Germany, Switzerland, and Luxembourg. It was because of the connection to Robert that Jean-Pierre could visit England. It was also an opportunity for Pink and Jean-Pierre to get to know each other. So far, they hadn't had a chance to intimately know each other or hang out on their own.

They arrived at St. Mary's. Mr. and Mrs. Reynolds were waiting for them.

"This is Mr. and Mrs. Reynolds," Pink said. "Stella's mum and dad."

Jean-Pierre shook hands with them. "
Pleased to meet you, sir, ma'am."

"Delighted to meet you, Jean-Pierre," Mr. Reynolds said. "Are you enjoying your visit to England?"

"Yes, sir, thank you. I have a very good guide."

"Pink is a lovely girl," Mrs. Reynolds said. "She's like family to us. We're lucky to have her. She's been instrumental in bringing peace to Portsmouth."

"Let's go to the house and have some refreshments," Mr. Reynolds said.

They all went to the house in the back.
Inside, they sat down for some tea and snacks.

Mrs. Reynolds poured tea for them. "How much of Portsmouth have you seen so far?"

"We've only begun," Jean-Pierre said. "Your church is the first stop."

"I thought I'd begin the sight-seeing with St. Mary's," Pink said. "After all, it is one of the main attractions in Portsmouth."

Jean-Pierre said, "It is really a lovely historical church."

"Excuse me," Pink said. "I'll be back soon. I forgot something." She went out to the coach.

"Thank you, Jean-Pierre," Mrs. Reynolds said. "We're glad you like it. My husband will tell you the history of it one day."

Pink came back with a bunch of flowers for Mrs. Reynolds. "They're for you. I left them in the coach by mistake."

"Oh, thank you both," Mrs. Reynolds said. "They're lovely."

"You're welcome," Pink said. "I'm thinking of taking him around the shops today. He also wants to visit a tailor."

"I heard some of the best tailors are in England," Jean-Pierre said. "I want to take this opportunity to have some clothes made here. Do you have some recommendations?"

"Actually, they're all good here," Mrs. Reynolds said. "My husband goes to all of them to keep them in business during wartime. Business is much better now, since we've had peace here."

"I think I shall take him to the one Richard and Robert go to," Pink said. "Then, tomorrow, I need to go to Isle of Wight. I think I'll take him with me."

"After all these years, I've never been to the Isle of Wight." Mrs. Reynolds said.

"I'm going there on official business," Pink said. "We're keeping that area guarded. Just in case somebody tries to get in that way. maybe after the baby is born, you can come with us one day. When is Steven due?"

"A couple of months yet," Mrs. Reynolds said. "Oh, somebody woke up, I think. He likes his name. Do you remember he was moving around a lot when you were there at the Easter fair?"

"How could I forget?" Pink said. "He was definitely letting us know that he was there."

Jean-Pierre looked puzzled. "What are you talking about?"

"We're talking about the baby," Pink said. "If you mention his name, he starts moving around inside her stomach."

Mrs. Reynolds said, "You know Pink is very special. She can sense certain things. For instance, she said this is going to be a boy."

Jean-Pierre smiled. "I see. Is there something else you didn't tell me about?"

"Slowly you will know everything," Pink said. "I think we should get going before the tailor closes. Thank you for your lovely hospitality."

"Not at all," Mrs. Reynolds said. "Please come again. Thank you for the lovely flowers."

They got up and left for the tailor's shop.

PINK AT THE ISLE OF WIGHT WITH JEAN-PIERRE

The next day, Pink and Jean-Pierre left for the Isle of Wight. She had some official business to take care of there. All the girls, including Green's ex-girls, were happy to see her. She introduced Jean-Pierre to everyone there. She brought them some gifts, tea, and biscuits, which they couldn't get on the Isle of Wight yet. She alternated all the girls on duty there. One group came in to relieve the existing one. They went back to Portsmouth in the same ship as Pink. This was a fair system because there wasn't much to do on the Isle of Wight. But she had to leave the key people, such as Val, there always. If Green ever came back and didn't see Val, she would get suspicious. Adonai, on the other hand, volunteered to stay there permanently. He had his personal agenda to take care of if and when Green came back. All these things were new to Jean-Pierre. He was astonished to see Pink's organization and leadership skills. Sometimes he was lost as to what to think about it. Some events seemed like a fairy tale. But Pink thought it was good that

151

he had the opportunity to witness all this. He would know for sure what he was getting involved in.

The Isle of Wight was not as built up as Portsmouth. There were no shops or grocery stores there. Those who stayed got their supplies from Portsmouth. Apart from Pink's people and the soldiers, you would hardly see anybody there. Pink's girls were always on alert in case of any French attack. Their job was to inform the soldiers of any intruders. Soldiers were busy building roads and bridges there, according to Richard's plan. As the lieutenant governor of Portsmouth, he was also responsible for the Isle of Wight. He decided to build some infrastructure there, as it was getting more populated every year. He had commissioned Jean De Gisord to build some commercial buildings, houses, shops, and so on there. De Gisord was a merchant and owned a fleet of ships. He had been involved in building most of Portsmouth. Richard thought he would be the right person to design the town on the Isle of Wight, thereby also creating jobs in the area. De Gisord was grateful to return favors to Richard for saving his ships from the French attacks.

Pink sent a message to Richard and Robert that she could sense Green's presence near the Isle of Wight. Richard and Robert rushed there with one of their battleships. On Pink's order, all the soldiers were pulled off of their road-building project. Within a couple of hours, the whole place was on war alert. There were already two battleships permanently docked there. Now they were going around the island in opposite directions, passing each other halfway. They were on full battle alert. Richard's battleship was also docked there, as they had arrived from Portsmouth. The distance between Portsmouth and the Isle of Wight was only four miles.

They secured the Isle of Wight when they overpowered Green's hideout. Since then, they had been keeping enough soldiers there. Since Green's people had joined Pink, they had a large number of witches on guard there too. They were very useful in sensing any unusual activities with their special powers. They would be able to sense Green's presence or any other hostile presence from a hundred miles away. With their help, Richard was able to make the shores of Portsmouth and the Isle of Wight literally impenetrable. Since Pink's girls had joined forces with Richard, all the attacks by Phillip had failed.

If somehow they could capture or kill Green, Phillip would be even more helpless.

King Edward was very pleased with Richard's success. He not only knighted him at his wedding, he also granted him all the funds he needed to keep Portsmouth safe and to rebuild it to its glory.

Unfortunately, even with all the precautions they were taking to remain incognito, somehow Green sensed danger. They could see from a distance a ship approach and then turn around and head back to France. It would be useless to pursue her from this distance.

"That was a close call," Richard said. "Thank you, Pink, for being so vigilant. You should really be spending time with Jean-Pierre."

"No, no," Jean-Pierre said. "I find it very exhilarating. Knowing what she does, I'll get to know her better this way."

"Good," Robert said. "This way you can really get to know Pink before you get deeply involved with her. She's an extraordinary person with extraordinary powers."

"Robert, you're not helping here," Pink said. "You're not supposed to frighten him away. Also, I'm no more extraordinary than you two. I have some witch's powers—that's all—which I use for the good of all."

"Thank you, Pink," Richard said. "We're grateful for that."

"We all have some talent that we use for the good of all," Pink said. "We also help one another, like the way you and Robert helped me to get out of my curse. Our intentions matter."

Robert said, "I don't mean to frighten him, but, rather, to encourage him to use his own talent for the good of people."

"I'm nothing important like you all," Jean-Pierre said. "I'm just a chef, and I grow food on our land with my father. Now we do it in Belgium, since we lost our land in France. We ran away there for our lives."

"This is another example of how adversity is an opportunity," Pink said. "Because this adversity brought us all together. At the same time, Jean-Pierre, you are also very important—because without food, what would we all eat?"

"That's exactly right," Richard said. "You serve people with your talent for food, and we keep people safe. They are equally important tasks. I can't wait to try your cooking one day."

"We're lucky to have each other," Robert said. "Like Pink says, adversity brings good people together. Without that, I wouldn't have come to England and met Richard. We wouldn't have met Pink without her problem. And then Richard brought Stella to us, we wouldn't have met you in Belgium, and you wouldn't have met Pink—and it goes on and on. It's growing every day. Now I fully believe that our problems bring us to our opportunities."

Pink said to the girls, "Ladies, this is Jean-Pierre. As you can see, he's a very special person in my life. I want you to take his scent and be on the lookout for his safety from now on."

All the girls lined up. One by one they came and took the scent from his right hand by sniffing. Until now, they had seemed like normal human beings. Within a moment, they transformed into mythical characters. When they acted as witches, their true colours showed up. Each witch had her own hue in her body. They all turned different colours. When the sniffing ceremony finished, Pink said, "Thank you all for caring so much. I am grateful."

Val said, "You would do the same for us, Pink. We're grateful to you more than we can ever repay. It's because of you that all of us are free of our curse. We would be still living under Green with fear. Thank you for giving us a life with dignity, freedom, and purpose. We will do anything for you. You have inspired us to have courage and live to our own potential."

All the girls said, "Thank you, Pink. We love you."

Pink said, "I love you too."

Jean-Pierre said, "I suppose this is something else you would tell me later."

"Maybe Richard and Robert will tell you the rest," Pink said. "Richard is the one who started all this."

"Now, now," Richard said. "Blame me for everything." They all laughed. "One thing I want to mention is that we must always remember to learn from our experiences. We cannot be judgmental without knowing someone well. Who would have known one of the most beautiful girls was hiding behind the atrocity committed by the Green Witch? Now we are ready to give our lives for one another. Although it was difficult, I persisted in following my grandfather's advice. He said that you can find a lotus blossom in the midst of a pile of cow dung. The way you look at things, it changes the way you look at it. Ladies and gentlemen, may I present my lotus blossom." He pointed at Pink. "Miss Pink."

Everyone stood up and clapped their hands in a well-deserved standing ovation for Pink.

Chapter 25

RICHARD AND STELLA MOVE INTO THEIR NEW HOME

Six months later, Richard and Stella received the long-anticipated good news from the contractor, de Gisord. Their house in Arundel was complete and ready to move into. The gardeners were putting landscaping down as the finishing touch. Some of the palms and trees saved from the big Easter fair were Seaforthia palms, wisteria vines, and ferns. Richard and Stella were happy to give them a permanent home. Also, the whole garden was adorned with typical English flowers such as Tudor rose, rhododendron, foxgloves, lavenders, irises, calla lilies, geraniums, fuchsia, freesias, and various fruit trees in the back garden like apples, pears, peaches.

Image 9: Freesia flowers behind the house in Arundel.

At Richard's request, the head landscape architect, Nicholas Walker, created an entire field of Freesias. That was located on the west bank of the lake, facing the master bedroom and ending on the horizon. It was visible from the balcony of the first-floor master bedroom. In the morning light through the bay window of the master bedroom, the view of the back garden, beginning with the arbour with wisteria blossoming, the plush green playground, the lake with the glass house, and ending the entire picture with the rainbow colours of the freesia, covered entire west bank of the lake as far as the eye could see. Though meticulously placed and designed by the master gardener, it retained the natural, carefree flow of the entire landscape in such a way that it seemed unspoiled and untouched by human hands. This was a surprise gift to Stella by Richard.

Image 10: She was wearing freesias on her hat.

He remembered the day he met her at the Easter fair. She was wearing a delicate bunch of colourful freesias on her hat. That picture of Stella and the colourful Freesias was eternally etched in his mind. He wanted to keep that most beautiful and meaningful memory of his life alive by this garden. Later he found out that Freesia represented strength. It was ironic to think that at that moment of his life, he needed strength the most. It was amazing how the universe brought forward the right person at the right moment with the right energy. Since then she had continued generating strength for him.

Their favorite pastime was to walk through the field of freesias barefoot. Richard had adopted this practice from his training with maha guru in Ajanta, India. In the Kama Sutra, kellie (teasing to arousal) would begin in a garden prior to entering the bedroom. They would walk barefoot in the field and sink knee deep into the delicate colours of the flowers while the fragrance filled their lungs, energizing them from head to toe, thus arousing their entire bodies with sexuality.

It was a small, stately mansion with fifty bedrooms in three stories and an equally big basement for the kitchen, storage facilities, and staff quarters. The whole mansion had several escape routes for fire and/or any other emergencies. Richard had learnt the importance of escape routes from the experiences of the French fire attacks. That was how Alex's parents and sister had gotten trapped inside their own home when the French firebombed Portsmouth. Richard had prioritized with the architect, Mr. de Gisord, to make sure that no one would get trapped during an emergency, whether it was manmade or a natural disaster. He had designed the mansion very ingeniously, with sufficient escape routes. Even the basement had four independent emergency escape routes where the majority of the staff resided. Later he installed fire escapes to all the buildings in Portsmouth.

There was a circular drive at the front entrance. The coaches would enter through a humongous gate and exit through a matching gate on the opposite side. Both sides of the driveway were lined with Seaforthia palms. There was a front porch for dismounting the passengers at the front entrance of the house, with marble steps and columns, to enter the main foyer of the mansion. The entrance doorways consisted of twenty-foot-tall double doors. Hand-carved doors were decorated with stained glass and ornate, shiny brass. At the same time, these doors were extremely strong and secure from any intruder's attack. When they were locked, it would literally take an elephant to knock them down.

The doors led to an enormous hall. Two semicircular stone-and-marble staircases led to the upper floor's balcony. Two large lions on either side of the porch entrance depicted strength and courage—also

Stella's birth sign, Leo the Lion, as she was born on August 1. Before the porch in front of the house, there was a plush green carpet of grass with a large, stylish Italian fountain in the middle with lotus blossoms supported by their dark-green, waxy leaves wavering, with trickling water drops from the fountain. That section was framed by the driveways leading to the main gates on both sides of the fountain. The front of the house was facing to the east.

The coaches entered the driveway from the northern gate and exited through the southern gate. In the southwest corner were parking spaces for the visitors' coaches. Beyond that, there was a row of garages and stables for horses, six garages for their own coaches, and six others for the guests' coaches. In the northeast corner, there were stables for their two elephants, Raja and Rani, and separate stables for Blackie the horse and five horses for their own riding. A large wall had gates big enough for the elephants' and horses' access. This wall separated the front of the house from the back of the house for privacy.

At the back of the house, polished stone steps went down the entire width of the house to the back garden. Two smaller lions framed the back doors. A ten foot deep verandah expands to the steps leading to the back garden. The back garden begin with an arbor extending two hundred feet to the west. Wisteria vines were growing on both sides of the arbour, covering the entire length of the arbour. By each side of the arbor, there was a green plush carpet of grass ending at a border of white roses. In the middle there was a large circular flower island with matching varieties of seasonal and perennial flowers of various colours on both sides. Adjacent to the carefully manicured border of white roses, there were the tall boundary walls on both the north and south sides of the back garden, extending beyond the lake.

The whole mansion was sitting on a hundred acres of land. That was part of the ten thousand acres given to them by the king as a wedding gift. Five hundred feet from the end of the arbor, five steps down, was the beginning of the lower mezzanine ground, which led to a small lake of two acres. There was a glass house built on the lake, accessible by a bridge, which would be used mainly for afternoon teas. There was a small rowboat parked by the side of the bridge, accessible via stone steps. This was a surprise gift by Pink to the newlywed couple. This boat was specially designed by the architect, De Gisord, at the request of Pink. It was fitted for a romantic dinner or picnic for a couple and had a beautiful canopy for privacy and protection from the weather.

Just beyond the lake, in the middle of the green field, there was a special circular hangar for housing a large balloon, which was a wedding gift from Robert and his family. The roof of the hangar could be opened by a special mechanism of rope and pulleys. It could be operated by a single person by winding the rope on a large spool with a handle, similar to a ship's anchor's mechanism. The architect DeGisord used his knowledge of shipbuilding for this purpose. It was designed in such a way that one could fly the balloon without having to drag it out of the building. Farther west, beyond the hangar, there was a designated open space for landing. This was marked with a huge black-on-white cross for easy visibility from the balloon. There were two other equally big hangars for Robert's and Jean-Pierre's balloons when they visited Richard and Stella. This would be a regular occurrence for them. After the long trip to Ajanta, India, with Robert, Richard already had flying experience of over a thousand hours. He was an expert navigator and pilot. It would be ideal transportation for them to visit France, Belgium, and other distant countries such as India.

In between the lake and the arbour, there was a large, plush, elevated area of green grass for playing games. There was an ornate wrought-iron fence separating the lake and playing area, for the safety of the children. The entrance gate to the lake was always locked so that the children could not access the lake without adult supervision. Before that, the arbour and the back garden were on an elevated area. The mansion was built on the highest elevation of the ten thousand acres for a purpose. The safety of the house was ensured from flood in case of torrential rain.

They had ordered their furniture before the house was completed so that they could move in as soon as the house was ready.

Their full staff consisted of a butler, cooks, serving waiters, launderers, gardeners, and stable keepers, including elephant keepers. Besides all this staff, there was a doorman always present at the front entrance of the mansion. There was one gatekeeper assigned to each gate.

Richard and Stella moved into the new mansion with Richtella. Richard would still need to be in the Portsmouth office every day. Although the distance was only about twenty miles from the new house in Arundel and that took only about forty-five minutes by coach, he felt better being in Portsmouth until things were completely under control. On weekends, he would spend time in the new house with the family. Robert and Pink would still be at the Portsmouth office. Richard would be maintaining both the houses. He would stay in Portsmouth with his whole family and move back to Arundel every weekend. They maintained a minimum staff at the Portsmouth house. They would be settled in the new house for about three months, and then they planned to have a house opening party there. It was important to have celebrations similar to the Easter fair, which was always good for the morale of the people. They would feel that life was back to normal in Portsmouth after long years of war.

The king was extremely happy with the progress in Portsmouth. After all, Portsmouth was one of the most important ports for business in all of Europe. Trading ships from all over the world were also starting to come back. Their housewarming would be an equally big celebration involving people from all over England and Portsmouth, as it was in the Easter fair.

RICHTELLA IS GROWING UP, BUT WITH SUPERPOWERS

Richtella was an unusual baby, to say the least. Since birth, he could fly to Richard's arms as if he were in a zero-gravity zone. Then, as he grew, he started to develop all kinds of abilities, such as talking to animals or summoning them when he wanted them. Also, Richard noticed that the baby was doing things exactly the way Richard would think about them or wish for. Richtella had a telepathic connection with him this way. In other words, the baby was a mind reader. For instance, one day Richard was thinking what if he could use the baby's power and send some bats in the middle of the night to frighten the French soldiers at their border in Calais? All of a sudden, the whole sky went dark with about half a million bats poised and ready for action. They were waiting for a command from Richard. Then, as if they had read his mind, they flew across the channel towards Calais. But Richard couldn't seem to hear what the baby was thinking about.

161

This boy was growing abnormally fast. At the age of five, he was five feet tall. This was a crucial age for him because now he had full power. He needed a lot of space to play and run around. There may be some truth in the saying that "the mind is more powerful than the body." In this case, the mind might be growing first, with the body following to accommodate the mind's ability. Obviously, his mind was growing faster than that of a normal baby.

King Edward's gift of ten thousand acres of land became very useful in this respect. Soon this private land became a haven and playground for Richtella. He needed that much space to try out his powers. Most of the time, he would play with animals and birds. His constant companions were Blackie the black horse and the two elephants, Raja and Rani. Blackie had been given to them by his grandparents, Mr. and Mrs. Reynolds. It was a beautiful, full-bred black horse. It was crossbred with an Arabian horse. Blackie had speed and beauty. The elephants were wedding gifts from the maharaja of Rajasthan. One wild eagle and an owl were also Richtella's constant companions. One of them was always on the tree outside his bedroom window, day and night. The owl would be there during the dark hours of night, and eagle would stay with him all through the daylight hours.

Stella also had special powers to communicate with animals. Whenever she wanted Richtella, she would send one of them to get him.

The land and the river were big enough for Richtella's favorite playground. It was also a sanctuary for many varieties of birds, ducks, and animals. When his father wished, he could call upon any animal or bird anytime, anywhere. For instance, he could send an eagle or an owl to spy for him and report back to him. He could send a large flock of bats to frighten the enemies. He could outrun his own horse and the elephants. He would rather play with these animals than with other human children. They were no match for him in any sense. Some human children came to play with him, especially those who liked the animals. But none of them matched his physical strength or abilities. But he seemed to have compassion for them. He would never show off his strength or special abilities to make them feel inferior.

This portion of the land drew a lot of spectators every day. When he played with the animals, people would come round to watch

162

his super abilities. For Richtella it was a normal day of playing. By now word had gotten around that Richtella was a special boy with superhuman abilities. A superman of the fourteenth century. People traveled long distances from all parts of England to watch Richtella's special abilities. Soon he became a legend. People loved him and respected him. He had been helping people all over Arundel and Portsmouth.

Slowly he became well known in every part of England. He would go up and down the country helping people in distress and when disaster struck. His horse, Blackie, and his elephants, Raja and Rani, would follow him everywhere. But when he needed to go somewhere fast, he would just run ahead of them, and they would follow him with the guidance of the eagles and owls.

For instance, if there was a fire in any part of Portsmouth, the eagle or the owl would notify Richtella. He would run ahead and rescue the children and others. Then Raja and Rani would put out the fire by spraying water on it.

He would jump across the river and challenge Blackie to do the same. Blackie would refuse by shaking his head from side to side. Blackie was no fool. He knew his limitations. He could swim, but this current was too strong for him. But to jump across more than two hundred feet was beyond the ability of any horse in the world. One of the elephants, Raja (the male), picked up water from the river with his trunk and sprayed it on him from the other side. Richtella jumped back across and playfully chased him away. Rani (the female) followed behind them, raising her trunk and tail in the air. The crowd laughed and clapped. He patted his beloved horse's shiny black coat affectionately and apologized to him for challenging him with that impossible task.

This kind of activity was easy for Richtella. He had acquired these incredible superhuman powers during his most unusual birth. Also, since he was 90 percent negative, he could see other beings with higher vibrations, just like his mother. His mother was the ancestor of Mrs. Griffiths, a.k.a. Maaculla, who was born seven centuries later. His sister, Rose, who was two years younger than he was, inherited her mother's 90 percent positivity and all her superpowers. The tradition began there. One girl was born of each Rose, and each of them was named Rose. Hence, Mrs. Griffiths's first name was Rose. She was the end of the line. She was childless, barren. Now we know the reason why she handed over all this knowledge to Saad.

Richtella's superhuman powers and strengths, though, remained dormant until there was an emergency. For example, if someone threatened, Portsmouth, his parents or him, or any animals, he would jump into action.. He had inherited Richard's temperament than way. On the other hand, it was difficult to calm him down once he was agitated. His mother could calm him down better than his dad. He listened to his dad to an extent. But his favorite aunt, Pink, and his mum could control his emotions more effectively. They would never let him go anywhere by himself. There was always someone there with him. Pretty soon, he knew everything about the military and their strategies and tactics. Stella would worry about that aspect of his abilities.

She said, "Richard, you can train him as much as you want. But I don't want our son to join the army and kill anyone."

"First of all," Richard said, "I am not training him forcibly. That's what he naturally wants to do. And second, he doesn't have to. I'm not going to let him join the army."

Soon everyone in Portsmouth was used to his unusual powers. Richtella had grown so strong and powerful. His grandfather, the priest of St. Mary's Church, thought it was a miracle. Many saints throughout the ages could speak to animals, and they had had similar unusual powers. Little did he know what Richard, Robert, and Pink had gone through to achieve all that. Otherwise he was just a normal young boy.

Stella and Richard noticed another unusual character trait Richtella possessed. Sometimes when he heard about wars and killing, he got extremely agitated and angry. When this happened only Stella and Pink could calm him down, with their amazing angelic and witch's powers. When one of them held him close, he became calm and normal again. With his 90 percent negativity, this was to be expected. He also inherited part of it from Richard.

Then again, with her 90 percent positivity, exactly the opposite was to be expected of Stella. They both were very powerful. But she was positive, and her power was permanent and was two hundred times greater than her son's, simply for the fact that the nature of negative power has always been destructive and therefore temporary.

On the other hand, the nature of positive energy was constructive and therefore permanent. She could stop any negative power, but she could not do any devilish destructive work because she was a positive power.

They had witnessed the two opposite superpowers come into being, both at the same time, by exchanging each other's energies—the birth of a devil and an angel at the same time. Being an angel and a devil are within each of us. Incidentally, Stella was the first Maaculla.

Chapter 26

RICHARD STARTS A PROGRAM FOR THE POOR

Portsmouth had grown with industries and businesses, and the demands for skilled labour had grown with it. To meet the demands, Richard started a program called Feed the Poor (FTP). In this program he invited the poor and the unemployed to be trained for suitable employment free of charge because he believed every person had the potential to be useful if he or she were inspired. He helped them find jobs according to their skills and interests. Those who were unskilled were being apprenticed in the various industries and docks. They had food and drinks when they came to the FTP office. This program was attracting people from nearby cities. Similarly, when it was done in the twentieth century, it attracted people from underdeveloped countries.

Portsmouth had surpassed its old glory and was on its way to becoming one of the major cities, second to London. Every month there were new hotels were being built, with bed-and-breakfasts to accommodate the surplus of visitors from around the world. They were arriving on ships. To accommodate that number of ships, Richard extended the porting docks all the way to Isle of Wight. Some inns and taverns were being built there too. Many other new industries were constantly popping up, and trained skilled labour force were being employed there. He had set up an office for the FTP program where employers could easily find employees there. In the same way, employees were finding opportunities by meeting with employers there. Thousands of jobs had been created. FTP was running out of people as the demand grew. They were advertising in the other cities for more people. Also there were small and big celebrations going on every week such as opening ceremonies for Inns, taverns, groceries etc. Everybody was celebrating because it was good for business. It also sent a message to King Phillip that life in Portsmouth was normal again and they weren't afraid of his reprisals anymore. At the same time, he had doubled up security all over Portsmouth, from the docks to every street. Security peace officers were visible and active twenty-four hours a day. He had also increased presence of soldiers and police in Isle of Wight. No one could come in or go out without being spotted by the security personnel.

PREPARATION FOR THE HOUSEWARMING PARTY

The housewarming party was going to be a big celebration. Open to all. Even bigger than the Easter fair. All of Portsmouth would participate. The bigger the better, according to the king and the people of Portsmouth. They were going to open the town hall, St Mary's and both the houses in Portsmouth and Arundel to be able to accommodate everyone. It would be open house to all throughout the day. People could come in and out of the party locations all day long. There would be music, dancing, fireworks, food, and drink for everyone. There were street performers and entertainers all over the civic centre of Portsmouth. There had been extra tents hoisted to accommodate the guests in both the houses.

The party would end at midnight. This was going to be a memorable celebration and the talk of the town for a long time to come. There would be guards everywhere. They would be able handle any small or big incidents. In a big event like this, there were bound to be some incidents and misunderstandings. These security people were trained to handle any problems, big or small, and with diplomacy. They were also ready for big incidents, such as a French attack and sightings of Green. In a word, they were ready to deal with any situation they might encounter. Richard alerted everyone, including citizens and visitors, not to let their own guard down. By doing that he raised their solidarity level very high indeed.

GREEN ABDUCTS ROBERT AND BRIGIT

When Richard was busy with his new home and Pink was busy with Jean-Pierre, Robert was left alone with his family. He was also busy introducing Brigit and his own family to the people of Portsmouth and was showing them around. Portsmouth seemed a very peaceful and happy place. Only a year ago, no one would feel safe walking on the street. They would always be looking over their shoulders. It took a lot of effort to maintain it that way. There was the threat of a French attack, which was still in the backs of the people's minds, especially key people such as Richard, Robert, Pink, Father Reynolds, and other officials.

Green had disappeared for the time being. No one knew her whereabouts. There was a chance that she would come back from her hideout. All of her known followers had joined Pink. Green had her ways of recruiting new ones by bribing, blackmailing, or threatening them in many ways, or by holding them for ransom, such as the one she had recruited to attack Richard on the beach. It was good that she was in France then. But who knew when she would turn up again? That was why security had to be extremely vigilant—especially Pink's girls, who had the power-sense her presence, as well as other unknown threats that might be lurking around. They had Portsmouth covered. But once you were outside Portsmouth, these girls couldn't protect you anymore.

Robert's mum and dad wanted to see London. They had never visited before. Robert took this opportunity to introduce his family to the king. After all, he was staying in England as a royal guest. King Edward III was very fond of Robert and grateful for the work he had done for Portsmouth. He was aware of Robert's good intentions for France and England. His trip to Luxemburg might have seemed frivolous in the eyes of laymen, but the king was well aware that it was an act towards peace. In the same way, many people, English and French, regarded Robert as a traitor to his own country, his own people. He had been vilified by certain people. But King Edward was well aware that Robert's actions were for greater good of humanity. His vision did not recognize any realm or boundaries.

The king had invited all of them to come and visit London and stay in Buck House as his guests. Robert already had a room in the palace allocated for him. He stayed there when he came to London for official business. This visit was going to be a pleasure trip. At the same time, he was going to report to the king and update the situation in Portsmouth. Robert had gone to London using this same route many times. He was very familiar with this road. He could either use this road or go to London via a ship. It would take a little longer to go by road. Also, a journey by ship was not preferable after the last incident. However, this would be an interesting and scenic journey, and they would visit a few cities on the way for his family. They would enjoy seeing other parts of the country.

It had been a very pleasant journey so far. On the way they stopped in many interesting places, such as Cobham, Guildford, and Esher, for rest and refreshments. They met many of the locals there. Everyone knew who Robert was. They had all come to know him from reading the newspapers and seeing his pictures. They welcomed him and his family. They were greeted like royals. After Esher, their coach had to travel through a place called Thieves' Corner. Four roads ran from this junction, east and west, north and south, and created a roundabout junction. Once this had been famous for the notorious highwayman gang called the Robbing Hoods. They used to appear to unsuspecting travellers from out of nowhere and then disappear through the north or south road after robbing them. They never attacked anyone violently unless someone provoked them. But this was an old story, and it was water under the bridge, so to speak. One day the hoods disappeared. Nobody had seen them since. They were masters of disguise. No one ever knew their true identities. Some say they died in a violent confrontation. Some say they left the country and were living in Spain. Some say the whole gang fell into the Cobham gorge. Others say that they still lived locally among the people and no one knew who they were. That junction was safe now. Also, there were guards posted at a watch post there day and night for the safety of the travellers by the king's order.

Their coach entered the roundabout from the east side and was going round to the west exit towards Putney, just before London across the river Thames. But what was that? As they came round to pass the south road, they were confronted by a couple of masked men. There were no guards on duty today. This was in the middle of the day. Robert had made sure to leave Portsmouth early enough so that they would arrive in London before the dark. The masked rider was approaching their coach, followed by another rider. He ordered the coachman to stop. Another coach appeared out of nowhere on the north side of the roundabout.

The first rider came to the door of the coach and said, "Will Robert and Brigit step outside, please."

"Who are you and what do you want?" Robert asked.

"I am not a violent man," the rider said, "but if you provoke me, I can be. No more questions. Please step outside."

"Robert, be careful," Mr. Artoire said. "Don't get out."

"Dad, I am not going to endanger all of your lives." Then, to the rider, Robert said, "I'm coming out. What do you want with Brigit?"

The rider banged on the side of the coach. "I said no questions. Robert and Brigit come out, or else!"

"Here I am, coming out." Robert stepped out of the coach.

"Are you testing me, sir? I can easily set fire to the whole coach."

"OK, OK," Brigit said. "Here I am." She came out.

The second rider dismounted and tied their hands behind their backs.

"Follow me," the second rider said. He led them to the waiting coach. He opened the door and signaled them to get inside. They struggled to get in with their hands tied behind their backs.

A croaky female voice from inside the coach said, "Untie their hands, you fool. We haven't got all day."

The rider said, "Are you sure, Miss Green?"

"Sure I'm sure. They can't escape from me now."

He cut their hands free. There was a woman with dark clothes sitting inside. They both sat down on the opposite side.

The woman said, "Welcome, Robert. We finally meet. And Brigit—you thought you could escape me just because you escaped from Notre Dame."

"So you are Green," Robert said. "What do you want with us, Green?"

"Oh, just you wait. In fact, your family can go. They can take a message to Richard and Pink that I have you and Brigit. Phillip will be pleased to see you again."

"Why, Brigit?" Robert said. "You have business with me. Let her go."

"Oh, but I like controlling. I can control you with Brigit, and Richard with you. See? Clever, don't you think? Ha ha ha. Cut the guards loose, you fools, and send them to the king to tell him what happened here. Ha ha ha."

"You will never get away with this," Robert said. "Pink and Richard will find you, like they destroyed your hideout. Even Adonai is looking for you. You have no chance. Why don't you surrender and save all this trouble."

170

"We will see about this. Adonai is still alive? Ungrateful fool. After all I did for him?"

"I'm scared," Brigit said. "Is this the evil sorcier you told me about?"

"Scared? You should be," Green said. "Just don't come too near me, you goody-goody. You make my skin crawl. You ain't seen nothing yet. Evil it is. Drive on, driver. Let's go visit our friend Phillip."

RICHARD GETS NEWS OF THE AMBUSH

One guard went to Buckingham Palace to inform the king of this incident. The Artoires wouldn't be coming after all. The coach turned to go back to Portsmouth to inform Richard and Pink of the ambush. They would have to somehow intercept Green before she got to France with them. If Phillip got hold of Robert and Brigit, he would surely put them under the guillotine.

It took them two hours to get to Arundel. Richard and Stella were busy organizing everything for the open house party in two weeks. Richard came rushing out of the house when he spotted them coming through the driveway. Something must be wrong. He met them on the front porch.

Richard asked, as Mr. Artoire was getting out of the coach, "What happened? Why are you back so soon? Where is Robert?" He went round to the other side of the coach to look for Robert.

Mr. Artoire said, "Richard, we have bad news. We got ambushed by sorcier Green at Thieves' Corner. She took Robert and Brigit. She told me to tell you that she is going to take them to France to see Phillip."

Mrs. Artoire came out of the coach crying. "Phillip is going to kill them, Richard."

Richard held her close. "Not while I'm alive. She'll have to go to France first. Our ships will intercept her ship before she can get there. It's the only way she can go. She won't come through Portsmouth, for sure. Please stay with Stella. I have to leave and let Pink know first."

RICHARD GETS THE SUPERPOWERS

Richard always had one of Pink's girls with him. In case of emergency, she could telepath Pink, who was still on the Isle of Wight.

171

"Fiona," Richard said, "can you telepath Pink about the incident."

"I already did," Stella said. "She's on the way back."

"Thank you, honey." He kissed her. "Fiona, please stay here with them in case Stella needs help. Keep your eyes and senses open. Inform Pink immediately if you sense anything."

He alerted the guards and told them to close all the doors and windows.

Richard got in his coach and told the driver to go. He sat back anxiously, trying to keep control of his emotions. He had been trained by the maha guru how to handle a situation like this emotionally. He needed to use his gap. He needed to push all his feelings down into the gap.

The coach was running fast. He suddenly heard some noises in his head. It seemed as if many people were talking at the same time. He could hear one voice louder than the other voices.

"This is Pink, Richard.
Concentrate on me."

"Is that you, Pink? I can hear a lot of voices in my head."

"That's right. Focus on me to isolate my voice."

"How? I mean, how can I hear you? I'll try to focus."

"Just focus on me for now."

"I can hear you clearly. But how?"

"In case of danger, you are using Richtella's power. Your emotions rose to the right level. I told you, you will know when the time comes. From now on, you can use your son's powers."

"Can we talk for a while? Because I need to tell you a few things."

"As long as you keep your focus on me," Pink said. "But I already know what you're going to say. I've sent two of the battleships from here towards London. They will intercept every vessel coming from London going towards France."

"Thank you, Pink. What would I do without you?"

"Well, you don't have to think about that now. I am here and not going anywhere. Don't worry; I got my girls on the ships. I know how much Robert means to you and to me."

"I can't lose him now. I can't lose any of you. We've come this far together."

"I don't want you to be sentimental now," Pink said. "I want you to concentrate on Richtella's powers. You can use them now. Remember that every adversity is an opportunity. Unfortunately, this had to happen to Robert and Brigit to raise your emotions to this level to get your power. Remember ancient history? People moved mountains when they needed to save their loved ones. Now is the opportunity to destroy the entire French army."

"But how?"

"Remember, I told you that Richtella can call animals. You can call them now. You have all his powers. It's like being enlightened in a negative way. You can send millions of bats into their camps tonight to frighten the French soldiers away. You can send big snakes to sink their ships. You can send images to scare the men and the horses. You can send a million rats into their camp in the middle of the night. Normally animals fear us because they choose to flee. These animals will not have any fear of men anymore. They will stand and fight. The men will run for their lives instead. There will be nobody left to fight for Phillip. Before Green reaches France, we will have captured Paris. This is our opportunity. We can do all that without shedding one drop of blood."

"That's how Robert wants it," Richard said. "He doesn't want any killings."

"You can tell your horses to go faster, and they will run like the wind. Richard, you have the powers now. Stay in touch with your gap, the inner mind. Do not allow your outer mind—your ego—to take over with fear. Remember, you and Stella don't want any killing either. Now you can lay siege and capture Paris before Green or Phillip know what has hit them. And remember, you can speak to Stella too. She's had the power since Richtella's birth. Try one or two of the powers by the time you get to the port. I'll be there in few minutes."

"Thanks, Pink. I will. And Pink, I love you."

"I love you too. We're going to do it."

All of a sudden, the horses started to run very fast. The driver couldn't control them. His hat flew away. He shouted, "I can't control the horses, guv."

"Don't worry," Richard said. "They're under my control. Sit back and stay safe."

A half hour later, Pink joined Richard at Portsmouth port. He had applied everything Pink had suggested to him. By the time they arrived in Calais, all the French battleships were abandoned. By the next day, all of Phillip's soldiers had run away from Paris. Richard and Pink marched into Versailles and captured Phillip. They stood in front of the crowd from the balcony of the palace. Richard was addressing the people of the Paris.

"Dear Parisian friends, we are not here to conquer Paris or any part of France. This madness has to stop. This war between our countries must stop. We are here to remove your mad king and stop this unnecessary bloodshed on both sides of the channel. To prove it to you, we have captured Paris and Phillip without any bloodshed."

The crowd cheered.

"I know that the French people do not want war. We do not want to fight with French people either. We want to be your friends."

The crowd cheered again.

"Unfortunately, Robert is not here today to reiterate our intention. I promise you we will find him and bring him back to his beloved Paris. This is why I need to leave at this moment—to search for him. As you all know by now, he and Brigit were kidnapped by the evil friend of Phillip, Green. Please choose your king carefully next time. Perhaps Robert can guide you when he gets back."

One man from the crowd shouted, "Are you sure Robert is still alive?"

"We know he and Brigit are alive. This is Lady Pink, and she has special powers. She is much more powerful than the evil Green, because she has the power of love. She assured us that they are still alive. Green will not come to Paris anymore. She's hiding somewhere in London."

The crowd cheered again "Nous ne voulons pas lui ici. Nous ne voulons pas de Phillip. Nous voulons la liberté." (We don't want her here. We don't want Phillip. We want freedom.)

Richard said, "I know, good people of France. Let us have peace in our life rather than war. It's your choice now. This war has lasted over a hundred years. Is it worth it?"

"No!"

"Let us end this long war right here, right now. Let us live together as friends with love. Robert proved it to you. He risked his life to go to England. He became the ambassador of peace for the people of France. He could have gotten killed. But he is my best friend now and joined me to end this evil war. Ladies and gentlemen of France, Robert sends his love, and soon he will join you—that I promise. I kept my promise to Robert. I captured Paris and Phillip without killing one soldier. He risked his life for you all. Please excuse us now. We need to go back and find him before anything bad happens to him. We bid you au revoir. Viva France!"

The crowd cheered. "Viva France! Viva England!"

"You are welcome to come to England anytime. King Edward sends his best wishes to you all."

Chapter 27

THE SEARCH FOR ROBERT AND BRIGIT

With the fall of Phillip, they weren't worried about French attacks anymore. Their priority was finding Robert and Brigit.

Pink and Richard quickly left. Instead of coming to Portsmouth, they headed straight for London because that was where Green was seen last, near Putney. She was probably hiding in London somewhere. With the fall of Phillip, she couldn't go back to France. That was exactly what Richard wanted. If she was in England, sooner or later they would find her. Also, Green was not a fool. She would keep Robert and Brigit alive as her bargaining chip. She wouldn't harm them because they were her ticket to freedom if she got cornered.

They started their search in London. They also sent a few of Pink's girl witches there beforehand. They scanned every inch of London from all four sides—on the east in Crayford, on the west in Heathrow, on the north in Bricket Wood, and on the south in Waldingham. They were looking in every corner of London, from the outskirts to the centre, towards Westminster, Piccadilly, and the West End. Pink and Richard joined them in this extensive manhunt.

The next day all the girls reported to them. There were no signs of Robert or Brigit—or Green, for that matter. They asked the girls to stay there and continued searching. She couldn't just disappear into thin air. They also told them to focus on Robert and Brigit. That way Green would not sense them.

THE SEARCH FOR ROBERT AND BRIGIT IN PORTSMOUTH

They arrived back at Richard's house in Arundel tired and disappointed. But at least they gave good news to Mr. and Mrs. Artoire about the capture of Phillip. They hadn't had any proper sleep or rest for the last seven days. They were both also very worried about what she could have done to Robert and Brigit and where she could be hiding them. They didn't have any time to waste.

Pink immediately communicated with Val and Adonai on the Isle of Wight in case she tried to go back to her old hideout. They also alerted all their watch posts in Portsmouth in case she turned up there. It was difficult to pinpoint where she might have been hiding. That was why they needed to search every possible place they could think of, including Portsmouth. They couldn't do much during the dark of night. They decided they would take some rest for the night, and at the same time, Richard could spend some time with Stella and Richtella.

Stella said, "I'm glad you're staying home tonight. Richtella has been very quiet since all this has begun. He hardly wants to play. Normally he is very active. When I told him that I love him, he just looked at me."

"That's right," Pink said. "You did the right thing. He's focusing on his powers. He may still be a baby, but he's well aware of what's going on, and he knows you love him."

"I was wondering what has happened to him suddenly," Stella said. "I haven't bothered you before because you both are so busy. Thank God for that. Thank you for explaining that. My dad said it may have something to do with it too."

"I'd better go and see how Jean-Pierre is," Pink said. "I haven't seen him for the last seven days. I need to also tell him that I love him. He might be wondering what's happened to us. Have a good rest, Richard. See you in the morning," said Pink.

Pink left for Portsmouth after hugs and kisses with Stella, the baby, and Richard.

"I love you," Pink said.

Stella and Richard said they loved her too.

The next morning, Richard arrived at his office in Portsmouth at five o'clock. A few minutes later, Pink arrived with Jean-Pierre.

"Good morning, Pink," Richard said. "Good morning, Jean-Pierre."

"Good morning, Richard," they both said.

"I want to help," Jean-Pierre said. "There must be something I can do. They're my friends too. I'm so worried about them. Please let me help."

"Don't worry," Richard said. "We'll find them. Until then we can't do much. Pink said she can sense they're alive, and she's never wrong."

Pink said, "Actually, I can sense their presence stronger now since we got back to Portsmouth."

Richard said, "You don't think she might have doubled back here somehow while we were looking for her in London?"

"But how could she get through?" Pink asked. "We have guards everywhere, and the girls."

"Why don't you alert all the girls that you can sense them in Portsmouth?" Richard asked. "What's the harm?"

"I'll do that," Pink said. "And Richard, don't forget you have the same power now. Even more than any of us. You can concentrate on them as well. That way we can get a stronger signal."

"I'll certainly try," Richard said. "These things are still new to me. I'm not quite used to all this."

"Remember to focus on Robert and Brigit only," Pink said. "We don't want to alert Green."

"That's right," Richard said. "Thanks for reminding me."

About thirty minutes later, one of the girls reported she could sense some activity in her area.

"That's near where you rescued me, Richard," Pink said. "She's extremely cunning. She might have thought nobody would look for her there. This area is so remote that nobody is guarding there. That girl is the only guard close to that area. But she's close enough to sense them."

"Well, let's go and check it out," Richard said. "But how are we going to get there? It's very steep to climb there. It'll take some time. How could she get there though?"

"She must have had some help," Pink said. "That's how she took me there."

"This talk is making no sense to me," Jean-Pierre said. "If it's so remote and high, we could use the balloon. I learnt to fly with Robert. That's why we had to leave Paris—because Phillip wanted to use all of Robert's students as suicide bombers. I'm one of the pilots."

"Thanks, Jean-Pierre," Richard said. "That's a brilliant idea. We still have the balloon. Let's go. This is your chance to help. Just so you know, this is a lot of involvement."

Pink said to Jean-Pierre, "Are you sure you want to get involved?"

Jean-Pierre: "Of course. It's my duty to get involved. Phillip has destroyed our lives too. God knows how many other lives he destroyed. I'm grateful to you for capturing him. Let me help find Robert. That's the least I can do. France needs him right now. Just take me to the Balloon."

When it was not in use, they garaged the balloon in a special hangar converted from an old barn. They all got the balloon out of the hangar and quickly loaded it with fuel and some food and water. Within an hour they had lifted off the ground. Jean-Pierre studied the wind and started to navigate to the top of the mountain. The cave was near the top of the mountain where she had kept Pink. Richard also sent a group of fifty strong soldiers who were specially trained for mountain climbing ahead of them on the ground. He instructed them to stay out of sight until they got there. They could see from the balloon that the soldiers were already making headway in climbing. Pink knew that mountain like the back of her hand. Only until a year ago, she had been a prisoner of the curse there. That had been her home for life until Richard rescued her.

It took them only a few minutes to get to the top of the mountain. Jean-Pierre expertly landed the balloon near the top in an open space. From there they only had to go about a thousand yards to the entrance of the cave. They secured the balloon to a rock and a large tree.

Richard said, "You know, Pink, I think I can sense them now."

Pink said, "I told you you could."

"But why am I sensing hostility?" Richard asked. "I'm not focusing on Green."

"So am I," Pink said. "Let's go and find out. It could be because Green is near there. Or Robert might have fallen under her spell. Either way we have to be extremely cautious."

"Let's go," Richard said. "It's good that they are alive and well."

They arrived at the entrance of the cave. There was no sign of anyone there. They looked around.

"I remember this cave when from I first met you here," Richard said. "The only change is some more bushes and shrubs grown wildly. But look. There are some fresh footprints here. Maybe about ten or twelve people."

"I thought she had some help to here," Pink said.

"How did she get them to work for her? Did she bribe them with something they needed? Everyone needs something, I guess."

"That's not in her nature. More likely she's holding their family for ransom."

While they were talking and looking at the footprints, they felt a presence all around them. Out of nowhere about ten or twelve people surrounded them. Robert was with them. They all were holding some kind of weapon—bows and arrows, machetes, swords. They looked like some kind of makeshift vigilantes. They were all pointing their weapons at Richard, Pink, and Jean-Pierre.

"Robert, it's so nice to see you," Richard said. "Are you all right?" He walked forward to him.

"That's enough," Robert said. "Don't come any closer if you value your life."

"Robert, don't you recognize us?" Richard said. "Richard and Pink and Jean-Pierre. We're your friends."

"I told you, don't come any closer."

Another voice said, "Don't move a muscle, unless you want to be hung, drawn, and quartered. You're outnumbered and completely surrounded."

Fifty soldiers surrounded them. Robert quickly attacked one of Green's men near him, the leader of the group, and then ran to join Richard.

The other voice said, "Drop your weapons now. Drop your weapons, I say, and hands above your head."

They all dropped their weapons and surrendered.

Robert was hugging Richard, Pink, and Jean-Pierre. "I knew you would all come."

"Yes, of course," Richard said. "You would do the same for us."

"She took Brigit inside the cave," Robert said.

"Don't worry," Pink said. "I know this cave inside out. It comes out on the other side of the mountain. We have to get to her before she reaches the other side."

"Let's go," Richard said.

"Wait a minute, Richard," Pink said. "It may be a good idea to send one of your animals—no, no, a snake—after Green. She's scared of snakes."

"But what about Brigit?" Richard said. "She took Brigit with her. Won't it harm her?"

"The snake will do what you want it to do," Pink said. "It will not touch anything else or anybody else. Send a python. She'll freeze, and we'll capture her. Send the python from the other side to block the exit. She'll have no place to go but to come back this way."

Richard shut his eyes and concentrated on the snake. About twenty minutes passed with no sign of them.

"I hope it's working," Richard said. "I saw a big python's face with dark, glassy, piercing eyes staring at me."

"That will do," Pink said.

Robert said, "Maybe we should go forward slowly, just in case."

Pink said, "Shh...listen."

Moments later they could hear a faint female voice frantically calling for help. "Help...help." It was getting louder as she ran towards them.

"It worked," Pink said. "That's Green. Let's go."

"Be careful," Richard said. "It may be a trick. Why can't we hear Brigit?"

"I hope she's OK," Robert said. "Let's go."

"No, wait," Pink said. "They're almost here. I can hear the footsteps. Someone's running this way."

A few moments later, Green ran out into the open, tired and huffing and frightened. The soldiers took her in to custody.

Green was trying to run with her hands tied. "Run, run for your lives! There's a big snake coming. Never seen the likes of this..."

After another few moments, Brigit came with the snake, as friends, walking together. The python stopped before the entrance in the semidarkness of the cave. Her menacing eyes could be seen piercing the darkness of the cave. Brigit came out into the light of the day. Robert ran to embrace her.

"There's the snake!" She tried to run again.

They all laughed.

"It's time for python to say good-bye," Pink said. "She won't come out in the sun."

"Wait," Brigit said. She ran back to the python and hugged her. "Au revoir, python."

Jean-Pierre said, "How could she not fear this menacing-looking python?"

"She always had pet snakes since she was very young," Robert said. "She loves snakes. She knows their every move and mood."

"Perhaps she can see the beauty beyond the appearances," Pink said. "Don't judge a book by its cover. Behind this menacing appearance, there is a heart of gold. Do you remember how you found me, Richard?"

Richard said, "Why would God give someone an appearance so menacing?"

"Everything has a purpose in life," Pink said. "She will always remain that way until someone else needs her. It is the observer who becomes the observed. Brigit is being observed as a friend because she observed her as a friend. On the other hand, Green looks at her as a fiend, according to her own mind. It is always the intention that matters. Anyway, I'm going to telepath Stella with good news. She can tell Mr. and Mrs. Artoire the good news."

"Wait," Richard said. "Let me do it, now that I have the ability."

Soldiers were waiting for orders from Richard for the prisoners. It was time to deal with them.

Richard concentrated and cupped his hands over his ears.

The captain of the soldiers said, in a deep voice, "What are we to do with these blaggards, sir? Pardon the use of a swear word in front of you, Sir Richard. They're ready to be hung, drawn, and quartered, if you ask me, sir."

"Well, first of all," Richard said, "I am a grown-up person and the equal of you. Yes, you can use swear words in appropriate moments. Let me remind you, though, no soldier takes the law into his own hands. They are prisoners of the king now."

Richard turned to the twelve prisoners.
All twelve men went down on their knees, one by one.

John, their leader, said in a Cockney accent, "We are no more blaggards than any of the Londoners, sir. We are sworn to loyalty to the king and you, Sir Richard. It's just that our families are being held hostage by this Green person, sir. We beg your forgiveness."

"Is that so?"

"Yes, sir." John said. "She threatened to harm our family if we didn't follow her orders, sir."

"I'm not surprised. Where are your families now?"

"They're all being held in the East End of London, sir."

"If it's true, then I will set you free to rescue your families."

Pink said, "I've already found out from our girls in London that they're telling the truth."

Green said, "Are you going to set me free if I tell my girls to set them free?"

"Nice try, Green," Richard said. "Still leveraging your way out. You never give up your evil ways, do you? Besides, this is not the only crime you're accused of. You betrayed your own people. You betrayed all of England and the king. You're not going anywhere in a hurry, Green."

"Just so you know, Green," Pink said, "My girls have already overpowered your girls." She turned to the men. "Your families are free and waiting for you."

John asked, "Does this mean we're free to go now, ma'am?"

Pink said, "It's entirely up to Sir Richard."

"I'm going to let you go on your own recognizance," Richard said. "You have to promise me to go to the king's court next Monday morning to be properly pardoned. Do I hear a promise from each of you?"

All of the men said, "Yes, Sir Richard. We promise and swear on our families' lives."

"OK, then. Release them."

One by one, they said, "Thank you, Sir Richard."

John said, "With your permission, Sir Richard, we can finish off this Green ghoul for you, if you know what I mean, Sir Richard."

"No, I don't," Richard said. "Since when in England do people take the laws into their own hands? She will have to go through the king's courts, just as all of you are. Now go before I change my mind."

"OK, OK," they all said. "We're going, Sir Richard. We're grateful for your kindness, sir. God bless you, sir."

Then Richard said to the captain, "Give them some food and water before they leave. It's a long way down."

"May I have some water?" Green asked. "I'm thirsty too. I'm rather parched after being chased by this monstrous python. I have the same rights as they have."

"I heard this saying in India: monkeys don't stop climbing just because they're old," Richard said. "You sure try, don't you. But just so you know, we're not same as you are. You left your prisoners without

183

food and water to die. Yes, give her some water. And put her in the gondola."

Green drank her water. "But Sir Richard, I'm afraid of heights."

"Too bad," Richard said. "Nice try again, Green. I don't trust you with these men. You might try one of your tricks again."

Pink said, "Might be a good idea to blindfold and gag her so she can't use her power."

"Is that really necessary?" Green said.

"You said it yourself, Green," Richard said. "You're afraid of heights. This way, if you can't see, you won't get afraid, now, would you?"

Green gave a piercing look to Richard.

"By the way, Green," he said, "your evil power doesn't work on me. Now let's go, everyone."

The soldiers left with the prisoners. Richard, Pink, Robert, Jean-Pierre, and Brigit climbed into the gondola. Green was gagged and blindfolded and her hands tied behind her back. As the balloon lifted off, she flinched and let out a muffled squeal.

They all laughed.

Chapter 28

TIME TO CELEBRATE

It was time to celebrate. It started out as a housewarming party for Richard and Stella. They were getting ready to celebrate the inauguration of their new home. In the meantime, the infamous war had ended. During that process they had also put an end to the Green Witch's hostility permanently. So now it was no longer just a decadent housewarming party. It turned out to be the most important celebration of the century. Their housewarming party coincided with the ending of the long war and defeat of the King Phillip IV together with capturing the Green Witch. Those alone were significant enough, and they intended to make the celebration of the century. They didn't need to boost people's morale or build confidence anymore. This became a celebration of victory and freedom. The whole of Europe wanted to celebrate. They were happy to see the end of this long--drawn-out war. Then, gradually, every country in the world wanted to join in the celebration. That proved that even though this was not their war, people around the world were empathetic enough to want to end it. One day, this kind of global empathy would bring hope for total peace throughout the entire world. That was another example of how through adversity the universe brings people together. We just have to be aware of that and look for the opportunity. This is where our intentions are so important. This could be an opportunity to unite the whole world by inviting them to celebrate the peace initiative.

ROBERT AND FAMILY NEED TO GO BACK TO FRANCE

Robert, Brigit, and the entire Artoire family was moving back to Paris from Luxemburg. So were many other French people, such as Jean-Pierre's family from Belgium and Brigit's family from Switzerland. Robert and Brigit would come back to Portsmouth after helping their families move back to Paris.

Richard, Robert, Jean-Pierre, Pink, and Stella were in the house in Arundel.

"It is time for us to part, my friends," Robert said, "but we are only across the channel. I hope you can come to Paris when they coronate a new king. The French people owe it to you."

"Nothing would give me more pleasure than to see the peaceful, happy faces of the people of France," Richard said. "Also, life here will be empty without you, Robert, but I know your duty calls. I hope we can see each other at least once a week. Remember the housewarming party next week. I want your mom, dad, Adele, Roger, and Brigit to come too."

"Yes, yes, we all will be here," Robert said. "I'll bring Brigit's mom and dad as well. They all have come back to France from Switzerland. They're waiting to see us."

"Of course they're welcome," Richard said. "And Jean-Pierre, our new friend, please bring your family with you too. We could return their hospitality in Belgium."

"Of course," Jean-Pierre said. "Thank you for inviting us. My sister is going to stay in Belgium with her husband. We're going to keep our farm there. I'm going to open a restaurant in Paris when Pink and I start a family there."

Pink face flushed. "This is a surprise to me. But I would love to." She hugged Jean-Pierre.

Richard said, "We'll miss you all for seven whole days."

"It feels surreal now," Pink said. "Anyway, I'm sending three of my girls with you for protection. Also Richard is sending thirty soldiers to safely accompany you all to your homes. You never know. We can't take any chances. From now on no one should lower their guard. Always be prepared. We learnt this lesson the hard way."

They all would leave from Richard's new home in Arundel. Richard, Stella, Richtella, and Pink would accompany them to the ship at Portsmouth dock. Three girls and thirty soldiers were already on board the ship, waiting for them. They hugged and kissed each other good-bye and departed. Richard and Robert are both wiping their tears even though they were going to be apart only for a week.

Robert, on the ship, said, at the top of his voice, "Au revoir. See you next week, my friends. Je t'aime." There was the noise of the ship moving "I love you. The first thing I'll do when I get back is set up a regular balloon transport from Paris to Portsmouth so that we can be here in an hour. I hope Phillip hasn't destroyed my balloon warehouse. In that case I'll make them from the scratch if I have to. Richard, I will need an open port here in Portsmouth as well as the one at your house in Arundel for landing my balloons."

"I'll get to it straightaway," Richard said.

Robert said, "Je t'aime. Merci. I love you, and thank you. So long."

Jean-Pierre said, "Je t'aime. I love you. Au revoir. So long."

They were all waving at each other.

Richard had sent one of his battleships, which was fully equipped to deal with any probable attacks, to take them to Calais. Soldiers and girls would accompany each of the three families safely to their homes. They weren't taking any chances.

A WEEK LATER, SATURDAY—THE HOUSE PARTY

As mentioned before, this party was a nationwide party, not just Richard and Stella's housewarming party. The likes of this party had never been seen in England before. It was doubtful that it would ever be seen in the future. It was the long-awaited celebration of freedom from the grip of the war. Freedom from the fear, doubt, and uncertainty of the entire population of England and France. The loss of resources and particularly the loss of lives were immeasurable. How could a war last that long? It boggled everyone's mind. Whatever had fueled that war for that long must been pure evil energy. It had to be an insane mind and the ego of the king fueling it.

People who opposed the war, especially in France, got destroyed or driven away from their homeland. It had pulled apart the people of these two beautiful countries who were yearning for peace and tranquility. Never before in the history of humankind had any countries suffered the devastating effects of war for that long. Hopefully the entire world would learn from this example that "war is not the answer." At the end, neither the aggressors nor the defenders had won.

THE PARTY—1453 AD

The celebration of both occasions was taking place all over England, France, Europe, and the rest of the world. Who knew the celebration of Richard and Stella's housewarming would become a global celebration? Countries like India, Japan, and China, along with Middle Eastern and African countries, joined in the celebration with all of Europe. That simple but powerful gesture depicted the mentality of people of the world of the day that nobody wanted war.

Alex Spittle had written a song for the occasion. Alex was one of the extreme sufferers in this war. He lost his mum, dad, and sister in the firebomb attacks by Phillip. Losing his entire family and their house also meant that he became a homeless person at the age of fourteen. He would still be homeless if he hadn't met Richard. He procured special financing from the king to rebuild his house and those of many other affected families. His new song was already being played in every city in England. In every pub people were singing along with the song. That summarized the mentality of the day. It was their leaders and the politicians with their personal ambitions who led people to wars and destruction.

When Saad was very young, he asked his grandfather, why don't the two countries' kings fight the war instead of the soldiers? They got all the credit for it anyway. That way, many people wouldn't have to die. Imagine now, two presidents going at each other. Soon none of the politicians would want any wars.

Everybody was busy organizing for the party. On Saturday morning at 9:00 a.m., the party would begin. Richard would make an announcement from city hall to inaugurate the party. Friday, they were busy making final arrangements. Richard, Stella, and Pink were anxiously waiting for Robert, Jean-Pierre, and their families to join the celebration. But there was no sign of them. They were supposed to be there in Portsmouth by Friday. Worry set in, in Richard's mind, when they were still not there on Saturday morning. They were hoping nothing detrimental had happened to them. Richard remembered that Robert had told him to start the party without them if they were late. Nothing was expected to go wrong because all the enemies had been defeated. In fact, everyone in France was happy that nobody was there to instigate the war anymore. Even the Green Witch was in their custody. They weren't expecting any attack from any direction. They would have surely heard from them if there was any problem.

"Are you sure, Pink?" Richard asked. "There is no message from Robert or the girls? He's always very punctual. I've never seen him be late since I've known him. Are you sure you can't send him a message through your girls?"

Pink said, "I can't send him a message because he's not enlightened like you, and the girls are not responding for some reason. But don't worry, Richard. I can sense they're all OK. There must be an explanation for this delay."

"Without them the celebration has no meaning."

"I'm going to the dock. Their ship may be arriving right at this moment."

"We have only an hour left. I need you to be back here before the party begins. Robert said to start the party without them if they're late. Why would he even say that?"

Pink arrived at the dock early Saturday morning. There was no message from Robert. There was no sign of their ship either. Where could they be? The party must begin at 9:00 a.m. sharp. Thousands of people were waiting for Richard's announcement. At 8:45, there was still no sign of them. Richard just made a quick announcement to the waiting public in front of the town hall.

"Ladies and gentlemen, the party will begin at 9:00 a.m. sharp. Robert has never let us down before. There must be a reason why he's late..." His voice broke up. "I'll keep you informed in case he's not here by nine. Everyone please pray that nothing bad has happened to them. Pink has just left for the dock. I'm sure she will find out the reason for their delay."

The moment he finished his announcement, there was a big roar among the people of Portsmouth. Many were suggesting that they should postpone or at least delay the party. They should find out what had happened to Robert and the others from France first. It was unthinkable to start the party without them. Robert's sacrifice for the peace was immeasurable. They would rather wait for them.

A minute later Richard was receiving a telepath from Pink. He cupped his ears with both hands to hear her.

"I'm sure they're here," Pink said. "I can feel them very near, but the signals are coming from high above somewhere. I'm on the way back."

The moment she said that, something drew her attention to the sky. What was that in the sky? Another roar of the people, twice as loud, went up into the skies of Portsmouth, followed by a loud clap and laughter. She could hear them from a mile away. She slowed down her horse to look up. Everyone's eyes were on the sky. All of a sudden, out of nowhere, a hundred hot-air balloons appeared in the sky at exactly 9:00 a.m.

Five-year-old Richtella looked up and pointed at the sky. "Uncle Robert!"

Pink had just gotten back to the party. Richard and Stella looked up simultaneously and saw the entire sky was covered with different-coloured balloons—one hundred of them, that is the equivalent of "war that lasted hundred years. They were throwing rose petals on the crowd below. One of the balloons represented the British flag and the other the French flag. The rest of them were made of all the colours of the rainbow. Richard, Stella, Pink, and everyone was waving at the balloons.

Richard said, "I told you he's never late." His voice almost got lost in the roar of the crowd. "I pronounce the party to be officially open."

Everyone was clapping as they looked up. Tears of joy were running down their cheeks at the same time they were smiling. This was an awesome moment.

The band started playing the song Alex had written for this party.

> Bravo! The war has gone.
> Bravo! Love has won.
> Now love, life—live the way you want, the way we want.
> Because love has won, because love has won, because love has

won.

> Oh, but when love is gone,
> No one to hold on
> And the cradle is gone,
> Nowhere to fall back on,
> 'Cause the war is on,
> The killing is on.
> Because there's no one to trust
> No one to be the winner in the end.
> Both sides got death and destruction.
> Love will always fend,

When war will kill and rend.
I hope you understand, war is not to depend.
'Cause the war is not the answer, my friend!
One people, one love, one life, earth one.
It belongs to none, belongs to everyone, not belonging to one.
So bravo! The war has gone.

CELEBRATION IN LONDON

King Edward III could not come to Portsmouth because the celebration was going to be held in London also. There were more than ten thousand people on and around the grounds of the palace.

The party was scheduled to begin exactly at 9:00 a.m., assuming that Richard and Robert were on the way from Portsmouth. He had no idea that Robert and his family were supposedly late.

Robert landed the balloon momentarily to pick up Richard and his family. They left for London immediately after they picked up Richard, Stella, Pink, and Richtella. King Edward III was waiting for them. They had already sent the two elephants, Raja and Rani, with Blackie the horse to Buck House palace the previous week. The king was looking forward to meeting Richtella and witnessing his unusual abilities.

The balloons were appearing in the sky of England as a symbol of peace this time. Robert had deliberately created this event to prove the point that energy could be used for construction instead of destruction, according to the intention of the user. It is the choice we make throughout life. This long war had given some valuable lessons for people to think about. This was the celebration for the lessons being learned by all mankind. The most important one was that when people from both sides took action for peace instead of following orders to kill one another, they initiated the thought of peace and put that intention into their gap and left it to the universe. The change had taken place in people's minds to bring about peace in their world. In the future, before any of the madness of war could begin, people would think about it. That was why it was important to pass along this history to future generations.

As the celebration continued in the palace, King Edward was waiting for Richard and Robert to come. He had no idea how they were going to come. The last thing anyone would expect was for them to appear in the sky via hot-air balloons.

All of a sudden, the crowd on the ground roared and were looking up into the sky. Everyone was pointing at a group of doves flying. Richard was using Richtella's power to communicate with birds and make a giant heart formation in the skies of London. Thousands of doves had joined to form this heart depicting love and peace. At the same time, on the ground, two elephants were following Blackie the horse. The crowd was parting to make way for the horse and two friendly elephants. They were all following the hundred balloons that had just appeared in the sky.

As Richard and Robert's balloon neared the palace, the king was clapping with excitement. At that moment something most extraordinary happened. In view of everyone, Richtella jumped out of the gondola and landed on the back of Blackie. He raced toward the entrance of the palace, where the king and everyone was waiting to receive them. The doves were also flying just above the balloons in a formation of a giant heart. This was probably the most spectacular show the King had ever witnessed. Blackie was now standing in front of the King. Richtella was standing on his back. Two elephants on both sides of Blackie. Richtella bowed at the King. Simultaneously the horse and the two elephants bowed. The King forgot his position for a moment and was clapping and jumping up and down like a child. He had never witnessed anything like this. At the same time, he opened his arms for Richtella. To his surprise, Richtella flew across to him. No one had ever seen any king ever behaving like a child in front of the public before.

Robert and rest of the balloons landed in the back garden of the palace. They were ushered by palace staff to the front of the palace at the king's court. The celebration was already underway, with fireworks, music, dancing, and so on. The arrival of the doves, balloons, Richtella, elephants, and Blackie the horse made it twice as entertaining and exciting. Everyone was very happy. They forgot their differences and hugged each other, starting at the king's court and spreading across the entire country. And from there to all of Europe. And from Europe to the entire world. When people are inspired, that's how love spreads across the world. People of the world were ready for that moment.

MAACULLA PART II—PRESENT DAY

Chapter 29

THE REAL STORY

Mrs. Griffiths, a.k.a. Maaculla, once told Saad that the stories she told him in the previous pages might seem rather fictitious and farfetched to many, while no one could explain why and how was it that suddenly the infamous Hundred Years' War ended.

As a matter of fact, that was the real story of how that long war had ended. The story was full of romance, sex, adventure, courage, friendship, and love. But the main reason that war had ended was the mass awareness of energy shifting towards positive. The story about to be unfolded in front of us is similar to "Part One" in principle. The only major difference is that the life of Saad and his family, together with the life of all the present-day people, will be directly involved with this story, as the future survival of human race is at stake.

SAAD CANNOT AVOID THE RESPONSIBILITY

Almost fifty years ago, Saad had learnt about these events. Now he had to live through and act upon upcoming events that would be an intricate part of his life and that of everyone around the world. Saad deliberately had not looked back or enquired about Mrs. Griffiths, a.k.a. Maaculla, since he left Portsmouth in 1969. He was fearful of facing or taking responsibility for the events of her predictions. He assumed that the greater the distance he created between him and Portsmouth, the further it would be from him in his life. His intention was to avoid everything she had told him so far. He had no idea that Maaculla had planned this all along too. She was well aware of these present-day events then. She was eighty-five years old in 1968, when Saad first laid eyes upon her. According to the legend, she left her body fifteen years after Saad left Portsmouth, on her hundredth birthday.

Now he found that he had unknowingly transitioned himself into the midst of these events, one after another. He was witnessing Maaculla's predictions, which had begun to unfold into reality one by one, right in front of his eyes. Worse yet, now it involved his own life and the lives of his family and everyone else around the world. Although it seemed that no one was directly involved in or responsible for events such as severe weather, earthquakes, the melting of polar ice, the rising of the seas, pollution, rising crime, terrorism, wars, genocides, unscrupulous and dishonest politicians, unrest among the people of the world, and so on, the effects of these events were becoming apparent in everyone's life day by day. No one might seem directly responsible for these man-made and natural disasters. But since everyone's energy had tilted towards the negative, everyone was unknowingly responsible for what was happening around the world.

SAAD TRIES TO DISCOURAGE THE MASS AWARENESS OF NEGATIVITY

We always believe and expect negative things to happen. Our minds are infected by negative energy, whether we realize it or not. Willingly or unwillingly, we all accept these occurrences as part of our lives. Ninety-nine percent of the daily news is negative. We hardly hear of any good news. At the beginning of time, it was the other way round. Consequently, there is a mass awareness of negativity in people's lives and minds. It has spread across the whole world like a viral epidemic. How's that possible? It happened so slowly and evolutionally that we didn't feel it coming. No one remembers consciously or willingly accepting any negative thoughts. It's like a secret conspiracy at work while everyone was busy with our modern way of living. This viral awareness of negativity has gradually crawled into our minds. It took hundreds of years to progress to this point. Consequently, it seemed like a normal way of life. We have reached a point of no return.

During the seventies Saad got so concerned about this epidemic of negativity that he decided to publish a newspaper called *Good News Daily*. He would publish only good news in it. But you guessed it right and probably are thinking, who would be interested in it? Yes, no one was even interested in reading it, let alone agreeing with the principle of it. With this extent of negativity, our bodies and minds have gotten riddled with new diseases that we may not be able to cure because they are originating in our minds. It's like your computer getting maliciously hacked. Now your computer is acting so erratically and uncontrollably that nothing can be done but replace it with a new one. But unfortunately, with human life it is not possible.

Positive energy, on the other hand, knows only how to construct. It will continue constructing endlessly. Unfortunately, we

196

need both energies in our human life. It's like fire and water. We need both of these in our lives. But it is always good to have a good balance.

IT IS OUR INTENTIONS THAT MAKE THE DIFFERENCE

You can imagine why young Saad wanted to run away from her as far as he could, to California. But he could not escape from her influence. On the contrary, he became part of her plans more so there. She wanted him to experience the diversity of life there.

Maaculla told him that the universe will separate good (positive) people from bad (negative) people. He can see that bad people from around the world are joining forces together. But he hasn't noticed any movement in the same direction among the good people. Maaculla also said that there are good and bad people in every race, religion, and colour. The good people need to be separated from the bad people to combine energy. But not from their religion, ethnicity, country, or choice of lifestyle.

The trouble with the negative energy is that it will eventually destroy the host. That's why it is always short lived. It is the nature of negative energy to destroy. It doesn't really care whether it destroys its own host or his adversaries or everything around it. She said to Saad that in the same principle, forgiving someone is the most selfish and self-serving act one can do. By getting rid of that negative energy (whether feeling of victim or revenge) from within, you will only protect yourself from being destroyed. If you embrace negative energy of any sort, eventually it will destroy you. You can't really swallow poison and hope others to die.

It is the intentions of humans that make them good or bad. Maaculla smiled, watching Saad's confused face.

SAAD CLOSES ALL HIS BUSINESSES TO WRITE THIS BOOK—2000

By 2016 Saad had lived in California for more than thirty-five years. Every year he visited England, where he grew up. He had started his restaurant career in England. After living in California for all these years and doing business there, he still couldn't completely separate himself from Maaculla. Now he realized that she wanted him to be in

California to understand their diversity of thinking. During his stay in California, many changes had taken place around the world. The Berlin Wall was destroyed, the EU was formed, China become the number-one global economy, and India and Brazil were catching up with them. America had elected a black president. America's embargo with Cuba had been lifted. Then there were negative things, such as North Korea threatening a nuclear attack, the 9/11 disaster, nuclear energy plants in Japan and Russia melting down, and the entire Middle East and Africa being in turmoil. The United States was about to build a wall between America and Mexico. He was witnessing one adversity after another. New challenges, such as pollution, global warming, erratic weather, earthquakes, crime, terrorism, and so on were becoming more and more prevalent.

And yet it was most ironic to see all these people living together in California from different countries and ethnicities and flourishing, people who once might have been considered enemies of one another during their stay in their native countries. It proved Maaculla's point that people in general liked to live in peace. And that was their intention. We saw similar examples of it in the fourteenth century between France and England.

He finally realized that he could not avoid Maaculla in spite of the distance. After fifty years of trying, he decided to close all of his highly successful celebrity-based restaurants and concentrate on writing this book.

A LESSON FOR SAAD—1968

When listening to Maaculla, Saad would fall into a trance, neither asleep nor awake. One day he was half awake, listening to her as if he was dreaming. Suddenly he felt a sharp pain on the left side of his chest, just below the ribs. Maaculla had jabbed him with her right middle and index fingers. He just stared at her as the pain spread across his entire body like an electric shock. Both of his eyes filled with tears. The pain was so severe that he could envision that blood might run instead of tears, followed by his eyes popping out from their sockets. It was so sudden that he could not react or even screw his face with pain. He just made an automatic short squeal, "oof" ("owe" in Sylheti). He'd no idea she was capable of creating that kind of pain. He continued to gaze at her as the sharp pain proceeded to numb his entire body moment by moment. He had no option. His entire being froze at that point. He wished he could close his eyes because tears were going to run down his cheeks. But nothing was moving. His body and the entire universe around him had become paralyzed, incapable of moving, talking, seeing, or performing any other physical activities. Life stood still like a flat photograph, silent and immobile!

Saad never asked her why she hit him so hard on that day. Maybe he didn't dare. He just walked around with a deep-blue bruise where she stuck her fingers at the bottom of his ribs for next three months or so. He continued to come and listened to her like a compulsion.

Another three months passed. All of a sudden she asked, "Do you still feel the pain?"

Saad, startled, shook his head no.

"I installed an energy there. Can you feel it?"

"I can feel something there."

"This is Deemagh."

Saad looked at her blankly.

"You will need it when the time comes," Maaculla said. "You will use it when challenges come to your life. I want you to focus there now."

Saad could feel that same intense pain as he focused. His eyes filled with tears again.

"I know it hurts," Maaculla said. "It's only physical pain. Your emotions will rise. The pain will dissipate over time. But the feeling will stay."

Saad nodded.

"I want you to feel the emotions there—anger, disappointment, sorry for yourself, victim or frustration. Can you feel it?"

Saad nodded.

"I want you to grab that feeling with your mind. Can you do it?"

Saad nodded.

"I want you to change that feeling to feeling 'good.' Just change it to 'good.' Don't make a statement like 'I feel good.' Just change it to 'good.' Can you do it for me?"

Saad nodded and smiled.

199

"Never make a statement. Always change it to 'good' when a challenge comes to your life. This energy is yours now. Use it."

Saad smiled.

"Everyone has this energy in them. Sometimes it needs awakening. Some people are lucky; they're born awakened. They don't know the difference, though. They think everyone thinks the same way. The other ninety-nine percent of people are not born that way. Regardless, we all have the energy within us.

"Remember, feelings come before the outcome or the circumstances. Most people think that their situations or the circumstances gave them the feeling of good or bad. No, it's the other way round. It is their feelings that have attracted this situation and circumstances which may good or bad.

"Remember this and keep 'the feeling good' in your gap. All the outcomes in your life will be in your favor, no matter how unfavorable they may seem at first glance.

"The reason why you don't make a statement like 'I feel good' is that your gap works like the needle in a compass. It simply points to the future outcome. Your future begins with the next moment. If you make a statement that 'you feel good,' it's already a 'past.' It is already in the yester-moment. In other words, what just happened now is a result yesterday's energy.

"You asked me how will you remember all this or deliver the message to the people. Use the gap all the time. If any desires or frustrations come, put them into the gap and turn them into good. All the outcomes will be in your favor."

Chapter 30

In Hyde Park Corner, London, on a Saturday morning, Saad had arrived from Los Angeles the night before. He was walking in the park with his family. He liked listening to speakers at the Speakers Corner, with diverse subjects. They stood on the grass and spoke whether anyone listened or not.

One man, apparently a Vietnam veteran from America, supporting himself on a wooden leg, was speaking to a small group of listeners. Saad could hear his voice, which had an American accent. Saad stopped to listen to what the man had to say. He told his family to go ahead, and he would meet up with them in Selfridges later.

The man said, "As the human race, our days are numbered if we carry on like this. We have to change to save the world for future generations. War is not the answer. We need to visit other countries to meet the people, regardless of their size or ethnicity or religion. We have to make peace, learn their cultures, do business with them, exchange knowledge with them. Not go there to conquer them and take their wealth or bully them. Believe me, people in foreign countries don't want war. They are friendly people. They believe in different religion. They look different. That's OK. The same God has created them. We need to empathize with them. We need to accept them. It's the politicians who want to keep us divided so that they can control us."

A group of young bover boys and girls started chanting, "Yank, go home." One of the boys went behind him and pulled his wooden leg. He was groveling on the ground, trying to get up, while another boy was pushing him down with his foot on his back.

Saad intervened. He went into the middle of the crowd told them to stop it or else.

They all turned round to face Saad. One boy said, "Or else what, old man?" He advanced towards Saad.

Saad threw him on the ground and pushed him down with his left foot. He looked around and said, "Anyone else, before I call nine nine nine?"

Saad let go of the boy.

201

The boy rubbed his arm. "You broke my arm, old man."

"No I didn't, but I could oblige you. And I'm proud to be an old man." He walked towards to the boy.

The boy ran away, following his friends, who were already in the distance. Saad overheard the boy saying, "Honest, I couldn't see him coming at me. He was fast..."

The rest of the crowd was clapping. One man came forward to help the American up. He asked Saad, "How did you do that? You're not so young anymore."

Saad smiled. "Did what? I have no idea what you're talking about."

He scurried away.

Saad overheard the American say, "Believe me, I've seen this kind of move before. They can do impossible things...they use the power of the universe."

Saad just shook his head and walked on.

SECURITY CAMERAS AND SCANNERS ON THE ROADS AND SELFRIDGES

There were security cameras on every street corner in London monitoring every face passing by. Computers immediately used a facial recognition system to identify known criminals or terrorists. It could process thirty thousand faces per second. In the event it recognized any person of interest, it would alert the police, Scotland Yard, and MI6.

Saad approached the large stone doorway to Selfridges. There was a security scanner similar to those at airports. Two security personnel, one on each side, greeted and ushered the line of people. These scanners were everywhere. They were in hotels, shopping centres, airports, government offices, meetings, concerts—anyplace where large numbers of people gathered. These scanners were specially designed to detect any biological weapons such as viruses, fungi, chemicals, and so on. They could also detect any conventional weapons, such firearms, bombs, and knives. If they detected anyone with a weapon of any kind, that person was restrained and handed over to the proper authorities.

The question here is, Are these sophisticated systems making our lives any safer, and are they reducing crime or terrorism? It seems that our expenses are getting bigger every day, while there is no sign of slowing down crime or terrorism.

SAAD IN LONDON—PRESENT DAY

Saad was visiting England at the request of the Paddington Research Hospital. In early sixties, when he was a student there, he was involved in medical research. Because of his hypnosis and philosophy background, he was given a scholarship grant to go abroad to study the mental energy levels of patients who suffered from epidemical diseases such as cholera, Ebola, smallpox, and so on. His report concluded that 100 percent of the patients who were infected by these diseases had a high level of fear prior to contracting the diseases, which led to a high level of acidity in their bodies.

SAAD'S REVISIT TO PORTSMOUTH—PRESENT DAY

After his family left for Los Angeles and after his meeting with Paddington Hospital, Saad was waiting for the next meeting with a few European doctors in Brussels. Until then, he had couple of days to spare. He decided to visit Portsmouth. This was where he had had his first encounter with Mrs. Griffiths, a.k.a. Maaculla, in 1968, almost fifty years ago. She was the one who had told him all this would come and what to do about it. Saad felt it was time for him to do something about it, as he could not avoid the consequences anymore. He was getting anxious, as Maaculla's predictions were coming to reality one by one. She had told him that she would be there in spirit when the time came. But she had never mentioned if he would be able to communicate with her at the time of need.

He was using his time on hand to visit Portsmouth in case he could see any signs from her. He planned to visit Albert Road and good old St Mary's Church, now Portsmouth Cathedral, where Maaculla's story began in the fourteenth century. Maybe she would communicate with him somehow. She had been dominating his life for last fifty years or so anyway.

He had checked into a bed-and-breakfast on Albert Road during his stay in Portsmouth before. He had no idea how to communicate with Mrs. Griffiths. She had been dead for nearly fifty years. He remembered her advice—when you are totally lost and haven't got a clue what to do, just feel or choose; deep inside your gap, you want to feel good. Then leave the rest to the unknown.

The next morning at breakfast, he met a group of people who were going to Portsmouth Cathedral. He remembered that Mrs. Griffiths, a.k.a. Maaculla, used to come to Sunday Mass at Portsmouth Cathedral. The pastor informed him that she was buried in the cemetery that belonged to the cathedral. He also told him that a strange but wonderful phenomenon had started occurring, centering in the cemetery. It had spread almost all over Portsmouth now. He had a distant look as he spoke.

"What is it, Father Brown?" Saad asked.

"Here, come with me, since you are the only one who has ever asked about Mrs. Griffiths."

They went outside, and Father Brown pointed at the cemetery. "Look!"

Saad could see the whole garden was full of roses. He looked at Father Brown. "So you have a nice rose garden?"

"Yes, but we didn't plant all these. In fact, we didn't even have any rose bushes. In just couple of weeks, our entire garden and the cemetery filled with roses. Our gardener said he has no clue where they all come from. He's afraid to even touch them. It's a miracle."

Saad looked around. "In just two week? Looks like they're fully grown, well-manicured rose bushes!"

Father Brown was excited. "Yes, and there's more to it. But first, how do you—or, rather, how did you know Mrs. Griffiths? Why are you asking about her grave? She has no surviving relatives. She left her entire estate to the cathedral. No one has ever asked after her before."

"I met her in 1968 and stayed with my business here for nine months. She was my landlady. Then I left Portsmouth in1969. I never came back here since."

"She died in 1983."

Saad looked shocked. "Exactly on her hundredth birthday!"

Father Brown was surprised. "How did you know that?"

"She told me she would."

"Really! Yes, but Saad, the strangest thing is this rose phenomenon starting from her grave. It's spreading across all of

204

Portsmouth, now you're here asking about her. Are we witnessing a miracle?"

Saad's voice has changed; he's emotional. "We're witnessing more than a miracle, Father Brown. The survival of the world depends on..."

Tears were running down his cheeks. "Father Brown, please show me her grave. I need to be there on my own."

Father Brown had a strange look on his face. He pointed at her grave. "You can't miss it. It's full of Tudor roses. The smell will guide you there."

Saad, without wasting any time, walked towards the grave as father Brown looked on. He disappeared from Father Brown's sight as he neared the grave.

Saad comes back from the cemetery after an hour with a beaming smile on his face. Father Brown was still standing there waiting for him.

Saad said, "Of course, Father Brown. Her first name was Rose. So was her mother's name, and her mother's name and on and on. There were seven Roses in all until Mrs. Rose Griffiths.

Father Brown said, "How do you know all this? It's a miracle!"

Saad smiled. "You know, you sure sound like Father Reynolds."

With that, Father Brown broke down, knelt in front of Saad, and kissed his hand. He was physically shaking with excitement. "

How do you know father Reynolds's name? He was the first pastor of this church in the fourteenth century. Please tell me who you are. I've been having strange dreams for the last two months." Tears were running down his face.

Saad looked around. "Father Brown, you're embarrassing me. Please get up." He pulled him up.

"Would you come to our house for a cup of tea?"

"Of course I would. Do you live in Father Reynolds's house behind the Cathedral? I know where it is."

Father Brown was more surprised. He didn't know what to say. He just led Saad to the house as he kept turning and staring back at him.

Chapter 31

MAACULLA'S MESSAGE TO THE POPULATION—1968

Maaculla said, "The human race has come a long way. We need to use our intelligence more wisely and intensely now. For example, we need to use our resources more positively for constructive work rather than for wars, destruction, and division. We have come to a point where no one is more powerful than the other. We have proved it again and again throughout history that having a war with others does not get us anywhere. It happens when one side gets greedy, jealous, or bigoted, or is just a bully. We continue destroying one another's lives, property, and resources. Yet all sides complain of lack of energy, resources, food, medicine, and so on. Many are homeless and starving, even in the highly developed countries.

"There is something wrong with this picture. Examples of this we have seen in our history again and again. Neither side wins in the end. Both parties are using negative energy, though one side may be defending themselves. Both sides suffer unimaginable losses of lives and resources. We saw that in *Maaculla* Part One how one side became greedy, bullying, and blinded by their unfair ambition. They continued on the same path for over a hundred years. They could have achieved any desired ambition a long time ago with their own resources. As I mentioned before, that negative energy eventually destroys the host itself, because the nature of negative energy is to destroy. While we are busy destroying others, it proceeds to destroy us, the host too. It doesn't know any other way. The other side has no choice but to defend themselves, yet indirectly they have attracted this into their experiences by fearing.

"As a result of these continued war experiences around the world, the skills of war, strength, and technology have grown in the negative aspects. We have been competing with one another to make bigger and stronger weapons, though maybe out of fear or aggression. We have developed weapons of mass destruction, biological weapons, nuclear weapons, and so on. The truth of the matter is, using any weapons like this against one another is suicidal, to say the least.

"While everyone always has rhetoric about wars, conflict, and division, no one has so far tried to introduce peace around the world.

Because conflict has been the easiest way to unite small groups of people—to stand against others. But now it has become global. That means annihilation of the human race is inevitable if we ever use these sophisticated weapons.

"The time has come to unite the entire world and restore peace before we destroy one another and hence the whole world. In order to unite the whole world, we will have to have a common goal. To have a common goal, we must have a common enemy of mankind that threatens the entire human race as it stands. Only then can humans forget their differences and join forces together to fight this enemy. But who or what is that enemy, and where is it?"

MAACULLA'S PREDICTIONS—1968—THE EFFECTS OF NEGATIVE ENERGY

Negative energy does not only destroy its own host. It destroys everything around it. When mass awareness becomes negative, you will notice the following and more:

1. There will be too much rainfall in some areas, and some areas of the world will have too little rainfall, resulting in a shortage of water in those areas. As a result, these areas will turn into deserts. The flooded areas will be permanently overrun by water, resulting in lost lands. The loss of land or the shortage of water didn't matter in those days when there weren't enough people living on our planet to feel these effects. People just migrated to more habitable areas.

2. Excess water will come down from our poles, and many countries will go underwater.

3. Crime will be out of control everywhere. There will be more jails in the world than schools. Crimes will be committed by law enforcement members as well as criminals.

4. There will be unrest and chaos everywhere among the people. In the name of religion and politics, small groups of people will make their own rules, and they will impose them on others.

5. War will break out everywhere. There will be the threat of nuclear war. The bombing of Nagasaki was only the beginning. There will also be the threat of biological and chemical warfare.

6. Natural disasters such as volcanic eruptions, earthquakes, floods, tsunamis, tornadoes, tidal waves, snowstorms, and so on will be more frequent.

7. New incurable diseases will be prevalent all over in spite all our medical advancements.

This is just to name a few major events. There will be too many elements for humans to deal with at once. All this will happen because our energy will have shifted too much towards negativity. When the mass awareness of negativity rises to that extent, there will be noticeable man-made and natural disasters. People and nature will turn negative and out of control at the same time because they all consist of the same two energies.

CRIME AND WARS ARE IMPLAUSIBLE

Maaculla said, "In the olden days, wars were fought with old-fashioned weapons. Today, fighting any war for any length of time costs millions of times more in computers, planes, ships, technology, and modern weaponry. If the enemy does not beat us, the cost of the war will certainly make the country bankrupt. So you see it is not feasible in any sense to have any war, big or small. Imagine what would happen if a couple of superpowers started a third world war. Also, today, all the counties around the world have all the ethnicities living together. This is a normal part of life and business. Imagine asking an Indian American to take up weapons against India or asking a Jewish pilot to bomb Israel. It is unfair to even ask. The universe very tactfully has shuffled people all over the world so that we won't fight with one another anymore. Maybe the universe is coaxing us to live in peace `

"The same argument can be applied to crime. When criminals commit crimes, it costs us property and lives. Then, if we catch them, it costs us even more. Taxpayers have to pay for police, court costs, and incarceration expenses. The economy has become the biggest retribution and reward in our society now, and for good reason."

THE BENEFITS OF A CRIMELESS AND WARLESS WORLD!

Maaculla said, "If we can just eliminate two things, crime and war, from our world, we will have a surplus of resources to fight any man-made or natural disasters such as diseases, food shortages, energy shortages, global warming, rising water, climate change, tornadoes, tsunamis, earthquakes, and so on. Living symbiotically, we can make this happen. If all of our needs are taken care of, we don't need to go to war or defend ourselves. To do that we need the collaboration of all countries, big and small. There are endless benefits to a crimeless and warless life.

"The most recent example is that when Japan and Germany were defeated, it was a good thing for them. They flourished in business, industry, technology, and so on, and became the number-one economy in the world—only because they didn't have to (or weren't allowed to) maintain armies and defense. They put all their energies and resources into business and commerce and became successful regardless of the size of their countries. In fact, they invaded the whole world again, but with commerce. This time we welcomed their invasions. All this happened just by giving up one aspect of energy wastage—wars. Imagine what could happen if they could eliminate crime as well. This is the perfect example of how the whole world could benefit beyond our imagination by giving up war and crime. We should have learnt a valuable lesson from these examples. Instead we've been spending more money by maintaining a presence of armies in those countries we defeated.

"Similarly, criminals commit crimes, and we all pay for it. While they were benefiting by leaps and bounds, we were paying even more for it. It costs fifty to eighty thousand to keep an inmate in jail. You can guess how much it costs the taxpayers every year. There is no sign of crime being reduced. On the contrary, it is increasing by leaps and bounds. Our system is actually encouraging crime indirectly, maybe because a government looks good when crime creates more jobs by employing more police, social workers, security people, lawyers, courts, judges, and so on. Then there are industries that benefit from crime, such as the suppliers and manufacturers of police uniforms, cars, radios, badges, computers, security cameras, and so on.

CAN WE ELIMINATE CRIME?
Maaculla said, "We may not be able eliminate crimes magically, but we can begin by saving what we spend on criminals. Make the inmates useful and productive. Make them earn and pay taxes like the

rest of the population. Let them pay for their own upkeep in jailing, health care, living expenses, hobbies, and so on. Teaching them skills and how to use them in a productive way can help them in productive careers rather than a career in crime. By making them productive, a government can save all the resources they spend on the crime.

"There is no one who can obviously be blamed for increasing crime. We used to blame poverty. But we can see that crime in the higher and richer places is more prevalent. Some people are criminals, whether rich or poor. In today's society, there are more thieves and rapists among the rich and powerful people than the poor. Of course, it's more obvious in the poor than in the rich.

"Human society has accepted crime from the beginning of time. We've punished them, jailed them, banished them, and even put them to death. Nothing has decreased or eliminated crime. On the contrary, there is no sign of it slowing down. It's there, so we have to protect our society, and we keep spending our resources on it. In fact, in the United States alone, we have more jails than schools. It's supposed to be the most advanced country in the world. Crime has become so expensive that no government can afford the luxury of having crime anymore. The truth of the matter is that all the countries around the world will have to continue maintaining their defenses against crime."

MAACULLA INTRODUCES A NEW PHENOMENON—MACULAE

Just recently a new disease or phenomenon has started to spread rapidly across all nations without discriminating against any country, the rich or the poor, the religious or the nonreligious, black or white, in any geographical area. So far scanners and computers have failed to detect this phenomenon called maculae. Scientists and the doctors at the CDC and hospitals around the world are totally baffled. They have no clue how or what's causing this, let alone how to cure or protect the people. One can only guess whether it is biological or a malicious weapon of some kind. Scientists are calling it maculae because it is similar to skin spots as maculae. Unlike normal ones, though, these bat-shaped maculae can be very dangerous. If unattended they become life threatening. Medical treatments are ineffective against this.

Medically, the only thing they've been able to determine is that the victim's acidity, or pH level, shows very high. Normally the body's acidity is treated with calcium and other antacids. But none of them has been effective against it, especially when acidity is as high as 10, which is much higher than the normal pH of 7. A higher pH creates a higher probability of bat-shaped maculae disease condition. The basis of all disease is acidity. But with this particular maculae, 50 percent of the cells being in acidosis is normal. It is totally unlike any other disease condition.

With normal maculae, which are known to scientists, the condition first appears on the skin as discolored spots with no particular shape or size. With this particular one, the spots appear to be more or less the same in size and in the shape of bats. The other peculiarity is that when negativity rises in the host's mind and stays that way for a while, the flesh starts to rot and fall away, exposing the bone. Unlike regular maculae, this gradually becomes life threatening if the negativity continues in the mind of the affected person.

A POSSIBLE CURE FOR MACULAE

The only way this new disease can be treated is by increasing positivity in the mind. Some relief or slowing down of its progress has been achieved by prayer, meditation, and turning into a positive, good person. Amazingly, it reacts more to the mind than medications. So far, no physical or medical treatment has been effective. If one wants to cure oneself before it turns deadly, he or she will have to become a positively, good person.

That is the way Maaculla planned to balance the mass awareness of negativities in the whole world—by making maculae as the common enemy of the negative people. In other words, good, positive-minded people would have nothing to worry about. Maculae affect only negative-minded people, regardless of country, race, or religion. If your intentions are negative, then you are a bad person; hence you are prone to maculae.

Normally, it is impossible to know who is a bad person and who is good person. But now, a bad person with harmful intentions will have no escape from this. The mass awareness of negativities has risen so far that one more thought of negativity will trigger bat-shaped maculae on that person. Their own negative energy will turn against them. At first they will be branded and exposed by contracting maculae. The bat-shaped spots will appear all over their faces and bodies. The more they continue being negative, the more the maculae will intensify. But once they turn back into positive-minded people, they will be cured instantaneously. That way, Maaculla intended to separate good people from bad and eventually force people to be positive.

MAACULLA USES MACULAE TO SEPARATE GOOD FROM BAD

Maaculla said, "The balance of our energies has tilted too much towards negative. As a result, just one more thought of negativity will trigger a person to self-destruct by contracting maculae. These people will be branded by this condition, as the bat-shaped spots will appear all over their skin. Everyone will know by looking at them that they are negative-minded people. It will affect only the negative, selfish, greedy bullies, bigots, criminals, terrorists, and dishonest people. These people will be zapped hence branded by their own negativities. They will come down with these bat-shaped maculae. If they choose to remain this way, it will become life threatening, and eventually it will destroy them. They'll have no one to blame for it but themselves. No one will have to punish them or persuade them or even cure them. It is their own choice that will destroy them or cure them. If they choose to become positive-minded people, they will instantly heal themselves."

SYMBIOTIC IS THE WAY

Maaculla said, "If you observe our nature carefully, you will notice that the entire world runs on a balanced equation. One part is dependent on the others. From the smallest to the biggest living beings, all depend on one another. They live off one another. The most obvious example of this is that we live off the oxygen the trees expel, and in return trees live off the CO_2 we expel from our lungs. Similarly, even the smallest bacteria live off one another. We can learn from nature's example. We can do trade with one another, exchange knowledge with one another, and so on. That way we can spend all our resources on knowledge, art, business, science, technology, medicines, and space research instead of on weapons, wars, and crime."

Chapter 32

THE LAWS OF THE UNIVERSE

Maaculla said, "Back to the laws of the universe. The law is that whatever you feel or visualize or picture will be attracted into your life. Most of the time we focus on what we 'don't want.' And this 'don't want' turns up in our lives. It's no good wishing something and fearing at the same time, thinking, 'I don't want to have this in my life.' This means that if you want peace, then wish for 'peace.' It's no good fearing and wishing 'no war.' When you think 'no war,' you are thinking out of fear. When you think 'peace,' you are desiring peace. And that's the law. Straightforward and uncomplicated. Consequently, the responsibility lies on you what you wish for. Most people try to be good and expect rewards for it. Even the most angelic people can end up with the worst of luck, harboring fear within themselves. At the same time, most a-holes are making successes of their lives. The universe doesn't understand human logic. That's why it forgives readily as soon as you are doing the right thing. It doesn't judge you for your past or present record—your sins or good deeds."

MAACULLA PRESENTS PROJECT SYMBIOSIS

Maaculla said, "If only we observe carefully, we can find an abundance of evidence depicting why things are the way they are in our nature. There is also evidence of deliberate plans supporting the events that have followed one after another through billions of years. It could have happened the following way: At the beginning, when the earth got covered with water after the dry desert period, all land went underwater. Earth began to cool down, and some water got stored as ice on the poles. And some water evaporated as the sun hit the other areas. Hence, water is stored as clouds as they float around the earth, supporting our atmosphere above earth's surface. Distributing excess water this way has exposed higher grounds, with mountains, hills, and flatlands. The lower craters remained as seas. It sure seems like a deliberate plan for these events to form land, rivers, mountains, and seas, thus allowing life forms to thrive on the land and water. These are big events by the universe, over billions of years. Incidentally, a human life-span is not long enough to experience or comprehend the impact these events have on human life. We rely on the records and evidence our pundits have left behind as recently as only few hundred years ago.

"The time has come, though, for humans to take the responsibility to make our home planet more habitable as needs arise. We have the knowledge, technology, and resources needed to make it possible. Project Symbiosis is the right project for this purpose. All we need is the cooperation and collaboration of all the people. We all know that's not going to happen soon. We cannot wait until all humans become civilized enough to willingly participate in a global project like this. We are too busy disrupting and wasting our energy and resources on the negativities of egos, wars, prejudices, crime, and so on. By then we may not have a world left to work on. That is why I plan to compel people to cooperate and collaborate.

"In order to change the effect of negativity in our world, I have laid out some plans for Project Symbiosis. It is always wise to emulate nature. You can see the laws of the universe at work in nature. It has designed our world so that we can help one another and depend on and exchange one another's knowledge and experience, and so on. So by joining PS, you will have decided to be a positive person. On the other hand, lying, cheating, bullying, bigotry, and taking advantage of people, controlling them, and so on for selfish reasons turns you into a negative person. We have tried the negative ways many times in our history, and it has never worked permanently. It brings us to the verge of conflict and war every time. If we follow these plans of PS—Project Symbiosis—we may be able to save our world and hence the existence of the human race. Alternatively, doomsday is knocking at our door, Maaculla said.

"Saad, it may sound confusing to you now because many of these things haven't visibly begun to happen yet. But in the future, you will be here to witness all this. You will need to pass this message on and educate the people."

Saad had a nervous look on his face.

WHAT IS PROJECT SYMBIOSIS?

According to *The Oxford Dictionary*, "symbiosis" means interaction between two different organisms living in close physical association, typically to the advantage of both.

It doesn't mention conflict because conflict is opposite to symbiosis. It is antibiosis. In our case we can create this symbiosis effect by interacting with one another, to the advantage of us all, by emulating nature. The universe has provided us all the raw materials, and we have to build our own habitats using them.

The principle of symbiosis is to exchange one another's excess resources. This principle can be applied to the rainy areas supplying their excess water to the deserts. And in return solar energy can be supplied from the deserts to the rainy areas.

During the building of infrastructure, large, water-carrying conduits can be laid out under the roads. At the same time, electric cables can be installed by the side of the conduit in a separate channel to carry solar electricity from the desert to the rainy states. A similar infrastructure principle can be used throughout England with their drain and water distribution system and electric supply lines underground. This will need to be done on a much larger scale. Also, in the near future, technology will be developed to export solar energy to areas of the world that need it.

In the same way, all the desert lands can be cultivated into habitats for humanity by transporting water through these conduits under the roads to deserts. Then all the excess water from the sea can be relieved when it rises from the melting of the polar ice. It is also a good idea to put back the majority of the salt into the sea, to keep the balance there and prevent the freezing of the seawater into ice. Evidently, most of the desert lands belonged to the sea once.

This way a symbiotic effect can be achieved, with deserts supplying solar electricity to areas that need it, and in return, excess water from other areas will supply water to the deserts.

Maaculla said, "Imagine that! I think the universe is hinting at us to be symbiotic in every way." We can be symbiotic with one another by exchanging knowledge, technology, science, medicine, foods, art, and so on instead of being antibiotic and wasting our resources and intelligence in competition, conflicts, greed, jealousy, bigotry, and wars. Let us embrace symbiosis as part of our life. With every country and project in the world, we can employ symbiosis. Hence Project Symbiosis. And hence a symbiotic world. Maybe this is why the universe designed our earth this way. You will notice that in one part of the earth, wheat grows better than in other parts. Likewise with rice, vegetables, fruits, herbs, coal, oil, iron, minerals, salt, gold, diamonds, marble, granite, sun, rain, and on and on. Every area has its own strong point. In the same way, every race and ethnicity has its own strong point. By exchanging, we will become symbiotic in nature, and we all will have access to all the knowledge, experiences, and resources of the world. We will do that by sharing and not by depriving others.

THE EFFECTS OF ANTIBIOSIS

Maaculla said, "Right now, the population of the world is living in antibiosis, the exact opposite of symbiosis. They are repelling one another and depriving one another. When the negative energy rises high enough, that creates mass awareness of negativity to the extent that it destroys the host and everything around it. In this case, the host is the entire human race. Our negative energy level is so high that one more negative thought will tip the balance completely and start the destroying process. If we continue towards negativity, it will eventually destroy us, the hosts."

In many ways, our so-called civilization is wasting resources. If we were really civilized, we would have learnt from our mistakes and would not repeat the same mistakes over and over again. The story in *Maaculla* Part I depicts the sort of mistakes we have been making. It obviously illustrates that war does not pay any dividend on any side. We are wasting our energies with wars. All these things happened in the fourteenth century. Did we learn anything or any lesson from it since? Obviously not. Otherwise we still wouldn't be having wars and conflicts in many parts of the world now. The only problem is that nowadays, we have developed the kind of weapons that will eliminate the entire world. There are countries already threatening to use these weapons. Their mentality is that if they don't exist, they don't care if the rest of world exists or not. Do we really want to go in that direction?

LIVING WITH SYMBIOSIS

Maaculla said, "We need to learn to forget our differences and live together. I have planned for Saad to have that firsthand experience by living in California. There you can see different races living together and creating art, movies, books, technology, medicines, engineering,

217

businesses, inventions, foods, computers, software, space technology and so on. They don't belong to just one race or ethnicity. They come from different parts of the world. Once, when they lived in their own countries, some of them might have been considered enemies of others. But the same people live together in California with love, respect, harmony, and, most of all, empathy for one another. We can extend this example to the entire world and bring the best out of everyone to share with one another. This proves that people around the world want peace, given a chance."

THE PLAN FOR SYMBIOSIS IS A PLAN FOR PEACE

Maaculla said, "So far in our human existence, we have always had the rhetoric of wars and conflicts. No one has ever come out with a definite plan for peace and presented it to the whole world to live together peacefully. No one has ever explained the benefits of living in peace. There was no definite plan ever. Without a solid plan, nothing works."

Project Symbiosis is one such plan, and it provides a single goal that is equally beneficial for everyone in every country in the world. It provides benefits to every country and every race, rich or poor. In fact, no one has to be poor when everything will be provided by this project. It explains the advantages and disadvantages symbiosis and antibiosis.

On the other hand, some natural disasters are unavoidable. We have a constant battle in fighting natural disasters such as tsunamis, earthquakes, floods, tornadoes, melting of the polar ice, and rising of the water level, to name a few. We can deal with these natural disasters more easily and efficiently when we don't have to spend our resources on war and crime. We already have seen in the examples of Japan and Germany how they have flourished without having to spend their resources on defense and wars.

Maaculla promises that even natural disasters can be controlled by shifting our energies to positive. In order to do that, we need to understand the root of the problem, which is that our awareness has tilted too much towards negative.

ELIMINATE CRIME WITH PROJECT SYMBIOSIS

Maaculla said, "Then there is crime, which is another major way we are wasting our resources and energy. If all our jail systems, courts, and policing were effective, then we should have less crime in our world. But the exact opposite is true."

With Project Symbiosis, we can make these inmates productive by making them work there. Criminals are mostly overactive physically and mentally. Once we introduce to them the right jobs, they can be extremely productive. Finding the right inspiration for everyone could be a very useful tool in this respect. At the same time, we can save those resources we spend on our criminals and inmates.

THE UNIVERSE IS INFALLIBLE

Saad had been thinking to ask the most obvious question for months. He didn't want to sound stupid, so he tried to think out the answer himself. "If the universe is infallible, there must be a reason why it allows all these negative things to happen, such as disasters, the killing of innocents, injustice, wars, crime, bigotry, bullying, and so on. Some of the occurrences seem so unnecessary and unfair."

Maaculla said, "The answer might surprise you, Saad. The universe has given us the freedom of choice. It is too big to care about minute things such as human existence. We have the responsibility to survive or be extinct. If we don't get along with one another and escalate to an ultimate war by using weapons like hydrogen or atom bombs, our existence will be at stake. We may be extinct like the dinosaurs. Does anyone care about dinosaurs anymore? It is totally our responsibility to survive or be extinct. To understand what goes on in the universe, one has to understand its plan."

THE FUTURE OF SEX—ANOTHER PLAN OF THE UNIVERSE

Maaculla said, "In the same way, we are probably misunderstanding the universe's plan to change from two genders to one gender. Who knows what the plan of the universe is in this respect? What if the possibility of one gender diminishes in numbers or completely dissipates? Consequently, human propagation may completely stop. Maybe that's why we see more and more transgender people born every day, assuming they are the bi-gender rendering of humans to come. This way, in the future, both partners will have the opportunity to bear children.

"The other thought is that with one gender, there is little possibility of abuse of the weaker sex. Maybe that's why it's making us get used to same-sex partnerships. To reiterate, the universe doesn't make mistakes, no matter how surreal it seems to us at first look. It's ignorant to think otherwise. Everything has a meaning to it, whether we understand or not. Visionaries and avatars in the past tried to tell us what lies in our future. They could perceive it with their higher vibration. Maybe that's why da Vinci painted a picture of a perfect human as one. He had combined a man and a woman's body as one. Was he referring to a bi-gender? Could he foresee the universe's plan of human rendering to come? Who knows? On the other hand, he could have easily painted a perfect man and a perfect woman separately. That would have been more logical thinking. An avatar like da Vinci may think in a way that defies logic. Human logic is like human ego—it's limiting, to say the least. Think about it."

This is just an example of how we could easily misunderstand the universe's plans.

Chapter 33

WHY MACULAE

Maaculla said, "Negativities are happening in our society constantly. There is no way anyone can monitor every crime and every negativity that goes on in our world. When we catch someone, we need to prove their guilt. During that process we spend billions of dollars worldwide for police, Scotland Yard, MI6, the FBI, courts, and so on. That's why I'm introducing maculae to our world. There is no need to monitor or catch anyone in a negative act. If someone does any negative act, regardless of how secretively, it will appear as bat-shaped maculae spots on their faces and all over their skin, thus branding them. The more they try to hide, the more intense it will get. That way, they themselves will voluntarily admit it to save their own lives. It is their own negative energy that will start destroying them. Imagine that—we never have to think of catching people, searching for them, or proving their guilt. We won't ever have to fear or worry about getting robbed or victimized, cheated or lied to in any way whatsoever. Complete peace of mind."

Saad just looked blankly. He didn't know whether to believe her or not.

"Don't worry," Maaculla said. "The necessary help will come to you at the right time. You'll find the opportunity in the problem itself."

She continued. "It's not to be confused with Maaculla, the nickname you gave me. It's most ironic that you gave me a similar-sounding name, because you have no idea what maculae are. Do you? Well, again you will witness it when the time comes."

The percentage of negativities will rise so far that one more thought of negativity will trigger maculae. For now all you need to know is that the negative doers from every aspect of life will be branded by a skin condition called maculae. It affects only the people with negative intentions so that everyone knows who they are. They will not be able to plead not guilty or deny it. There is no need for lie detectors either. Everyone will know from their branded faces with bat-shaped spots. Their own negativities will start destroying them. As you know, the purpose of negative energy is to destroy, and eventually it destroys the host, whoever harbours it. For this particular purpose, it will just appear on their skin in the shape of bats to begin with. Like tattoos. Normally, maculae are harmless spots on the skin in any shape or size. But when the bat-shaped ones stay long enough, they will get deeper, and the flesh will fall off the bat-shaped spots, exposing the bone. This will only happen if that person continues being negative. It will become extremely painful and life threatening. On the other hand, if they decide to turn back to positivity, they will be cured instantaneously. It's as if God is always forgiving, but only when they repent. I will give you the formula for the cure later. No doctors or hospitals will be able to cure it because it is coming from their own mind rather than an infectious virus or germ from outside. Only they will be able to cure themselves by applying that formula.

WHAT'S THE PURPOSE OF ALL THIS?

Maaculla said, "The big question here is, do we humans want to wait for that day to come that will compel us to cooperate and save us from our own annihilation? The purpose of this is that when humans around the world do not cooperate willingly to find a common element for the entire human race, they must be compelled to do so. Then they will be united to fight for this purpose. This purpose is maculae. It needs only the cooperation of negative-minded people. Maculae is the ideal instrument for this. Their own energy will cause this to happen. No one else need be affected by it or blamed for it. They say we are our own worst enemy. They might not dare to think of any negativities, because their own negative thoughts will trigger their own destruction by triggering maculae. This will be the beginning of another human civilization. It will compel them to be united and be one human race, regardless of their differences. Right now, there is no other way to get the cooperation of all the people of the world."

Maaculla continued. "You may not be able to understand or notice that our world is going in the wrong direction right now. Only I can feel the energy shift that is taking place, because I can perceive higher vibrations. Just as I could see the brown-suited man's spirit. Believe it or not, our world is shifting towards the negative. No one will understand it even if I try to explain it to them right now. They would think I'm imagining all this. It needs to run its course and let the whole world experience the effect of negativity first, for them to be able realize it. By then I won't be here, but you will. You will have to tell them what I am telling you. As the mass population harbour negativities, it starts affecting our environment and our livelihood and our health and, in the end, our existence.

"Incidentally, it's also ironic that you gave me a nickname that rhymes with Dracula. According to legend, he was 100 percent negative energy. That's why he was so short lived. His own negative energy destroyed him."

Chapter 34

SAAD IS HUMBLED BY ALL THIS—PRESENT DAY

Saad wanted to apologize to the leaders, experts, and scientists of the world for having the audacity to present this plan as a layman. He was simply a messenger who was delivering an important message to the world. No disrespect was intended for the learned experts of the world.

Having said that, we realize from our past experiences that there is no hope of uniting people and educating them to combine their energy and live together with love and peace. We have no way of knowing who is telling the truth and who has good intentions for the common good. We can only wish there were a system that would separate good people from the bad. Well now there is. Maculae are that common factor that will compel all humans to think positively. At the same time, we will recognize who is negative and who is positive by branding the negative doers. This will separate good from the bad. It will not discriminate based on their race, colour or ethnicities, rich or poor. At the same time, it will give a chance to the negative people to turn positive.

MEETING WITH THE LEADERS

After trying to put all the people together for a year or so, Saad was very discouraged with the responses he had received from leaders from around the world. That reminded him of what his grandfather once said: you cannot put all the frogs in one basket, even to save them from their demise, because their nature is to jump in and out, especially when they have options to jump in and out at will.

As a last resort, he invited a few ex-presidents who were considered to be the most popular and respected leaders of each country from around the world, particularly President O, who has just finished his last term as the president of the United States of America. Maaculla had told Saad to look out for a leader who had a nondescript racial and religious profile. He would be neither black nor white nor brown. His birth had resulted from the union of two of the biggest religions in the world. He would have no enemies in any country. He would have experience in governing the biggest country in the world. He would be well respected in his own country and all the countries in the world. He would be secretly and openly admired and trusted by the majority of people who encouraged positive energy. Most of all, he would be available at the right moment. President O fit into almost 80 percent of the descriptions she gave. Incidentally, he would be mostly recognized by his father's race, especially in America. His mother's race would be irrelevant to them. The Americans were still highly prejudiced against women, more than even blacks. Unlike Europe, they hadn't elected a woman president yet for the same reason.

He also invited philosophers, writers, philanthropists, businessmen, Jewish leaders, black leaders, Chinese leaders, Indian leaders, Mexican leaders, and so on. They were also well known and respected in all countries.

Diplomacy was not going to work. It never did. Straightforward talk with honesty was necessary here because everyone knew that diplomatic talk always has a hidden agenda. This needed to be in the interest of everyone equally and not as an individual country or race or religion. He had explored every resource he could think of. He was hoping to prove Maaculla was wrong when she said, "If it hasn't happened yet, it will never happen. By then it may be too late to do anything about it. So it's now or never."

After his term finished in the White House, Mr. O wanted to keep himself busy doing some humanitarian work. So he readily accepted Saad's invitation to join the Project Symbiosis. He put together a team of ex-presidents with O, C, and Cl, who were powerful and greatly respected by all countries for their humanitarian work. He also wanted to use their philanthropy together with the strength of their foundations to make a jump start of the Project Symbiosis. At Saad's request, groups of three or four would go to different countries where they would be welcomed and respected. O, Cl, and C would go to North Korea. The other groups would go to China, South Africa, India, Europe, and so on. Their job was to persuade all these countries to join Project Symbiosis. They all welcomed the fact that for the first time, someone was talking about the globalization of the effort for peace and progress for the human race as a whole. We as the human race had tried making progress dividedly as separate religions, countries, and so on. The rhetoric of wars and conflict have been more common than peace talks in our world. The result was that we were back to square one. Instead we were on the verge of self-annihilation.

SAAD PRESENTS PROJECT SYMBIOSIS AS THE ANSWER

1. Saving on defense: Most countries spend 80 percent of their budget on defense when one in five children are starving, even in the United States. When we have peace around the world, we save resources from wars, conflicts, weapons, and the military, and we spend these resources on food, shelter, comfort, education, medicine, science, and advancement. Imagine that no country in the world has to worry about invasion, terrorism, or genocide. All countries will be united, which will bring peace. No country will threaten another with nuclear weapons or any weapons.

2. Saving on jailing: If you look around, you will notice that our jails are already overcrowded, even though we have more jails in the United States than schools. America is supposed to be the richest and most advanced country in the world. Even in this country, the system is about to go bust simply because the number of criminals is rising and the costs of maintaining jails are also increasing. Conversely, the system is failing because crime is not reduced or discouraged by it; rather, it's encouraged by it. In the United States alone, each inmate costs the taxpayers approximately $50,000 per year. It doesn't make any sense, because we spend that much money to take care of his livelihood in the jail. These resources can be and should be spent on elderly war veterans and poor people who need food, clothes, medicine, education, and shelter. There are elderly people dying even in America because they don't have money to buy heating oil in the winter. This distribution of resources could be distributed more fairly. Criminals are the ones causing harm, and they're being looked after by our tax money. They should be made to pay for all the damages and their own upkeep.

Project Symbiosis is the right project for this purpose. The benefits of Project Symbiosis are endless. By making the inmates work for their upkeep, all countries will save money on security, jailing, court, police, and so on, thereby stopping the recycling of criminals. This way, the criminals have to bear the cost for all these. Imagine a crimeless society.

3. More land to live on: About 29 to 30 percent of the earth

consists of land—that is, approximately 196,935,000 square miles, or 149,000,000 square km. Out of that, we use 3,096,621 square km. of irrigated land. The amount of rainfall determines the value of cultivable land. If there is five inches or less rainfall, an area is considered desert land, meaning it has no cultivation value. About 60 percent of Africa and 70 percent of Australia are desert land. That means about 35 percent of the whole earth's land is desert now.

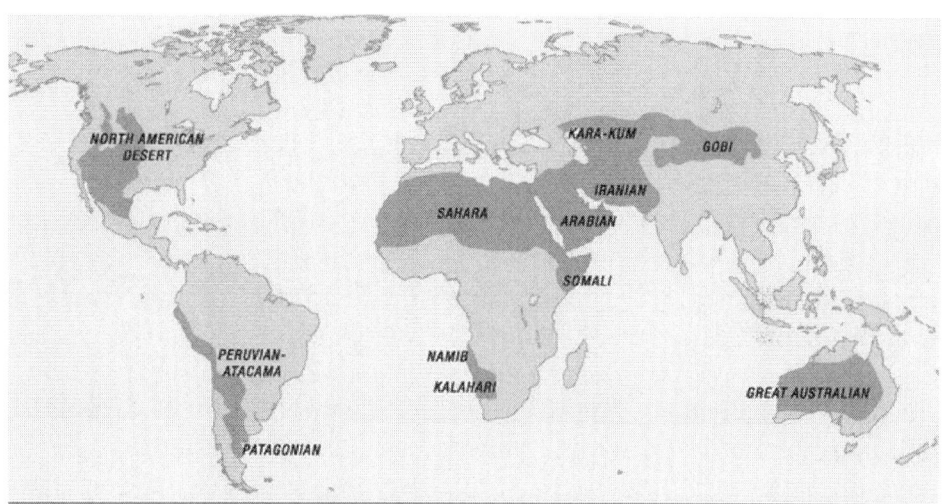

Image 11: Aproximately 35 percent of earth is desert land.

What does it mean? At the beginning, none of the lands were livable, cultivable lands. Humans had to make the land suitable for their needs. Now we are facing bigger challenges, more global challenges. If humans around the world combine their resources, knowledge, experience, and ingenuity, they can meet any challenges. At this moment, Project Symbiosis is the only answer to all human needs. Irrigation with Project Symbiosis will convert the deserts into cultivable land. By joining PS, we will have extra resources and manpower to build on the new habitable lands we will gain from this project. This will create new frontiers for people to live on, now and in the future. We will have more land to accommodate the influx of populations and refugees, grow our food, and build industries, cities, and dwellings. At the same time, we will solve the problem of rising water through the inevitable melting of the polar ice. We will transport the excess water from the seas to deserts through large conduits, canals, and rivers.

4. More energy: Instead of abandoning the deserts, we will use resources from the deserts. We will have an unlimited supply of solar energy from the deserts, thereby creating less pollution. Soon we will develop technology to export this energy to the needed areas.

5. More resources: We will have more resources to spend on research technology, science, medicine, space, and so on. The standard of living for all humans will rise when we don't have wars, jails, and security. No one will starve or be denied medical treatment or homes. With PS more people will be needed, thereby creating a shortage of people rather than overpopulation. We will have no need for birth control. We would rather encourage births.

6. More freshwater: Through the PS system, we will take water to the deserts from the rising of the seas. When this water evaporates from the desert areas, clouds will form, and rain will come down with freshwater to restore the balance of the water. Some water will evaporate and stay in clouds, so we will enjoy more habitable land.

7. A peaceful world: Imagine a world without any crime, hunger, war, lack of anything. Every human need is taken care of. United, we will spend all our energy and resources for a better life. We will then have enough resources for positive use and employ our workforce in positive industries such as food, beauty, health, education, art, space, transportation, hospitality, technology, and so on.

8. More resources to combat natural disasters: When a natural disaster threatens our world, together we can defend against it. For example, we will have enough firefighters and technology to combat natural forest fires and more resources and technology to combat natural disasters such as tsunamis, floods, earthquakes, and so on. At the same time, Maaculla promises that when all people of the world become positive and our mass awareness of positivity increases, it will affect our environment positively and the natural disasters will be dwindled to a trickle.

9. More resources to combat disease:
When diseases such as plague, Ebola, SARS, smallpox, cholera, malaria, TB, and cancer threaten our lives, together we will have more resources to find a cure for it in all parts of the world. We will have enough funds and resources to combat, research, and contain them.

When positivity becomes more prevalent in our minds, many diseases may disappear on their own, just like bat-shaped maculae. Most diseases are caused by our own fears and stress—in other words, by our minds.

10. A bright world: Imagine a world without crime, never having to worry about the security of your home or getting robbed, murdered, cheated, mugged, or hijacked—a world without crimes, war or boundaries. You're free to roam on every continent with no fear of terrorism or political or religious reprisals.

It may sound too farfetched at first glance. A world without poverty, disease, lack, bullying, or bigotry can be blissful in every way. The universe has given us enough resources for everyone. Look around and think about it. We have used our intelligence to make great progress in every direction. Just to wish for a peaceful world has become against our nature. As Maaculla said, "We have to fight this inner war with ourselves holding each other's hands to end all wars and crime forever."

11. The future: And lastly, when we put our resources and ingenuity together, we may be able live on other planets. In that case, we will need more population rather than less. We'll also need more water to transport there rather than have excess water here, and we will receive from the melting of the ice.

Instead of thinking in old-fashioned ways of getting rich and successful individually, we will grow rich and successful all together as a whole human race.

Also old fashioned ways of acquiring energy from coal mining by inflicting inhuman dangerous work for miners and by destroying earth's core. It was necessary once but we have better choices now. These workers can be trained for healthy and humane careers. Some politicians don't care about the health of these miners or their lives or the earth's core. We don't have to know who has good intentions and who hasn't. The maculae will brand negative ones automatically.

Right now human ingenuity is either deterred or redirected to wrong and negative causes. We saw examples of all that in *Maaculla* Part One. Most importantly, when fear is eliminated from the human spirit, there is no limit to what humans can achieve. Right now fear is implemented by governments, corporations, and religions to control people. By controlling humans, they're creating limitations. Instead, set the human soul free and see what people can do. Only the sky is the limit, literally. Human intelligence is destined to reach beyond the stars.

These are only a few of the major and obvious benefits. After years of conflicts and wars throughout human history, we should have learnt by now that we are heading in the wrong direction. We will never have peace on earth, and we will never be united if we continue on the present course.

Now imagine that something like the bat-shaped maculae is really possible in our world. We wouldn't have to worry about any of this. No one would dare to think of any negative intention. We would be protected from all negativities automatically.

This brings us to the point: are humans going to cooperate?

Chapter 35

A VISIT TO NORTH KOREA

At Saad's request, the three ex-presidents, O, C, and Cl, go to North Korea.

North Korea's leader, Kim Jong-un, was very upset with America. He angrily presented a copy of the movie called '*The Interview*', in Korean.

"How could you allow this?" he asked. "This is an insult to the Korean people."

They all exchanged looks. They didn't expect that.

O said, "We're here to talk about world peace. This is only a movie for the entertainment. We think of it as a humor."

"This is no humor," Kim Jong-un said. "This is a threat to us Koreans."

C said, "We all need to forget about what happened in the past in order to believe in a common goal. In America, we believe in freedom of expression. They can do as they feel. But a cheap movie maker does not represent our country."

"Maybe you can learn from Korea," Kim Jong-un said. "We have control of 100 percent of the people here."

Cl saw that the conversation was going the wrong way. "Supreme leader, with all due respect, we are here to discuss a very important subject, Project Symbiosis. The whole world is afraid. The human race is in danger of becoming extinct, and that includes the Koreans also. We must all cooperate to survive."

Kim laughed. "They should be afraid. You give them too much freedom, and they destroy themselves. We know how to keep them under control."

O looked at his watch. "Supreme leader, I think you are right. And I think we should sit down another time and talk in more detail when you have learnt more about Project Symbiosis. We have to catch our plane to go back. We have to visit many other countries for the same project. Thank you for seeing us. It was enlightening. Thank you for the delicious dinner.

"We're leaving the papers for you to look at. It's called Project Symbiosis, PS for short. Please get in touch with Saad when you're ready. He's not a politician. At his request, we all joined this project. Instead of sending it with a messenger, we wanted to personally bring it to you, because we believe in it. This is not a political agenda by any means. Thank you."

They all got up, shook hands, and left quickly before the conversation could go any further. Their limousine was waiting for them outside the presidential palace.

C said, "I hope he doesn't take it the wrong way, O. They're a very proud people. I'm not surprised that they are upset over a movie."

Cl said, "This is the last thing you do—laugh at them. They think you're bullying them because you're a more powerful country."

O said, "I know. I dealt with them on a few occasions too. They always feel intimidated. It doesn't take a lot to upset them. I trained myself and my staff not to smile in their presence. Always keep a solemn face. Otherwise they think you're laughing at them. That movie didn't help our relationship. But I can't sit there and admit that this movie represents our country, our government."

C said, "I think you did the right thing, avoiding an altercation."

"I agree, O," Cl said. "It's best to avoid confrontation, and that's what he wanted. To start an argument."

"Well," O said, "let's see what other countries have to say."

EXPERIENCES WITH OTHER COUNTRIES

They had a similar experience in China. They were accused of falsely blaming China for counterfeit bills and Internet hacking. Saad had warned them that some countries might have defensive attitudes when they approached them. But China finally understood the value of working together for a single goal, peace.

Bangladesh said, "We're a poor nation. How can we take part in a massive project like this?" They were willing to receive any help they could.

At least didn't find an excuse not to join.

India, on the other hand, welcomed the project and agreed to help out as much as they could. They would do anything they could to bring peace to the world.

Pakistan didn't like the idea. They thought they would lose control of the people (as if they had any control now). They didn't see the benefits of helping countries such as Bangladesh or Africa. They wanted to know, what was in it for them? If their Arab allies agreed, then they might reconsider. They were also very suspicious of the West. Maybe the west had conjured up some kind of trick to gain control of them.

Most of the Arab countries simply didn't trust the West, meaning Europe, the United Kingdom, and the United States. But the Arab nations might be interested in helping if other countries were to turn to Islam and follow Islamic rules. This was exactly the opposite of Project Symbiosis. You didn't force people to make a personal choice.

The Israeli government didn't want to join, period. They thought they would have to become friends with Arabs. It was like trying to mix water and oil. It would never be stable. They laughed at the idea of turning into an Islamic state. "We strive to go forward and not the other way around. We're doing fine without their help." But many Israeli people expressed that they could live in peace with Palestinian brothers and sisters.

African countries were also very suspicious. They thought it was some kind of secret invasion plan. They felt they would lose control of their deserts. Once the white people took control of their deserts, they would invade Africa again. They had bitter memories of European control in South Africa and French, Spanish, Portuguese, and British control over parts of Africa. Then there was the Arab oppression in parts of Africa that is still going on.

Japan was very eager to know about the project. They were willing to participate any way they could. Anything to save their already limited lands.

ALL IS NOT LOST

They had most interesting meetings with several countries, especially North Korea. They were on the way back now, on their private jet having a relaxing drink. They called Saad on a conference call to let him know the outcome of their meetings so far.

"Good morning, Saad," O said. "We thought we'd call you to let you know we are on the way back."

"Brace yourself, Saad," C said. "Most of countries declined our requests to join."

"You know what, Saad?" C said. "Most people wait until the last minute, until they're desperate. They don't believe in prevention."

O said, "We're running around to save everyone from disaster."

"I would like to thank you all for your incredible adventure," Saad said. "I can assure you your effort is not a complete loss. We have at least some countries willing to participate in PS. That's all we'll need for now."

O said, "But you said we needed 100 percent of the people's cooperation."

"Exactly," Saad said. "We will follow Maaculla's method now. We will start with the ones we have and keep announcing the progress and the benefits on the world news. The rest of the countries who refused will want to join, one by one. They're waiting to see how we get on. They won't want to miss out. Humans like emulating others. Then we can negotiate our terms with them."

O said, "You should have been a diplomat. I could have used you."

C said, "Yes, yes. We could use a man like you."

"Sorry," Saad said. "This is not my idea, I'm afraid. Maaculla is guiding me. See you in Washington soon."

Chapter 36

ATTACK ON THE THREE EX-PRESIDENTS

Coming back from visiting North Korea, the private jet carrying the three ex-presidents had just landed at the Washington airport. They were hoping to meet with the present-day president the next day to discuss their experiences and to invite the US government to join Project Symbiosis.

They entered the airport building. They went through the security scan like everybody else. They wouldn't have it any other way. All three ex-presidents were walking together and waving to the people and the cameras. They came out of the airport terminal and were walking to a waiting car. Three men rushed towards them and stabbed themselves to death with their own blades about fifteen feet away from them. It looked as if they wanted them to witness their hara-kiri. The FBI and airport security rushed to the scene and shrouded the ex-presidents with their own bodies. All these events were caught by news cameras. A minute later, they were rushed to the waiting limousine. They were taken to a safe house, where Saad was waiting for them.

All three of them were wondering what had just happened.

"Don't worry; I was expecting that," Saad said.

"What do you mean, Saad?" C said. "Those men just killed themselves!"

"Yeah," Cl said. "What's that in aid of?"

"These are our American people committing suicide!" O said. "What for?"

C asked, "How do you know they are our American people?"

"I know these guys," O said. "They're ex-FBI agents. They got fired because the last time when I was in Korea, they were found partying with cheap girls while they were on duty."

Cl smiled. "Girls! That's no reason to commit suicide. They're lucky they weren't put in jail."

"I can assure you," Saad said, "they did not commit suicide there."

O said, "We just saw them stabbing themselves in front of our eyes. You weren't there, Saad."

235

"Yes, yes," Saad said, "but they thought they were stabbing you guys. I'm sorry to say that." He looked at their faces. "You see, they were hired by the North Koreans. They didn't want to do it in Pyongyang. They wanted to make it look like some disgruntled Americans killing ex-presidents."

O was disbelieving. "But it sure didn't look like that."

"Let me explain this part," Saad said. "It may sound like science fiction or ridiculous to you. If you remember, I spoke to you about deemagh. When your body is loaded with deemagh, in the presence of negative energy, it projects an image of you about fifteen to twenty feet away from you. It creates an illusion for the assailant that you are not here; you are over there. Only the assailant with negative energy can see that image. His own negativity blinds him. He's thinking that it's the real target, and he attacks the image instead. But, of course, there's nothing but empty space there. So when he stabs with all his force, it actually comes round to his own body. Maaculla explained that to me. It's like stabbing in the water. There's no solid object to resist the velocity of the hand with the weapon; hence one will stab oneself. She uses their own negative energy against themselves. Gentlemen, you are protected."

O said, sarcastically, "Saad, since you put it that way..." He smiled and looked at the others.

C said, "Yes. They were about fifteen feet away from us."

"How do you think I felt when Maaculla started to tell me all these in 1968?" Saad said. "I never thought any of this was for real either. Now I can see all this is happening for sure, and so can you. I'm excited and fearful at the same time. Gentlemen, I must leave right now. I have to go home and meditate. I think Maaculla is already here. I've been waiting for this moment for almost fifty years. I have to be sure. Good-bye. Sorry; I have to go."

Saad rushed to the door.

The ex-presidents exchanged disbelieving looks.

Saad said, from the door, "I'll explain later, when I know more. Have a good rest. You'll need it. Bye."

"There's more?" Cl asked.

Again they exchanged looks at one another.

That brings us to the point when everyone experiences Maaculla's presence!

SAAD IS MEDITATING (to ask for help from Maaculla)

Saad was at home in Los Angeles. After hearing about what Kim Jung-Un said and the attack on the three ex-presidents, he lost all hope that every country would join PS. He felt responsible. He didn't want to stir up more negativity around the world. We had had enough of it as it was. He sat down to meditate that night, wishing he had kept in touch with Mrs. Griffiths, a.k.a. Maaculla. Who knew that someday his conversations with Mrs. Griffiths would actually come true? She had passed away, or left her body, by now. After all, she was eighty-four years old in 1968, when Saad first met her. Each Maaculla supposedly lived for one hundred years in human life. Father Brown informed him that in 1983 she had departed. He hoped she could hear him somehow with her superpowers. After that incident at the airport, he was almost sure Maaculla was there in spirit. Otherwise, how could one explain what had happened there? It was good that he could remember what Maaculla had told him about deemagh.

Saad meditated: "Mrs. Griffiths—I mean Maaculla—directly or indirectly, you gave me an impossible responsibility. I have failed to persuade all the people to unite. It is for their own benefit and for the safety and future of the human race. But most people don't seem to take it seriously. Don't they realize how important it is? We are running out of time. Frankly, I feel grossly disappointed with my fellow humans. You are right; I am wrong. Everyone agrees and understands and shakes their heads when I explain Project Symbiosis to them. They all agree that it makes sense, but I have no satisfactory commitments so far. I don't see any hope in the near future. I have probably another twenty-five years before I complete hundred years in this life, when I will leave this world. I hope you can hear me. You warned me this might happen. But I thought I would try anyway. I cannot think like most people. I felt that I wanted to at least try to explain the graveness of this situation. We are human; we don't give up that easily. That's why we are still here, much longer than our predecessors, dinosaurs. I had better respect for human intelligence before all this. The universe gave us free will. We are using this free will to destroy ourselves. If you do hear me, please give me a sign. I'm sorry I didn't get in touch with you in the last fifty years. I didn't take these things seriously. Now I can see things are happening as you said. I am lost as to what to do next. I feel responsible. I await your guidance. I feel that before I die, I need to know that the human race will continue living here on earth and prosper. All humans, not just a single group, race, or country. All people living together in peace and harmony. All my life I felt that you were always with me and guiding me through my lonely journey. I've never felt for a moment that I was alone. Please respond so that I know that I didn't waste a half century of thinking and analyzing your words, preparing and anticipating for this day. Please show me a sign."

He finished his meditation exactly in one hour, every morning from 4:00 until 5:00 a.m.

Karen knocked at the door. "Honey, are you done? You have to see this. There's a news flash. I think Maaculla is here."

"What?" Saad said. "What are you talking about? She can't just appear. After all, she's dead, at least physically."

They both rushed to the living room.

"What's that smell?" Saad asked. "I recognize that smell. I smelt it fifty years ago."

"Honey, that's the smell of the Tudor roses that you brought from England. We have unusual blossoms outside. You can't see the leaves through the roses."

"Wait a minute. I remember her first name. Her first name is Rose. I saw this same phenomenon in Portsmouth."

Karen just looked at him.

Saad continued. "Mrs. Griffiths—I mean Maaculla. Her first name is Rose. She told me only once, in 1968, her first name. I always called her Mrs. Griffiths. She always had this rose fragrance on her and in her house."

They arrived in the living room.

Karen said, "Honey, this is a BBC news flash."

On TV, a reporter was saying, "There is a new phenomenon on the horizon. It's a skin disorder called maculae—discolored spots on the skin. Maculae is the scientific name for this condition. But this particular one is unusual, these spots resemble the shape of bats. Doctors and scientists are puzzled. They don't know what to call it now. Bat-maculae? Baculae? Actually, it's quite a serious matter, because it's spreading all over the world by leaps and bounds. It first appeared in North Korea after the three US ex-presidents left Pyongyang.

"Their supreme leader, Kim Jong-un, is infected by it. They're blaming the Americans for some kind of biological weapon attack on the supreme leader. The entire Korean army, air force, and navy have also come down with these bat-shaped maculae. They're ready to attack."

Saad said, speaking to himself, "But who are they going to attack? It's only speculation that the United States is responsible for it. How is anyone going to explain that their own negative energy is destroying them? How am I going to explain to them? Who will believe me? Only Maaculla can set an example to convince them. But how? Maaculla never prepared me for this. I hope she will guide me through this now. I also have to convince the rest of the world. It's not just confined to Korea. It's happening all over the world."

Karen just looked at him and listened. She had heard him talk like this to himself all the time for the last fifty years. She thought he was thinking aloud.

This brings us to the point: are maculae a real threat?

WHAT'S HAPPENING TO THE PEOPLE?

People are coming down with this new disease called maculae. The phenomenon has become prevalent all over the world. This is new because it appears on the skin in the shape of bats. The normal maculae are a kind of discoloured spots on the skin. It is relatively harmless. But the bat-shaped maculae are exactly the opposite to that. When it stays on the body long enough, it gets deeper, and the flesh starts to rot away. Eventually the rotten flesh falls off, exposing the bone. Then it gets very painful and ends up killing the host, similar to the Great Plague of 1738. Which killed fifty thousand people.

Unlike the plague, though, it is not infectious or contagious, and it's not confined to one area or two. It's widespread, covering the whole world. These maculae are not bacteria related. Hence it is not curable by any medical treatments such as antibacterial drugs or antiviruses.

239

On the other hand, it can be contagious in the mind in the sense that if some other mind makes a suggestion of negative thinking or fear, it can pass on to weaker-minded people. In that sense it can be contagious from one mind to another. For the same reason, it can be cured only by the host, by becoming a positive-minded person. The host's intentions must be good. The host must be free of any kind of negative energies.

Saad and the other members of Project Symbiosis had to convince the rest of the world that these bat-shaped maculae were a real threat and that this was their own negative energy attacking them. That was why doctors and scientists could not help these victims of self-negativity. Only they could cure themselves by choosing positivity, by giving up the path of a criminal life, by choosing a life of honest living, by being nonprejudiced, and by accepting everyone regardless of their differences, living with love and respect.

But how would anyone explain something so outrageous as bat-shaped maculae? Nobody had ever heard of anything like this before. The fact that it was there and that it was bat-shaped and resembled tattoos—that was out of the ordinary, to say the least. It was not a biological weapon attacking them. It was coming from within themselves. It was their own negative energy manifesting into a self-destructive condition.

According to the painting *Definition of Humankind*, the balance of negative energy had tilted towards negative. The balance of negative energy had risen to 75 percent instead remaining at the normal balance of 50/50. This imbalance had taken place so slowly and gradually that it had taken several thousand generations to come to this point. That is why one life-span is not long enough to notice these changes. As a result, there was a mass awareness of negativities all over the world.

At the same time, it was being very selective. Certain people were not affected by it at all. Even in the same family, some people were affected and some not. That was why it was very puzzling to everyone—because in the same family, not everyone's energy levels are the same. Some can be more positive and others more negative.

Since it was not contagious, other members of the family might be completely safe. Animals and children under twelve were not affected by it at all, although animals avoided being close to people who were affected, simply because the animals could recognize negative-minded people who had hostile or negative intentions. Scientists and medical doctors came to the conclusion that there was no bacteria or virus causing this epidemic. It just randomly affected certain people, so it seemed. It was similar to genetic predispositions—in this case, the disposition of the mind. The CDC was trying to quarantine the affected individuals, although it was not a contagious disease. So what was the purpose of quarantine? People were jamming the hospitals anyway, even though the medical staff were helpless. Some of the medical staff were also falling victim to the maculae. People were afraid. They didn't know what to do or whom to turn to or what to think of it. Essentially, this type of maculae was a real threat indeed. The common denominator of the people who were affected was the negativity in their minds.

Seventy-five percent of the people in the world had been affected by this condition so far. It didn't seem to react to any medicine or treatment known to us. On the other hand, people who did meditation or who were just starting to do meditation were getting some benefits, or at least slowing the advance of maculae.

PEOPLE ALL OVER ARE CONFUSED

The North Koreans were threatening to use their nuclear weapons if this biological war was not stopped immediately. But who were they going to attack? No one knew who was doing this. They strongly suspected it was the Americans and the British. The ironic thing was that the more they threatened to attack, the more they were being negative, thus intensifying the maculae condition. The puzzling thing was that even the Americans and the British were not spared from this fate.

The same percentages of people in the United States, Europe, and Britain were being affected by this condition. It was not sparing any particular region or race, developed or undeveloped countries. By now it had become a total, universal condition. It was actually threatening the entire human race. Experts and doctors were trying to understand the cause of it. They were doing their usual sophisticated tests, x-rays, MRIs, blood tests, and so on. But so far, they had no clue.

The Russian people were angry with their government. They thought this was an effect of the radiation from Chernobyl. Again, the more they complained about it, the more severe it became.

The same thing was going on in Japan. They were blaming the government for not containing the Fukushima site. But when the people got angry, it seemed to intensify.

The worst-affected countries were North Korea, the Middle East, Afghanistan, Syria, Pakistan, Israel, Iran, Palestine, and the parts of Africa where religious and political bigotry and terrorism were more prevalent. Fear, doubt, suspicion, and distrust had infected everyone's minds there. They thought they were being attacked by the West with some kind of biological weapon. But the reports showed that more or less the same things were happening to the West too.

In reality, no one knew where it was coming from. They were just blaming one another. But it spread to every country, big or small. It was attacking every human indiscriminately. By now it had created such havoc that if they had to quarantine people, they would have to quarantine the whole earth. There was no safe place left. Nobody had gotten cured from this maculae outbreak so far. Perhaps this situation would persuade the people of the world to cooperate and unite and fight this debilitating condition together.

IS THERE A CURE FOR MACULAE?

Just to reiterate, Maaculla and maculae could be confusing to everyone. Maculae was the skin disorder everyone knew about. But Maaculla was the nickname given to Mrs. Griffiths by Saad when he met her, and it meant "mother of the world" in his colloquial language of Sylheti. The reason he called her Maaculla was because she was exactly the opposite of Dracula. Dracula was a being with negative energy, and Maaculla was a being with positive, angelic energy. The nature of these two energies were that one was destructive and the other constructive.

We normal humans are also made of these two energies, although the percentage is different, at 50/50. Hence the devils and angels are within us. At the same time, we also have the choice of being more devilish (negative) or angelic (positive). That is to say that we can also increase either of these two energies at will by making that choice. We can choose a dishonest or criminal life or vice versa. Therefore we can assume that the enemy can be and is within us. When the whole world got zapped by maculae, it was our own individual negativity that caused this condition to appear. It became so widespread because the mass awareness of the whole world had become negative. Consciously or unconsciously we made this choice to tilt the balance of our energies to negative. Now, only we ourselves could change that balance back to 50/50. No one else could do that for us. Having said that, we can also say that no one could vindictively change our energy to negative to spite us or harm us. Hence, blaming one another was neither healing us nor killing us. It was up to us individually to change the balance of our energies back to normal, or else.

The only way it could be cured was by individually choosing positivity. Also, only one person out of seven billion people in the world knew what was going on. He was the only one who had the formula for the cure. It was given to him by Maaculla before she passed away. He was the only one who had the responsibility to educate everyone as to how to cure themselves and how to protect themselves from maculae. This person was Saad. Maaculla had prepared him for this day when the outbreak of maculae will be prevalent. But he had to accept this responsibility, unwillingly, in 1968. At that time he wasn't even sure if it would ever come to a reality. He was just listening to her as if she were telling him a story. He knew that he could get deeply involved if it ever came to fruition. At that time it was OK to listen to her. But now it is time to take action.

Nobody expected maculae. No one even expected this epidemic to threaten the whole world, the entire human race. Nobody could actually make any such connection or imagine that maculae would compel them to cooperate and join the PS. It would be the first project in the history of humanity that was truly global. It would need the total cooperation of the whole world; otherwise, we would face the annihilation of the human race.

Saad remembered Maaculla's words—that an epidemic would threaten the whole human civilization.

This would come from an individual's mind.

This would be the ultimate war of wars.

This would be a war for peace.

This would be a war without any weapons.

This would be a war without a visible enemy.

This would be a war fought by every single person in the world, not just soldiers.

This would be the war to end all future wars.

This would be the war to love one another.

This would be a war that would benefit us all.

This would be the war that could not be avoided by anyone.

This would be the war that would ensure the survival of humanity.

This would be the war that would be fought by holding one another's hands instead of guns.

This would be the war to build our future.

This would be the war to embrace one another instead of killing.

This would be the war without bloodshed.

This would be the war of positive intentions.

This would be named the War of Maculae.

This would be the last war in human history.

The maculae's cure must come from within one's mind. The cure itself sounded very simple, but to execute it or apply it to oneself was another story. One had to fight one's own nature. No doctor, psychologist, hypnotist, guru, or hospital could treat it. The cure was within one's mind. One had to fight a war within to change one's mind to love. One had to change one's energy level to positive. The only way it could be done was by becoming a positive person, an empathetic and loving person. And the only way one could become a positive person was by not allowing any negative thoughts inside one's mind. Only the stronger minds would be able succeed by overcoming their own nature.

Maaculla said, "Human—material—experiences can be achieved at their peak only with the energy level of fifty-fifty. In other words, you are neither negative nor positive. That is to say that you have fallen into the gap. When you are in the gap, you are indifferent. You are neither frustrated nor happy with life. That is the state of 'being.' When you are in the 'state of being,' you are connected to the field of all possibilities. For example, that's why a wise teacher would say, if you want money, don't feel deprived of it or falsely pretend that you are a rich person. Because in the field of all possibilities, there is no such thing as deprived person—or a rich person, for that matter. That's how you match the vibration of the field of all possibilities—only when you are indifferent and you are in the gap of negative and positive vibrations. Our emotions use the negative and positive vibrations for good and bad feelings. The whole universe is created with two sides. Left and right, back and front, up and down, light and dark, and so on. Physically you have two sides too. For instance, imagine your left hand being the receiving hand and right hand being the giving or spending hand.

"The universe is very clever, don't you think?" Said Maaculla.

Saad just looked at her blankly.

Maaculla said, "The universe has made our life very simple in that sense. It is a simple matter of choice, what you want to become. Not by your words, but by your deeds. We have been choosing negativity in every aspect of our lives for a long time. If we look around, we can witness the insurmountable amount of negativity going on all around the world. Every day, we see all the negative news of rape, murder, accidents, fire, disasters, deceit, fear. We have come to a point where a little bit more negative thought can topple the balance. It materializes in one's body as maculae. That's the beginning of destruction. And as it continues to increase with the negative energy, it destroys the body completely, simply because the nature of the negative energy is to destroy. So it is our own energy that is killing us. On the other hand, only our own energy can save us."

YOU MAY NOT HAVE CHOSEN TO BE NEGATIVE

Maaculla said, "After generations of negativities in our lives, we now inherit our tendency towards negativity. Thus it has become automatic for us to be negative, and we don't even realize that we are negative. We think this comes automatically, so it is natural and normal. We are not responsible for the consequences. But the universe doesn't work like this. It works like mathematics. If the balance of energy varies, it will behave that way. Two plus two is always going to be four. There is no exception. Mathematics doesn't work on exceptions. Once the energy level inclines in one direction, it will go in that direction.

"Humans, on the other hand, work on logic and emotions. We can put up with the ups and downs of life, and it's OK with us. But imagine this: if Earth diverges just one millimeter from its orbit, it may disappear into the unlimited space of the universe, leaving our solar system, and it may take a trillion years for it to come back this way. In that case, without the sun, everything on Earth would be frozen. Or it may get vaporized by another sun a trillion times larger than ours on the way.

"The universe will not function with human logic or emotions. The human life-span is so short lived compared to these heavenly, infinitely big events that it is too insignificant to impact the universe. It definitely matters to us, because emotionally, we feel we want the human race to live as long as it can. When mass awareness becomes negative, it definitely affects our bodies and our own environment, hence our experiences.

"That brings us to the point how we can get rid of maculae."

RETURN OF THE SEVEN MAACULLAS

Maaculla had already told Saad how to cure this condition, in 1968. At that time he thought Mrs. Griffiths was just telling him a story. Now he realized that this was as true as human existence. This was the only way to save the whole world. But Maaculla herself couldn't be consulted anymore. She had passed away almost fifty years ago. He hoped and prayed that he could receive some sign from her spirit. No human would ever be able to perceive Maaculla now, because she was 100 percent positive energy. That meant she was an angel. That included Saad himself, even though he had met her once when she was a human as Mrs. Griffiths.

When all seven Maaculla spirits arrived on earth, humans around the world could see the signs of their arrival. Each country saw its roses blossoming in very unusual ways and numbers. No one had ever seen roses growing in this abundance before for no apparent reason. For instance, England's national flower was the Tudor rose. So the Tudor roses grew boundlessly in England now. It was difficult to see the green leaves through the red roses. And the smell overwhelmed the air in the United Kingdom—likewise in China, India, Russia, Africa, Australia, and so on. So the whole world was covered with roses.

Incidentally, the maculae, on the other hand, was not a sign from Maaculla. It was the people's own imbalance of negative energy that was causing it. Maaculla had told Saad that something like this would happen when negative energy became dominant.

The world was on the verge of extinction. The choice was either a nuclear war or get zapped by the condition called maculae. The cause of both was our own negative energy. Although we couldn't see her or hear her, Maaculla was here to help save the human race from extinction and at the same time stabilize the environment. All seven Maaculla spirits were here on earth, but we couldn't perceive them with our physical senses. The only way we could get the benefit of their arrival was by allowing them into our lives. And the only way that could be done was by believing in them. This act alone was the beginning of the positive energy. They arrived on all seven continents. We could feel their presence through the fragrance of the roses on each continent.

Saad was the only person who knew what to do next. He had to describe to the people of the world the cure for the maculae. The cure for human extinction. The cure for our habitable environment. That was a responsibility even a seasoned politician would decline. But Saad had no choice. He had been chosen and prepared for the last fifty years for this moment, willingly or not. How was he going to do it? Why would the people believe him? Who was he, anyway? It seemed we didn't have the luxury of asking these questions anymore, when no one knew what was going on or how to cure them. Even the most learned and educated scientists and scholars had no idea what was going on! Any news of a cure should be welcomed by everyone. Had Maaculla planned it this way?

Something must be done, or we would face extinction!

THE CURE

Just as Maaculla had predicted, unbeknownst to all of us, what had happened to our world was that the balance of our energy level had shifted to the negative. In our mass awareness, we thought of negativity most of the time. Even if we didn't participate in negative acts such as terrorism, crime, prejudice, and lies, deep inside our minds, we expected them to happen. That made us just as negative as those who were doing it. One Indian philosopher described it this way: "Those who do injustice and those who tolerate them are the same."

Our energy was in the normal ratio of 50/50 negative and positive. Most people are born that way. But now, the mass awareness had shifted too far to the negative. So now, our energy balance was hanging at the edge of destruction. Just one more negative thought could trigger the maculae (or destruction) in our body. Eventually it would destroy the host. That is the nature of the negative energy. You cannot convert negative energy into positive. You just allow more positive into your life to survive and prevent destruction. No one else and nothing else is to blame. Our own choice of energy is bringing this predicament into our lives. Also, no one else could cure it and prevent it from coming back. It was the individual's choice.

The actual cure was very simple:

The Maacullas have provided us one rose for each person in the whole world. That is why we can see the sudden abundance of roses growing all over the world.

Hold one rose in your cupped hands.

Then smell its fragrance with a deep breath.

Then say in your mind, "I am transcending from my limited world of emotions, ego, and logic to the source of unlimitedness, in the gap."

Then say, out loud or in your mind, "See no evil." You make a choice to see no evil, whether it is yours or others'.

"Hear no evil." You make a choice not to hear any evil, whether it is yours or others'.

"Speak no evil." You make a choice not to speak of any evil, whether it is yours or others'.

From now on, you live by these simple laws (or choices). Not by just loud words, but by your deeds. Every time you see, hear, or speak of evil, you feel it in the deep inside your mind. Change that feeling into "good feeling." Never use "I." Just feel good. That's it.

From now on, live by these three simple choices—not just by words, but by our own deeds.

Maaculla had reiterated to Saad many times during her conversations with him: "In the past we could get away with these choices, a little more of negative or vice versa. Through the generations, the mass awareness of the whole world has tilted so far to the negative that we cannot indulge ourselves with just one more negative thought anymore. It's like one single straw that will break the camel's back. In other words, no more participation in or thoughts of or gossip about supporting wars, terrorism, genocide, apartheid, prejudice, discrimination, bigotry, crime, deception, racism, hate, competition, jealousy—wasting energy and resources on the negativities. No more expecting or wanting to see, talk about, watch, or listen to sensational news. It only applies to the negative thinkers and doers. The good or positive-thinking people have nothing to worry about. That's how the universe has separated the negative bad people and the positive good people. A world without negative thoughts. A world united, with one race, one people. Working together for a better world. And to begin this new journey, every country in the world will participate in Project Symbiosis. Who knew it would be that simple to unite the whole world!"

But how can just one ordinary man, a layman, educate seven billion people and save them from annihilation?

SAAD REMEMBERS

Maaculla told him, "The cure for maculae is very simple. It's like the cure for any other disease that threatens lives today, such as cancer, diabetes, arthritis, and many other new diseases that are popping up. Doctors and scientists are baffled. They can't find a definite cause or cure for them. They're just speculating and treating the symptoms. It's same concept and logic that they apply to crime: you can't eliminate it, but it employs people. It's good for business, so it's OK. For example, after spending years and years and trillions of dollars on research, they don't even know which part of the body cancer is prone to hit or a definite cause of it. It's not like containing a smallpox or cholera outbreak. Cancer can appear in any part of your body, from your head to your toes. It doesn't need any excuse, such as smoking, because the root of all these new diseases is the energy fluctuation. Until they deal with the root of the problem, they may fix only one symptom after years of effort and the loss of millions of lives, and then another will pop up. It's like the surface of a balloon is weakened. When they fix one leak, another will pop up with the pressure of the air inside. Needless to say, one has to strengthen the surface instead of just going after the leaks."

It's about time that scientists recognize the power of the mind. Saad remembered Maaculla's words about placebos. Do you ever think about why placebos work at the same rate as the real drugs? You will notice that people with strong minds and beliefs make both placebos and real drugs work at the same rate. In other words, drugs have no value in the curing of a disease, just like placebos. That is why no one can explain how the same drug can heal one and kill another. It's the people's own beliefs that heal them. Humans are already self-contained for curing their own challenges.

It's a long story, but in short, your genes are equipped to dictate the body's condition. Your belief system sends a command to the part of the gene that is responsible for this action. This command or message originally must come from you (feeling "good"). You might have noticed that even brothers or sisters don't share the same fate in health, prosperity, relationships, happiness, and so on, if that matters, because individually they send different messages to the gene. Each of us is responsible for his or her own destiny. You are not just the experiencer of the reality; you are the creator of the reality. That's why some people can cure themselves of deadly diseases without any help from doctors or hospitals.

But the command alone is not enough to trigger a cure. Along with it, a lifestyle of exercise and ingesting live food into the body sends the necessary and correct command to our genes. For instance, eating just one fresh apple can send eight hundred positive messages to our genes. But eating processed apple chips will send zero messages.

Incidentally, Maaculla mentioned that our natural food doesn't come with labels. That means any food that is processed and has a label on it is a dead food. Unfortunately, today we are seeing more and more dead food on the supermarket shelves. Eating dead food is not going to send any message to your genes.

SAAD DOESN'T THINK HE IS THE RIGHT PERSON

When Mrs. Griffiths told Saad that he would have to teach all the people of the world how to change from their negativity, with a nervous and despondent smile he told Maaculla that he didn't think he was the right person for the job. He simply didn't have the efficacy for this humongous task. He had grown up with a most astonishingly divergent point of view.

Saad's father tried to prepare him for life as best as he could. He told him how life can be a struggle to make ends meet. For example, you may not have enough cloth to make your suit. It only covers one buttock. When you pull one side the other cheek gets exposed. Needless to say his father spent his own life the same way he always preached, believing there was no way to avoid this fate.

Once again Maaculla assured him that when the time came, he would get all the help he needed. Always look inside the problem to find the solution. He believed Maaculla then, thinking this was only a story, even though most assuredly she made an indelible impression on him. So why not? But now he realized that slowly and surely it was beginning to happen in reality exactly the way she had described it to him. There was no way he could avoid or abdicate the responsibility for this. So now he was thinking, where is the help she promised? It was time to get nervous, especially when he was witnessing what was going on all over the world. People were dropping like flies. It was on the verge of annihilating the only intelligent and thinking life form on earth.

His own daughter got sick with this proliferating disease called maculae. He was hoping and praying he could cure her before something dreadful happened to her. He was having difficulty concentrating, worrying about his own daughter. But where was Maaculla when he really needed her? He wished he had been more adamant about refusing to listen to her. But somehow he had been powerless. At the same time, he realized that he had to do something about it right now.

Chapter 37

FINALLY, GUIDANCE FROM MAACULLA

That night Saad sat down for meditation. But his mind was full of concerns and fears. He found it difficult to concentrate. He found himself talking to himself.

Maaculla, please give me guidance. In this chaotic world, how am I going to relay your message to the people of the world? I have no idea where to begin. I'm afraid to think how people are going to react to all this when they're fearing for their lives. After all, it's a question of life and death. They might even think I'm the terrorist who has caused all this.

You've brought me this far, and I know—I mean I hope—you can hear me. Unfortunately, my vibration is not high enough to perceive you. You gave me a sign of your presence with the roses around the world. Now I need your guidance more than ever. People are dropping like flies. Nobody deserves this fate. Please help, so that I can at least relay your cure to them and start saving lives. Please, Maaculla, I don't want to lose my own daughter.

Immediately after he finished his meditation, the phone rang. Their daughter, Saaren, was in the hospital quarantined. Saad had given her the instructions for the cure prior to sitting down for meditation. He was anxiously waiting to hear from her.

Saaren was excited. "Daaaad!"

"Yes, Boo?" Saad said, calling her by her nickname. "Are you all right? Did you apply the cure?"

Saaren was more excited. She could hardly contain herself. Her voice was trembling. "Dad, I'm cured!" She started crying.

Saad was controlling his own emotions. "Oh, that's good, Honey Boo. We're so happy. We're coming now. Don't cry; don't cry."

Saaren's voice was breaking. "Dad, I want to come home."

"Yes, yes, honey," Saad said. "We're going to bring you home. Don't cry. Don't cry, honey. Mummy and I are coming right away."

Saad realized that this was another sign from Maaculla. She had planned this incident, placing Saaren in the hospital, surrounded by thousands of people and media, and curing her there. That way, everyone would witness her getting healed by applying Maaculla's cure.

By the time they got there, all the media were waiting for them. Saaren was the first person to be cured of the deadly maculae. Word of the cure had gotten around the entire hospital and all the media. People were acting very aggressive. They wanted to know the cure. The proof is in the pudding. Now they would believe him. Saad had no idea that Maaculla had planned this all along so that he wouldn't have to do anything. The media would do all the announcing for him, all over the world. That's why we have media, and that's why we have the Internet and social media. Now the cure would become viral. Who could have known that Maaculla had planned it this way all along?

Saad looked up and said, "Thank you, Maaculla. Thank you, thank you. You are a genius." Tears were running down his face.

That brings us to the question, what was Saad going to do next?

Chapter 38

Saad was at the hospital where his daughter, Saaren, was quarantined. She had just gotten cured of maculae spots, with the help of Maaculla's simple but powerful instructions. Her flesh had filled in. The other quarantined patients had noticed that she was cured and walking out of the hospital with her Dad. They wanted to know how she had healed herself. Some of them recognized Saad from TV.

One voice from the crowd said, "I recognize you. You're the guru who was telling us how to cure ourselves."

By then the word had gotten round the entire hospital. Everyone was gathering around Saad and his family and the media.

They didn't need to call the media because they were already present, 24-7, to report any development.

Suddenly all the cameras were on Saad and his family. He was nervous, but he remembered Maaculla's words: Every problem is an opportunity in disguise. You can take this moment and turn it into a benefit. A smile came across his mind.

He quietly said in his mind, "Thank you, Maaculla."

This must be an opportunity to let the whole world know the cure. Just prior to this, as you know, he had been wondering how on earth he was going let everyone know, let alone convince them.

Again, quietly, he said in his mind, thank you, thank you, thank you...Maaculla. And then, loudly, "I love you."

All of a sudden, his nervousness disappeared.

He went in front of the cameras. "Good morning, everyone. I have some good news to share with you all."

The crowd was demanding, tell us how to cure ourselves of this curse. How did your daughter get cured?

Saad said, "Listen up, everyone. It concerns every person in the world."

The crowd gets impatient. They came one step forward.

The security guards were busy keeping the crowds under control and away from Saad's family.

Saad said, as loudly as possible, "There is no one who can cure you."

The crowd got angry and started to advance towards him and his family.

Saad shouted, "Listen to me. The miracle of healing is within you. It's a long explanation, but in short, you have to give up negativity from your mind. It's your own energy."

The crowd reacted angrily.

Saad raised his voice one notch more. "You want to be cured, don't you?"

The crowd groaned affirmatively. "Just tell us how."

Saad said, "Then listen to me. You may not believe it, but I've waited almost fifty years to deliver this message to you." He paused.

"As I said, nobody but you can cure yourself."

The crowd got very noisy. "How? How can we cure ourselves?"

Saad shouted, at the top of his voice, "Only you can cure yourself!"

One of the security guards had a megaphone. She handed it over to Saad.

He fumbled with it.

The crowd was still very noisy.

The security person took the megaphone back and pointed it at the crowd. " Please listen to Mr. Saad. He has an important message for you. If you listen to him, you can all go home soon, like his own daughter."

She held the megaphone to Saad's face.

The crowd calmed down.

"Listen up," Saad said. "You have all witnessed Saaren, my beloved daughter, cure herself." His voice broke a little. "I gave the instructions to her first to prove to you that you can cure yourself."

The crowd cheered

The cameras panned around the crowd of about four to five hundred people.

Saad said, "Yes, my friends, I love you too."

He made a namaste gesture towards the crowd and then touched his own heart with both hands. "I want you to know you are the first in the world to have this knowledge and the first to be cured."

The crowd cheered with joy.

The news cameras panned the crowd again.

"But we have a responsibility to share this with the entire world. And this is probably the first lesson: love everyone as much as you love yourself. This is a matter of mind."

One voice shouted from the crowd, "I love you, Saad."

They all joined him.

"And I love you more than you can imagine. You will soon realize this after you read all of the instructions on how to cure yourself.

"My wife has brought thousands of copies for you guys so that no one gets left out. She has them in the foyer. I want you all to do me a favor. I want you to form a queue calmly and respectfully, allowing everyone his or her place in the line. This is your second lesson: respect one another.

"I want to thank you for your kind patience. It seems like a lot of people are here, about four or five hundred. But imagine that we have to pass this along to our seven billion brothers and sisters all over the world. That is why it is available in the Internet, You Tube, Twitter, Pinterest, Google, Yahoo, Wikipedia, Face Book and so on.

"And this is your third lesson: share your love. Now I have hope for humanity.

"I'm going to read it out to the cameras so that they can broadcast it to the seven billion people around the world. Seventy-five percent of the seven billion people are already affected by these maculae.

"Ladies and gentlemen, here it is. Although it's only one page, it's a lot to remember. That's why my wife brought you the print version. It will be available in the foyer after this press conference. Again, please go there in an orderly manner. Let's make history, because you are the first, and your cooperation will heal our billions of brothers and sisters. From your example the rest of the world will learn and cure themselves. We are creating history today, one earth, one people. One love.

"Also, Amazon has kindly made it available for you all. They're allowing everyone to download it to any device, free of charge.

"It goes like this: 'The actual cure is very simple. Foremost of all, you need to set your intention. It should be always positive.

"'Hold one rose flower in your cupped hands.' That's why you have noticed by now that the Maacullas are offering an abundance of roses around the world. He repeated the whole instructions See no evil...

"That brings us to the point," Saad said, "of how to live after the cure."

Chapter 39

A NEW BEGINNING

The siege of the maculae was over. Everyone knew that as long as they stayed within the framework of positivity, they would be safe from it. Religions around the world were trying to teach the same principle and the equation of mathematics. Humans, being humans, every now and then, here and there some of the disbelievers would try to go back to their old ways of deception and negativity, as they had done before also with the religions. Now the universe had introduced a stronger and more global measure, so to speak—maculae. It would keep them in line, individually and instantly. Any wrongdoing would automatically get them zapped by the maculae. The good thing about maculae was that no one could hide them. In reality, it was the science and mathematics of the universe. You embrace negative energy, and it will consume you.

Imagine that no one can deceive you or tell a lie to you or you to others! No one has to catch a criminal or terrorist! Their own energy will destroy them. No politician can lie to us anymore. No lawyer can deceive people. No unscrupulous businesses can survive. Even small incidents—no mechanic can ever cheat you. No mortgage company can deceive you. No doctor can run unnecessary tests on you. No husband or wife can cheat on each other. No investment banker can deceive people. No phone company can overcharge the consumers. No religious group can interpret or mislead the followers. No lawyer or politician can manipulate the truth to win a case or the election. No one can even sit at home and think evil of others. No one can see, hear, or speak of negativity. The most amazing thing about maculae is that no one has to watch for crime, terrorism, deception, and so on. There's no need for burglar alarms or police or the FBI, CIA, or MI6 anymore. Bad guys get zapped by their own energy automatically. Then they come running back to the centres. Needless to say, there are hundreds of centres for maculae for educating everyone. They're called Maaculla Centres. Many of the churches, synagogues, mosques, and temples have also been converted to Maaculla Centres temporarily to accommodate people. This is truly a new beginning.

That brings us to the question, what lies in the future of mankind?

THE PROJECT SYMBIOSIS IN THE PRESENT DAY

Project Symbiosis (PS) is going full force. Crime around the world has dropped drastically. In fact, there are no more new crimes. All countries are participating in the project. They're sending truckloads of criminals to PS centres in deserts. Many criminals are volunteering, thinking they will be at least outside of jail. Only a handful of them are complaining, because they prefer the lazy life in jail. But jail is no longer an option. If you're convicted of a crime, you're required to serve in the PS. The severity of the crime dictates how long one has to serve there. These are the criminals from premaculae time, because there aren't any new criminals.

Deserts on each continent are being cultivated. Endless solar energy is being used to create clean electricity. No one has to put up with the inhuman toil of coal mining. As part of the infrastructure, European, American, Indian, Chinese, and Japanese knowledge are being used to advance the quality of people's lives. Now there are new cities being built in the desert. Huge rivers and canals have been dug from the sea to the middle of the deserts. Humongous reservoirs have been dug out to store the water brought in by the conduits. From there, underground conduits have been installed alongside the roads to distribute water to every corner of the desert. They also installed desalinization plants to trap all the salt from the sea water before it reaches the desert. Even prior to that, at the point of entry, they've installed grids so that no big animals can enter the river. Small fish are being allowed.

Agriculture experts from around the world have begun agriculture in the desert, now that water is available there with aquaponic systems. The new aquaponic system pumps water from a gigantic fish tank to equally big tanks where the plants are grown on the water. The fish waste supplies the necessary nutrients for the plants, and plant wastes goes to feed the fish, using the principle of natural symbiosis.

They've installed greenhouses for miles and miles, to grow vegetables and fruits and nuts of all kinds. Actually, the desert land is very rich with minerals, which are the building blocks of human chemistry. Evidence shows that it was under the sea once. Most of the greenhouses use soilless aquaponics. Also instead of soil, they're using coconut husks, thereby controlling bacteria and poisonous chemicals in the vegetables. They've built underground cold-storage units.

The new solar houses and buildings are extremely efficient. Lots of funds are available, since there are very few resources spent on war, crime, and so on. The unemployment rate is minus -10 percent in every part of the world. There are no homeless people in the cities anymore. Refugees from every corner of the world are finding homes and employment in the new desert lands with Project Symbiosis. Every country is now holding on to its human workforce. Many countries that have previously refused refugees are welcoming them now. It is ironic to see how in an instant our perspectives can change according to our circumstances. In some instances a shortage of human workers is being compensated for by robotics. They are being introduced in many major cities. Instead of birth control, every government is encouraging more birth now. Human laborers are rare in areas such as trash collection and recycling, city maintenance, gardening, auto industries, car washes, domestic chores, and so on. Humans resented working in these areas in the past.

We have excess resources in every country. Humans have to work only three days a week. They spend the other four days enjoying life with family, sports, and hobbies. There is no such thing as a weekend now. Everything is open all the time, 24-7. No stress, no diseases. Managers have been eliminated. People work on their own accord; otherwise, there is the threat of maculae hanging over their heads. By doing that, quality and production have increased 1000 percent. There's no more stressful crime-industry employment such as courts, lawyers, police, and guards. The need for this kind of employment has been eliminated by the maculae.

Nowadays, no one even laughs at others, let alone thinking of bullying, crime, terrorism, or wars. They get zapped by their own negative energy. There is no need for surveillance and security anymore. Each person is responsible for his or her own situation. No one ever has to worry about graffiti, crime, robbery, or getting mugged. All doors are left unlocked. We don't see any crime or high-speed chases in the news anymore. All cybercrime has been eliminated. It's safe on the Internet, as well as in our regular, daily life. No one can secretly plot any negative doings anymore, for fear of maculae.

The only thing we have to worry about is natural disasters. But natural disasters are becoming few and far between as our positivity increases gradually all over the world. In other words, our mass awareness is being established in positivity. We see fewer and fewer earthquakes, tsunamis, tornadoes, and so on. It only proves Maaculla's words that our environment is also affected by the mass awareness of negative energy. It was hard to believe it at the time.

The world has never seen such prosperity, health, and happiness. Employment is at 110 percent, meaning there is a shortage of workers. There is no need for artificial birth control.

JOBS

The time has come for people to feel enthusiastic about going to work. No one has to accept a job he or she doesn't enjoy. No more working two or three jobs to make ends meet. Now people work only two to three days a week, and everyone enjoys the work they do. They work because they want to, not because they have to. Women and minorities are in the same pay scale. No one can bully or take advantage of anyone. People all over the world work to live, not live to work.

At the same time, we've lost jobs in the crime, war, and weapons industries. New jobs have been created in positive industries such as computers, cell phones, communications, business, manufacturing, retail, agriculture, solar power, space technology, art, music, sports, movies, television, travel, hotels, gifts, and so on. People work fewer days for more pay to allow others to work. In the near future, they will probably work only two days a week to keep everyone employed. It's ironic that only a decade ago, people were complaining that powerful companies were cutting people to impress their shareholders, thus making two people work ten people's workload. Today people work of their own accord. They set their own hours. Sometimes they may work twenty-four hours or until their project is finished. They can stay at work with proper accommodations and food available twenty-four hours a day. Other times they may not turn up to work the whole week.

No one is supervising their work or hours. When work becomes pleasure, there is no such a thing as hard work, and there is less stress and fewer diseases. The overall health of the people has improved 100 percent, so we're saving on the healthcare industries as well. Hence a peaceful and happy family life. People are enjoying more with travel, entertainment, and eating out in the fine restaurants. As a result our entertainment, restaurant, hotel, and travel industries have grown a thousand folds. Workers earn the same salary working for Amazon as on Wall Street.

Governments have excess funds available for free job training and education, financing private businesses, and so on. In a decade or so, life on earth has turned around 1,000 percent in favor of the positive. No disgruntled people demonstrate against any company, government, party, or politician. People have peaceful and happy lives all over. All this is attributed to not having war and crime in our world, for fear of maculae.

TRAVELLING

People are travelling all over the world without worrying about costs or security. There is no need for passports or immigration control anymore. People are free to explore any country, any place in the world. They're tasting one another's foods, art, music, lifestyles, and cultures. Anyone can afford any hotel or resort. It's a matter of choice rather than what they can afford.

People all over have realized that there are more benefits in peace than in war and bickering. People are giving love and gifts rather than hate and bullets. They're exchanging cultures and enjoying one another's food and company.

PEACE

Finally, world peace has become possible. The change in individual people has made it possible. Now everyone realizes that peace is better than conflict. In fact, it is harder, riskier, and much more expensive to create conflicts and war than peace. Although at the beginning they were compelled to live in peace with others for fear of maculae, no one is complaining about it now. They've realized that living with others with a variety of ways of life is more fulfilling than hating others' lifestyles just because they're different. The same goes for others' food, sports, art, music, culture, industries, language, religion, sexual preference, and so on. People are inviting one another to experience their lifestyles. They're respecting one another's religions. They're appreciating one another's differences rather than trying to convert one another to their own ways of life. At the same time, they're open to changing to any new symbiotically beneficial ways. No one is laughing at anyone or bullying anyone in schools or workplaces. They're free to choose any place to live or any place to travel.

WEAPONS

Gradually, all weapons have been dismantled and destroyed. Some weapons are being displayed in war and weapons museums as symbols of a primitive lifestyle. People can't even think of owning or making any more weapons. This type of thinking has become a thing of the past. These museums are a remembrance of the way people used to think. Future generations can't even comprehend that at one time humans used to kill one another. They can't even imagine that people made weapons to destroy one another. They can't think of having an argument or disagreement. Making weapons and conquering other countries seems so primitive. They're shocked to see weapons of killing and destruction displayed in the museums. Is this for real? You can't even see this kind of primitive behavior in the movies or stories anymore. In the past small groups of criminals took advantage of religions and continued criminal savageries in the name of religions. It was almost impossible to control this kind of crime. Maculae has put a stop to all that.

Only in the last century people were having wars and conflicts around the world. What was all that about, anyway? Some countries wanted other countries' wealth and land and fuel. They fought over that. Both sides killed each other in the hundreds and thousands and millions. They destroyed each other's countries and their histories with it. In the end nobody won. Different people from different religions hated one another and fought with one another. Now everyone welcomes one another. They appreciate one another's knowledge and wisdom. There were conflicts, disagreements, and fighting all the time, all because they didn't like one another. The present generation cannot think what kind of mentality would hate instead of love. What's the purpose of it? There is no benefit in any kind of conflict. But in spite of all the education, religion, and experience, this kind of mentality continued for thousands of years. They could not see that both parties suffered heavy losses. They still continued fighting after losing property, peace, land, and, most precious, lives. They called themselves heroes. Wow, what a primitive lifestyle. One can't imagine even animals living that kind of life. We've come a long way since Maaculla put a stop to all this.

Even now some have fears. They've asked the inevitable question: What if some country such as Iran, Iraq, Pakistan, Israel, or Korea secretly start developing weapons in the hope of world domination? In fact, in the past this same fear has triggered many countries to make their own nuclear weapons for protection. But now, everyone involved will be zapped by maculae. Anyone who thinks of picking up a weapon with malicious intentions will be branded by maculae.

Chapter 40

ALL IS WELL—CONCLUSION

Maculae have become the protector and the guardian of the people from self-destruction. It will stay there, like the yellow lines on the roads, until humans learn to drive safely without the lines. With maculae, the universe has installed a system of crime and punishment inside each human instead of one system for all humans. In conclusion, humans have found a common enemy to fear. The enemy is within each of us. In other words, maculae (not Maaculla) have become our common enemy, or the common element to unite us and make us work together. Maculae work like a guardian. It is not physically possible to monitor every crime and every wrong doing or every negative thought. With maculae there is no need for overseeing or watching over any negativity. People are guided to choose positive awareness and lifestyles. One hundred percent of the humans expressed that they like this peaceful world now that they are introduced to this lifestyle. They feel that this is the true freedom.

Saad would like to clarify, in case the reader may have any question about why it was necessary for Maaculla to bring forth the metaphor of maculae, what kind of relationship they might have with it in the end.

Karen asked, "In the end, what kind of relationship do you think people would have with maculae? Because it seems that there is always a threat of falling sick with it. They will be always aware of this threat throughout their lives?"

Saad said, "This relationship will be similar to the one I had with Mrs. Griffiths, a.k.a. Maaculla. I was afraid of her, yet I continued visiting her. I was afraid because I felt she might impose another responsibility on me. But deep inside, I knew she loved and respected me as much as I loved her and respected her, similar to the way a mother and a child would feel. She would protect her child with a strong hand from endangering himself. But a child would never see that as a threat. Every time I reminded Saaren that 'Mummy loves you' after she was disciplined, she always said, 'I know.'

"I learned that from observing you—how you protected Saaren during her childhood. Even now you feel the same way, although you

265

respect her freedom now that she's an adult. I didn't understand that until I met you, because I had never had that relationship with my own mother when I was growing up. Because I never had a mother present during my childhood. Sometimes I wonder if Maaculla planned that too, like most of the main events of my life."

The threat of maculae will always be there, like a guideline similar to the yellow lines on the road. We will wait until we can eliminate yellow lines from the roads and still drive safely and successfully. From that day on, we will have no need to fear or worry about the maculae.

She will be protecting us, the fledgling human race, until we become mature enough to continue on our own. Hence Maaculla—the Mother of the World.

The choice is clear. Either humankind continues with its destructive thinking, or this could be the watershed moment for the fledgling human civilization's peaceful life. "Peace" is not just a word; it is a reality. Only you can make it happen.

The choice is yours!—Maaculla

NO, THIS IS NOT AN EPILOGUE. RATHER, IT'S A CONTINUUM…

Printed in Great Britain
by Amazon